The Human Element

Lauren Baker

Tea and Tales Publishing LLC

First Edition: August 05, 2025

Book Cover by Shelby Schena

Book Design by Tea and Tales Publishing LLC

ISBN:979-8-9988436-0-0

CONTENTS

To the ones who fight self-doubt each day and still create beautiful, needed things.
And to my favorite human beings in the world: **My husband** *and* **my son**.
All I can say is I'm forever grateful the Universe brought us together in this life, and hopefully in every other to come.

CHARACTER NAME GUIDE

LORELEI-LOR-Ah-LYE

DAEMON- DAY-Mun

SAMUEL- Sam-ULE

DEAN- Deen

MAGNUS- MAG-Nas

ZANUL- Zah-NOOL

RAPHAEL- Rah-FYE-elle

ARIEL- Ar-E-elle

LUCIFER- Loo-CIH-Fur

CATVYNIA- CAT-vun-EE-ah

VALAC- Val-ACK

XINLIN- ZEN-Lin

NYRIED- NEER-ee-Ed

SYLETH- Sil-ETH

MICHAEL- MIKE-ull

PROLOGUE

I'M FALLING.

I don't have time to think of anything else before I slam hard into...sand?

Despite my eyes being closed, I can tell it's bright. Blinking several times, my eyes begin to adjust and I see it: I am in a desert. To my left and right, there is nothing but sand as far as the horizon. But as I turn behind me, I see them. The Giza Pyramids. As a massive history buff I know them the moment they catch my gaze.

"Why am I here?"

Before being able to formulate a reason, my feet, on instinct, begin moving my body towards them. I'm quite a distance from them now, and although I think the sand will give me problems, seeing as I'm barefoot, I am able to practically glide over the sand towards the middle pyramid with not so much as a stumble. I am being pulled by this unexplainable force; I have to go to them. But why?

"You must open them."

This thought erupts inside my mind, like it was coming from someplace else. Or...someone. Open them? But that doesn't even make sense? Yet somehow, I know it's the truth either way. How I know-is the real mystery. After what feels like a lifetime passes, sand stretching for miles with no end in sight, I at last reach it- with a feeling of relief mixed with awe: the middle and largest pyramid of the three.

Standing just a couple of feet away from its exterior, I observe the stone directly in front of me. I lift my arm forward to place my hand upon it when before I could touch the magnificent structure, a thunderous crack causes me to jump, stealing my attention off to my left.

Up in the sky, I see a black blur hurtling towards me. Without a moment of hesitation, I sprint as fast as my legs can carry me over the difficult terrain, sand shifting uncomfortably beneath my feet as I try to gain footing and skid along the face of the pyramid.

Finally reaching the right side of it, and while attempting to catch my breath, leaning my back against the pyramid with a hand on my chest, I wait. Finding some courage, I take a step around the corner to see the blur hitting the side of the pyramid with an impact that makes the ground shake violently, a large chunk of the pyramid comes barreling down. The blur plummets into the sand, giving the earth another quiver.

The air begins to fill with dust from the debris and it blocks my vision from whatever has now damaged one of the Seven Wonders of the World right before my eyes. A massive sand cloud fills the air, and I quickly cover my mouth and eyes to keep from coughing.

As the dust begins to clear, I can finally see what caused such damage. Thinking it was a missile, or a plane crashing into the pyramid-only to discover as the dust settles-it's a man. A man who just brought down a massive piece of an ancient creation that has stood the test of time. But at closer inspection, this was no man...

My eyes first land on the large, black wings glistening in the sunlight. Silky-looking, with hints of green that pop when they shift and move, my eyes then move to where the wings connect: a muscular body, heaving as he tries to regain his breath. He stretches his arms into the sky, a bit sore, but otherwise unscathed from the impact.

How could he not have been killed from that fall? And what are with those wings?

Holding my breath, afraid one exhale could alert him of my presence, he looks at me, revealing his shocking emerald eyes. Face chiseled, with near luminous silver hair that meets his shoulders and whisps playfully across his face. A feeling of mesmerization and fear overwhelms me while I continue to watch him.

His eyes narrow, and although I'm still hidden behind the corner of the pyramid, all at once I realize I have been holding my breath for far too long and I have to exhale. As if drawn by magic, my body vibrating all over, I step forward and reveal myself from the side of the pyramid. Heart racing fast now, I keep my head down before bucking up the strength to face this terrifying, winged man.

Our eyes lock and the intense feeling from his piercing gaze reels me in like a helpless fish on a hook, until he finally blinks and I feel a release. Breathing slowly, I again see the enormous wings extended behind him spanning the length of his own body. He looks ready to attack or take off in flight. After several moments like this, he seems to relax a little, finally realizing that I was no threat, slowly letting the wings fold neatly onto his back. His eyes show a sense of urgency, and familiarity.

Yet there is no place I have traveled in my life that I have ever seen a man of his equal.

Confused, I continue to stare at him silently, waiting for him to say something. But there isn't a chance. Flashes of red and bright, white light crack in the sky above me. The noise is so loud, I cover my ears, but the cracks continue over and over. Dark clouds start to swirl in unison, blocking what is causing the light. As if on cue, the figure's wings whip back out and we meet eyes once more. Before I can ask who or what he is, or what was happening here, he is shooting back up into the sky, swallowed by the swath of stormy clouds above.

The now damaged pyramid standing guard like a watchful companion, begins to shimmer and fade into nothing. I reach out and try to bear my weight upon its rocky surface for support as the earth quakes again beneath my feet, but soon I fall to my knees as the pyramid disappears entirely—leaving nothing but a plume of dust lingering in its wake. Staring up to the last place I saw the man, the final thing I see is the sky illuminated by a chaotic flurry of colors that fade into abrupt blackness.

PART 1

CHAPTER 1

LORELEI

And then...a thud.

Lorelei's eyes quickly open after she knocks her head into the window, her head having slipped off her perched arm that was leaning against it. Wincing, she rubs her forehead where she knew a small bruise would surely form. Rubbing it gingerly for a moment, Lorelei looks out the window to see the Scottish countryside passing by. Clouds are hovering above the hills, barely caressing them, trying to cuddle up to the Earth for comfort.

The dream again. The same dream she's had for as long as she can recall. One she could never understand and that left her with a headache each time she woke from it. It always went the same: falling into the desert, seeing the pyramids, knowing she must "Open them," and usually it would fade out about the time she reached the pyramid. She never got to the part of the dream where she could finally understand what it all meant, or what happened next. But this one, this one was different. This was the first time that winged figure had ever been in her dream. He was fascinating, with eyes that shone like a flurry of green that made her suck in air.

Was it an angel?

Lorelei shook her head.

I wouldn't think an angel would have black wings.

She blinked as the headache sent a pang of pain across her head. Her mind couldn't even comprehend what she had seen in her dream enough to allow her to contemplate it now.

I'll come back to that newest conundrum when I've got more time. Besides, the psychiatrist said it was probably a mere fantastical dream. Nothing to read into. But then again, she always said that. She does say I have a very active imagination.

Either way, the dream was one of those perplexing things she dealt with throughout her life, one that never seemed to come with a full answer and always kept her feeling the worse for its existence.

Lorelei sighs, massaging her temple. Typically, she got used to the same dream for so long, she stopped trying to make sense of it. She'd pop a couple of Ibuprofen to help the dull ache in her head when she woke, and tended to ignore it. But in the back of her mind, she couldn't help wondering about its meaning. Especially, with a new and strange figure popping up out of the blue.

Perhaps I should go to a dream specialist one day, see if what I'm seeing means something more, or if it's just the extra glass of wine I had last night that caused the sudden change in the annoying dream.

Deciding it wasn't worth the agitation of deciphering the cryptic message of her nonsensical vision, Lorelei looks about her train cabin to see that she is no longer alone as she previously was when she first boarded. Not completely unexpected of course, but seeing as though she is going to the small city of Inverness, Scotland, she honestly didn't expect the train to be too full on this trip.

A satchel bag with the name "Addair" was etched into the leather strap that slung across the seat opposite her. It wasn't new, she could tell the strap had been worn down and one of the clasps on the front obviously hadn't worked for some time. Yet it seemed as though the owner kept it well cleaned and when it was bought, spent a good deal of money on it. Perhaps some sort of business man? She knew Addair was quite a common name in Scotland.

Lorelei let out a long, drawn-out sigh before looking at where a large notebook lay upon her lap. It was filled to the brim with pages of newspaper clippings, pictures, and articles printed from the internet, as well as small scribbles of half-cursive, rivaling a doctor's, that any other person wouldn't be able to make heads or tails of. For Lorelei though, this was her sanctuary. Her notes were her way to make sense of the world, her thoughts and musings, the places she could go back to for comfort. Although, too often, she herself had a difficult time decrypting the sloppy code she concocted. She flipped to the current page. For it being one of the bigger stories she was sure to tackle, she didn't have much but a couple of pictures.

Lorelei had been working as a writer for a small, obscure magazine called *"The Mythical Truth"* for about a year now. After graduating university in London, she wanted a job that allowed her to write and travel. The magazine was based out of London, but she was able to travel all over. She mostly wrote about myths and legends in particular areas and then would go to "investigate" or cover the story at those locations. This one was pretty exciting for her, as she has always been a bit of a history buff and believed that all myths had some essence of truth behind them. A notion her father instilled in her from a young age. Although often fantastical in nature, myths were an eyeglass into the past. How the people lived, their belief systems, what their woes were, and how people found comfort in the unknowns. It was a motto she lived by: not everything is as it seems. There's so much intrigue and lessons you can learn about human nature in these tales—which was often a fascinating topic of interest for her. Also an ode to her studious, truth-seeking father.

She was tackling the famous "Loch Ness Monster," which after a small amount of convincing, was allowed to go to Inverness to cover her own version of the story that so many know. Inverness is a small town where the story supposedly originated, as it lies along Loch Ness. Now, although it was highly unlikely she would find more to the story on the truth of an actual fabled lake monster that dwells there, her goal was to attempt to find a new angle on the legend that hadn't yet been covered, which like the words of her boss ringing in her ear, would be a long shot. But that was a fun bit of journalism, right? Plus, this myth was one of the crazier ones she would ever face—and what a fantastically entertaining story it was nonetheless! Either way, it was a chance to travel and write, which was always Lorelei's favorite things to do.

Mr. Fletcher, her boss, started *The Mythical Truth* about 15 years ago. He was a rough, staunch looking man in his 50s who always had a glass of bourbon on hand. Lorelei didn't actually know a lot about him or his past, but it was hard for a magazine—even an odd, down and out one—to take a chance on a new, young writer. So she was grateful to him for that. He allowed her to write about whatever myth or legend she wanted, as long as she was okay with just a small compensation on meals. Seeing as Mr. Fletcher himself lived in the flat above the office, and the fact that their magazine only had about a few hundred copies around London and a few other minute places around the globe each month, he didn't have much to offer in terms of money. After her father's death, she came by some inheritance he'd surprisingly saved over the years, that allowed her to maintain her flat in London and keep her living expenses in check, despite the lack of income from her job. On the side, she often wrote articles on varying subjects like travel, food, and life as an American living in England to several other online blogs who pay per article a fair price, which helped. She lived cheaply though, putting most of that inheritance away for savings. Her hopes were to buy a cottage in the English countryside one day. A dream that at this point, was years in the making. But she was content with her situation for now.

Lorelei wasn't the only employee at the office. There were two others. Paul Evans, a 35-year-old who has been with Fletcher since he opened. He was Fletcher's nephew, and resembling his uncle's adage of keeping bourbon on him, Paul always had some new diet craze he was trying out. He once asked Lorelei if she wanted to try his new protein shake he got in the mail that he swore was the tastiest protein shake on the market. When she tasted it, she smiled and nodded in eager agreement of its deliciousness as he then chugged one of his own, and then quickly spit it into the nearest trashcan when he turned his back. The other employee was Walter Cooke, 18, scraggly-haired kid who was as clumsy a person Lorelei had ever seen. Walter constantly had bangs and bruises on him as he knocked into the printer, the water cooler, the chair, and even tripping over thin air was a common occurrence for him. She wasn't particularly close to either of them, most of the time Paul annoyed her and Walter stared a little too much, but all in all, their company didn't bother her. Especially since she traveled as frequently as she could. Working there wasn't what she intended to do forever, but it was cushy and she enjoyed the research and historical conspiracy aspect of it.

After her father passed a month before she graduated, Lorelei didn't really have much to go back to the states for. She never really knew her mother, but from what her father told her, she wasn't meant to be the mothering type. Around the second year of her parents' marriage, her mom Claire, got into a pretty vicious car accident. It left her with a knee that would never be quite right again. Her dad said she was constantly in pain and began to take advantage of the painkillers. Her denial of her addiction really put a strain on their relationship, more than once resulting in her father attempting to take her to the hospital. But when they found out she was pregnant with Lorelei, she seemed to realize the wrong she was doing and put a stop to it. But not long after the birth, she began using again. This sent Lorelei's father to the brink, and to protect his only child, he left her. But it didn't seem to matter to her; most of the time she hardly knew where she was let alone remembered that she had a child in the first place.

So her father raised her, best he could, on a museum salary. Benjamin Alexander was a tall, lumbering sort of man, who always seemed to have what looked like peach fuzz on his face at all times. With the kindest blue eyes that could easily reassure and comfort you when you were feeling worn down or distressed, large, round glasses that sat at the brim of his nose snuggly, conforming to a lean, freckled face—he had the kind of look that made a person smile on command, for the pure sweetness of it alone. He worked in the archives of the Natural History Museum in Los Angeles.

Mr. Alexander always had a love and passion for history, which trickled down to his beloved daughter for whom his world revolved. Although a quiet man, he did his best to instill his love of history into Lorelei, who had a natural knack for memorizing facts and trivia. Her favorite memories were when he would have to work late, and although a bit reluctant, would bring her along. Lorelei adored going to the museum where she would play pretend archaeologist attempting to decode the bones discovered at an ancient burial site or an explorer trying to find the City of Gold. She also enjoyed watching her father work, quietly and with a gentleness she only ever saw elsewhere when he would tuck the stray pieces of blonde hairs behind her ears when he was putting her to bed at night.

As Lorelei got older, her father was her constant rock: between heartbreaks from silly boys, always showing up to her soccer games, and shouting louder than any other parent in the stands despite his usually quiet nature, and even fixing her favorite sausage and potato soup whenever she got sick. Lorelei never usually missed her mother because her father filled the space that was left there. It wasn't until the death of her mother while in high school due to her ever-growing addiction—was when Lorelei felt the blow of being truly motherless. Lorelei didn't cry at the funeral, but she saw her father did. Out of the corner of her eye, with the church beginning to empty as the service came to an end, she watched as her father walked back to the casket, assuming he didn't know people were still around. He leaned quizzically over the body of her mother, and she saw small drops of tears fall into the casket before he closed the lid. It was the only time she ever saw her father show any emotion towards the mother she never had. Lorelei hurt for her father at that moment. Even if her father never said it, and seemed to be generally happy, she knew then he was lonely for never being able to have the companion he so longed for. He loved her mother fiercely, and she knew it killed him when he had to leave.

Around the time of his death, they had just been speaking a few days earlier on video chat, discussing how her finals were going and his trip out for the graduation. He seemed in good spirits and was terribly excited to be back in London. He had always loved London, ever since he was stationed there for many years while serving in the Air Force. When Lorelei was young, he would tell her stories of the hustle and bustle of a city mixed beautifully with old and new; a lively place where it felt as if history could come alive there at any moment. It was from a young age that Lorelei dreamed of living there someday.

She never even thought that something might be troubling him, she couldn't tell he was distraught in any way. But that's how it goes most of the time, doesn't it? The person who smiles the brightest and always strives to make others feel good around them, are the ones who are hurting the most on the inside. If only she had known then, she still thinks she could have done something....anything. When she didn't get a call or text from him that he was boarding his flight to come a couple days before graduation, she immediately knew something was wrong. She contacted his neighbor, Florence, to go check to see if he was at the house. It was locked from the inside, but his car was still in the driveway. A couple of hours later, police found his body hanging from the stairway banister.

Lorelei never attended graduation, she cried for what seemed like weeks. She blamed herself for not staying home to be with him all these years. Guilt consumed her. The "what ifs" of whether she stayed in the states with him; if that would've helped keep him here. How blind she was to his torment. It ate away at her, and after the tumultuous feelings she continued to struggle within her life because of her mother's absence; and her own issues with depression; it sent her into a spiral. Hence the reason for the psychiatrist to help deal with the guilt of his passing and her own sadness of the loss of *both* her parents. It's been a year now, and although equipped with a much healthier view of the situation and on her feet with work—a crippling pain erupted in her chest every time she thought of him.

They both missed a woman who was never there; but should've been. She only wished she could've told her dad he didn't deserve what he went through either, that he was strong and he gave her the best life, and that she was so sorry he was suffering quietly for so long. The memory of their last hug as he left the airport back to the states a few months before her graduation tugged at her mind again.

It was a spontaneous trip around London together, reminiscing old times he had spent there in his Air Force days, beguiling the majesty of the city, the smile he wore the entire time—this was how she tried to remember him. It was a comfort to know their last time together was this beautiful and joyful, which eased her a bit whenever she felt the sickening, overwhelming sadness threaten to overtake her. But, she truly believed that whatever pain or loneliness her father was feeling, she was just happy he didn't have to feel it any longer. Sometimes she liked to imagine her parents, falling back in love somewhere starting over together in a paradise where neither could hurt or worry.

A swooshing sound alerted Lorelei and forced her to come out of her thoughts. A slender, but fit looking gentleman with short brown locks, and a smile that covered the width of his face, stepped inside the car and beamed at her.

"Oh good, you're awake. When I came into the car and saw you were sleeping, I tried to stay out to let you rest. You seemed absolutely scunnered!" His Scottish accent was thick, almost raspy in nature and sent what felt like shock waves through the train car due to its vivacity.

Lorelei didn't say anything but continued to observe the man, who obviously picked up on the fact she was confused by his phraseology.

"Apologies, tired, I mean."

With that clarification, he closed the door behind him and took his seat opposite her, picking up the leather satchel bag and placing it on the opposite side of him neatly. He was handsome, an almost devil-may-care flare about him that radiated each time he flipped his bangs off his forehead. He had a defined nose, but it suited his face, matching his high cheekbones. Wearing a navy sport coat and slacks, he crossed his legs before clearing his throat. An awkward air filled the car until Lorelei spoke.

"How did you know I wouldn't understand the word..." She paused, unable to remember the word he used.

"Scunnered? You gave the classic, "What the fuck?" look when I said it, so naturally, I assumed you weren't from around here." He chuckled, and Lorelei noticed it had a light, playful air to it. She felt a little flutter when she heard it, which made her smile in return, the awkwardness fading.

"I'm sorry for that, I think I was just deep in thought. I am a bit...scunnered."

She laughed as she said this, shaking her head. Was she really acting this flirty with a man she just met? Has it really been so long since she had been with anyone? These thoughts quickly scatter her mind, but she attempts to

16

shake them off and focus her attention back on him. He had to be a good bit older than her, but that never deterred her in the past. The last date she went on, the guy was about 10 years older than she was. She always assumed her father would've never approved, seeing as she was 22; he was a bit old school in that way. This man looked about late 20s or early 30s, and she watched as he picked a piece of lint off of his sleeve before meeting her eyes again.

"So, where are you from then?" He asked.

"Los Angeles, originally, but I've lived in London for years now."

"Oh, what brought you there?" He seemed to be genuinely interested, unlike some people who simply ask out of politeness.

"Schooling, I went to The London School of Journalism."

"A writer, eh? I was never very good at writing, I'm a numbers person myself. I work as a bank liaison. A bit more boring I can assure you." He laughed, the sound of his Scottish accent was refreshing, yet contained a robust sensuality hidden within it; which she found to be incredibly attractive.

Lorelei wasn't actually sure what to say to that, so almost blurting it out, she shoots her arm out quickly to shake his hand.

"I'm Lorelei, nice to meet you."

"Dean, Dean Addair. A pleasure."

Returning her handshake, it was firm and sent a tingle through her arm; like she had been lightly shocked, which she thought odd.

"Lorelei, huh? That's quite an interesting name. There is a legend about a siren called Lorelei, if I recall correctly."

Lorelei perked up upon hearing he knew a legend from which her name came from, and while closing her notebook and setting it beside her lap, she returned her attention to Dean.

"I work for a small magazine where we cover all sorts of myths and legends, I am definitely interested in a legend that has something to do with my name, if you're willing to share."

Dean smiled brightly, showing a beautiful row of teeth, excited that she wanted to hear the story.

"Well, it is said there is this rock on the Rhine River in Germany, where a maiden, so distraught about her faithless lover, threw herself from and died."

"Wow, that's just horrible, isn't it?" Lorelei laughed as Dean continued.

"Aye ken, right? Well she came back to life as a siren, who would sit upon this rock and lure fishermen to their deaths." Dean made his voice tremble in an attempt to be spooky, which made Lorelei laugh.

"Well," she said, "That is some tale, then."

Dean gave a small smirk and teasingly asked, "You don't plan on luring me to my early demise, do you?"

"Haha nope, it wasn't on my to-do list for today."

Is he flirting with me?

Lorelei couldn't help but think he was. Dean was incredibly charismatic and articulate, on top of the fact that he was pretty attractive with an air of maturity Lorelei hadn't come across in awhile. But he also seemed to be a bit of a spirited, fun-loving chap as well.

"I am here to write some stories on some of the classic Scottish myths. Inverness seemed like a good place to start. I'll only be here a week or so, but I think I can get a lot of writing and inspiration in that amount of time. You must be somebody who is interested in myths as well?"

"Well I wouldn't say I know much about them nowadays, but my mother adored them and would always tell me them as bedtime stories growing up. A few stuck with me."

Suddenly, the train's whistle blew, making her jump. Checking her watch, she didn't notice how much time had passed. It was already 6 o'clock at night. Soon the train was pulling itself into the train station, and with a lurch, it came to a halt. As it did, so did her time with Dean Addair. This realization was a little disappointing to her, seeing as how enjoyable the conversation she was having with him was. Dean looks out the train window and sighs,

"Ah, looks like we're here."

He also seemed to be disappointed that their conversation was to be cut short. Lorelei gathered her notebook and stowed it in her large, faded leather bag, the one her dad gave her when she started University—which resembled that of Dean's ironically—and grabbed her small suitcase from the storage bin above her seat. Dean stood up and kept the car door open for her as she smiled at him a final time.

"Thanks for making the end of the trip so enjoyable, Dean. It was nice getting to chat with you."

Before he could respond, she slipped past him and made her way off of the train. Stepping onto the train station platform, the beginnings of a brisk, autumn wind whipped through Lorelei's hair. Sighing, she adjusts her bag on her shoulder, looking around to see where to go, clicking the handle on her suitcase just as she realized her name was being called.

"Wait! Lorelei!"

Lorelei turns around and sees Dean running towards her, apologizing to the people he nearly runs into, until he is panting as he stands before her.

"Lorelei, I know you won't be here for very long, but I couldn't miss the chance to ask if you'd like to go for a bevvy with me this evening?"

Lorelei blushed, a sudden apprehensive excitement brightened her cheeks. She only hoped he'd mistake it for the brisk weather.

"Ahh...a bevvy, that one I know! I always loved that is the term so commonly used here in the UK. That would be great, Dean. I'd love to get a bevvy with you."

Regaining his breath, he smiles and lets out a comical "Whew!"

"Goodness, for having lived in the UK so long, at least you know that one! Tells me you're not one to shy away from a good pub, eh?" He paused a moment and twiddled his hands together; Lorelei found the gesture quite cute.

"I was a bit nervous to ask; I honestly wasn't sure you'd say yes. Where ya staying?"

"I'm staying at Drury Court."

Smiling he continues, "I know a pub near there, The Castle Tavern? How about we meet there at 8?"

"That sounds perfect!"

Dean looks all too relieved; she accepts his invitation, and he gestures to the street, allowing his shoulders to drop slightly as he speaks again.

"Let me get you a cab."

Lorelei shook her head and began looking down at her watch, unsure why she was overwhelmed with nerves at his chivalrous gesture. "Oh no, you don't have to do that, really."

"It's no problem, the least I can do considering you're making my entire day by joining me for a drink in a little while." He winked at her before pulling out his phone to order a cab, when one drove up only a moment later, which never happened that quickly back in London; Lorelei was thankful to get out of the cold. Dean walks Lorelei to the car and then grabs her hand, giving it a light kiss that sends shivers throughout her.

"I'll see you soon, gorgeous."

Lorelei smiles brightly, and steps into the back of the cab, Dean closing the door for her before the cab drives away. As the cab headed down the street, Lorelei felt like she could nearly pinch herself over the interaction with Dean.

Omg, omg...Calm down, Lorelei. It's just a date...A date with an extremely handsome man who seems to think you're a catch.

She could tell her pulse was out of control, and she could still feel the gentle kiss he left upon her hand. It was like electricity was shooting through her veins. She couldn't stop thinking about meeting up with Dean the entire drive to the hotel. When she arrived, she checked in, and made her way up to the 4th floor. The moment she was through her room door, she threw her stuff to the ground and jumped on the bed, screaming with excitement into a pillow.

Rolling over and spreading her limbs across the bed, she starts to think about what she might wear out tonight. Sitting up again, Lorelei stretches. Tentatively, she sniffs under her armpits, and to her surprise, still smells like her lilac soap from home. Figuring she didn't need to take a shower before going out with Dean, she places her suitcase on the bed before unzipping it. Rummaging through her clothes, she decides upon a black pair of jeans, some black suede boots with a medium-sized heel, and a baby blue sweater that showed a little more cleavage than she usually flaunted, which she felt quite confident in. Once having her outfit picked out, she grabs her leather bag, finding her small makeup pack at the bottom of it.

Turning on a couple of more lights in the room, she locates the remote for the television and clicks it on, putting it on an animal special where a British narrator was currently talking over a family of wildebeests tussling. She then goes over to the full-length mirror on the wall next to the television while she listens absent-mindedly to the man's soothing voice as he continues to discuss their mating habits.

Lorelei takes a hard look at herself in the mirror, and can see why Dean had called her "scunnered." She had massive dark circles under her eyes, a bit of her mascara smudged itself onto her eyelid and her hair looked like a rat had been living in it for about a week.

"Dear god, how the hell did Dean even want to take me out looking like this?" She said out loud to herself as she shook her head and ran to grab her hairbrush from her bag. Brushing out her hair as best as she could, she decided to go for a high ponytail, and once her fly-away hairs had been sufficiently taken care of with some hairspray, she began touching up her makeup, adding a little extra pop with some winged eyeliner. She figured she'd wait until right before she left to put on her favorite red lipstick, so she turned to go sit on the bed and watch some tv for a little while.

But the moment she turned, Lorelei felt an intense, instantaneous wave of dizziness wash over her. Grabbing her head, she closed her eyes tight hoping it would pass momentarily, but it only intensified. It was like a ringing in her brain shaking her very core. Before she could think of what to do, she blinked repeatedly, attempting to regain some control over her body, and thought she saw a swoosh of something moving through the hotel balcony glass door. She couldn't remember anything after that.

CHAPTER 2

LORELEI

Lorelei's eyes slowly opened, the ceiling fan in the room directly above her, she propped herself onto her arm and looked around the room.

What the hell just happened? Did I pass out?

Still feeling somewhat dizzy, she took her time standing up while letting her eyes catch up with her surroundings. She pulled the chair at the small desk in the room out to sit and let clarity overtake the confusion bubbling up inside her. Sitting there a moment without moving, steadying her breath, thankful for the dizziness subsiding. When she felt like she was back to normal, she remembered what she saw before passing out.

The figure of blackness that crossed the balcony.

Was it a play of her imagination as she was becoming unconscious? It had to be, but to settle her racing thoughts on the issue, she stood and walked over to the sliding glass door to the balcony, unlocked it, and stepped out into the chilly air. She looked around her, seeing only a small bistro table and chairs, a fern sat in the corner. Walking to the edge of the balcony rail, she looks over the edge, only seeing the darkness of the street below, with some splattering of light from the streetlamps. Nothing more.

*Must have been a lighting trick before I blacked out. I know I was tired, but I didn't think I was **that** tired.*

Lorelei walks back inside and closes the door behind her, then strides across the room and fishes for her cellphone from inside her bag. Lifting it out, she clicks the screen and nearly drops it when she sees what time it is.

"It's already 7:45?! Damn, I need to get to the bar. It's only a few blocks from here, but since I'm walking, I need to leave now!"

She rushes over to her bag and grabs her lipstick, slaps some on, making sure none of it was on her teeth, slips on her jacket, flattens down a couple more stray hairs, places her wallet in her jacket pocket, and then runs out the door. Her eyes were still adjusting, but otherwise she felt fine again. She wondered if she should get a CT scan, or if she was having a sort of fit of exhaustion, but with no other adverse effects from passing out—Lorelei decided it must've been a fluke. She noted to herself to keep an eye on it should it happen again.

When Lorelei stepped out of the hotel lobby door and onto the sidewalk, she checked her phone's GPS to make sure she knew where she was going, and then turned left into the direction of the pub. Stuffing her phone back into her pocket, she pulls her coat collar a little closer around her face and sets out on her walk.

She could hear her heels click upon the slightly dampened sidewalk, having recently sprinkled. Sounds of uproarious laughter came from a couple crossing the street in front of her, huddled together to combat the chill of the evening. Despite the consistent reassurances in her head about the incident, she couldn't shake this foreboding feeling. Lorelei tries to think back as to why she might have blacked out. Had she been dehydrated? No, she knew she had enough water that day. As various theories were making their way through her mind, a prickling sensation ran up her spine.

Looking up, the light from the street lamp in front of her began flickering wildly, and that's when she saw a dark figure heading her way. Had he been there this whole time? It was like he appeared out of nowhere.

Lowering her head slightly as she began to pass the man who was donning a dark grey hoodie that covered most of his face. When she glanced up at the last moment, just as they were passing each other, bright green orbs met hers from under the hood of the man's jacket. They flashed brighter the moment their eyes met, and she gasped. Before she had time to think, she whipped around to see where he went, but he was gone. Vanished entirely.

Her heart was pounding fiercely and she just stood there on the sidewalk in confused awe. The encounter made her shiver, goosebumps trickling along her arms, and she hugged them around herself for warmth—or possibly, protection. Turning back around, she continued on her way to the pub, hurriedly. All the while, she couldn't help wondering how the man disappeared on an open street. And what about those glowing eyes?

I must be more tired than I thought, I'm definitely seeing things.

Stepping into the pub, she was still visibly shaking and quickly found her way to the bar counter to sit. Fumbling to take off her jacket, she lays it over the back of the chair and rubs her hands together. Lorelei gets the attention of the barkeeper and orders a large ale, which she practically chugs, willing it to calm her already agitated nerves.

Taking a moment to turn in her seat, she admires the coziness of the tavern. It was a small place, with earthy, rich colors throughout. Varying glasses hung upside down from the ceiling behind the bar, creating a glowy, speckled display as the dimmed lights reflected off their pristinely, cleaned surfaces; resembling a disco-ball. Wooden tables and chairs lay about in an organized manner all around; people clinking their beer and wine with exuberant laughter, filled the already vibrant space with cheer and camaraderie. One of the many reasons why Lorelei adored traveling was to experience the medley of folks enjoying their off time together. People appreciating the joys of a good drink, hearty conversation, and music that muffled the sounds of whispering couples in corners beyond. Times were tough, but moments like this reminded her how glorious the world was and how lucky she was to be able to explore its depths.

It was already 8:10 by the time she'd finished her first beer, but Dean was still a no-show.

"He's probably just late or stuck in traffic..." mumbling under her breath, trying to reassure herself.

Another lager down and 30 more minutes later, there was no sign of Dean. Sighing, feeling quite defeated, she figured she could have one more beer before heading back to the hotel to wallow in her pity. As she begins waving to the bartender for another round, a man takes a seat beside her. Excitement rushes through her and as she turns to greet who she assumed would be Dean; to her surprise, it wasn't Dean at all, but the man in the hoodie she passed on her way here. His face was turned forward, but a few strands of long, silver locks draped out from under the hood. The bartender comes by again, her mouth agape, unable to articulate any words; trance-like, she reaches a hand and drags the dropped off ale towards her silently, as the bartender now looked at the newcomer.

"Aye, what'll it be then, lad?"

The man finally lifted his hood back, moving a piece of hair out of his face before responding.

"A pint of lager, thanks."

The man's British accent was a deeper, caressing sort of tone that could definitely make a woman weak at the knees or make a heart melt. But right now, it sounded worried and haggard. The bartender nods and runs off to check on other customers, but Lorelei couldn't stop looking at the silver-haired man at her side.

It's the winged man from my dream.

She couldn't believe it, but there he was, sitting right next to her in this little Scottish pub. Words wouldn't come, she just kept blinking, thinking perhaps she'd had too much to drink, or maybe her drink was laced with something and she was hallucinating. The barkeeper came back with the man's beer and he downed it in one go, wiping his lips off impatiently. Before she could muster up something to say, he spoke again.

"You don't have to gawk at me like that, it's off-putting, eh?"

Lorelei just stared at him. Struggling with the reality sitting before her, her voice finally found its courage when she responded in a mocking way.

"Off-putting? You're the one who's off-putting! Who the fuck are you? I...I saw you in a dream?! You passed me on the street and..an–"

As she starts to say more, he cuts her off, huffing in frustration and at last turning to face her. His emerald eyes were piercing and they made her feel frozen in time, just as they had in her dream.

"I don't know why or how for that matter, you saw me in a dream. But that isn't the point, we don't have time for you to wrap your lovely little head around all this, alright? If you want some answers, and you don't want to die, then you need to come with me."

Lorelei hadn't responded yet while he was already standing and pushing his chair in. He walked a few steps away from her and stopped, looking over his shoulder.

"You coming? Or do you actually wish for death, then, hm?"

The harshness of his tone made her heart start to pound once more. She looked around the bar fervently, hoping Dean would show up all of sudden and save her from this insane experience altogether.

The man rolled his eyes, walked back over to her, hands in his pockets, a seriousness washed over his face as he watched her eyes search the pub.

"He isn't coming, so don't waste your breath. Now, let's go."

What? How does he know...

Despite every fear in her body, she didn't think arguing with this man would get her anywhere, plus, he obviously knew far too much about her for her to not get some answers from him. Yet, she can't move. She only stares after him, fear gripping her insides. As she felt she might scream for help from this obvious lunatic, she was saved by the barkeep coming back.

"Aye, you gotta pay for that, son."

The kind man was standing, cross-armed behind the bar with a rag in hand, a stern look towards the mysterious man who stood behind her. The man walked back towards the bar and pulled out a couple of pounds, placing them on the counter, his eyes glancing back at Lorelei as the now satisfied barkeep sauntered away.

"Lorelei, we don't have time. You need to come with me, *now.*"

How does he know my name?

Lorelei's heart raced beneath her chest; not only did she see this man in her dream, but he was here in the flesh, knew her name, and was spewing nonsense that if she didn't follow him, *she would die.*

If there was ever a time for Ashton Kutcher from that pranking show to appear...it would be now. Or if I could just wake up again from this in my hotel room, peacefully having fallen asleep after an exhausting day of travel, please..

Coming towards her, the man placed a white-knuckled hand on the bar counter, turning her chair to face him abruptly. He was so close to her, she thought she could smell a musky cologne, the scent of citrus and pine, perhaps? He leaned in closer, his lips brushing her ear so only she could hear his next words.

"Please, I want to help you...but I can't do that here."

Swallowing, her breath hitching at the back of her throat, she forwent all logic, feeling that same immediate familiarity in her dream; the way he made curiosity run rampant. She needed to figure out what was going on. He stepped away, allowing her room to pack up her stuff, and finishing the last bit of her beer, she slips on her jacket. The man waits for her, and then follows behind as she leads them out of the pub. Once outside, she looks around once again, but still, no Dean. Sighing, she turns to the man who is beside her now.

"So, where should we go then?"

He doesn't answer immediately. He was glancing around in a protective way like a guard dog making sure nobody was near, before pulling her over to the side of the pub in an alley. He unzips his hoodie, he wasn't wearing a shirt despite how cold it was. His toned body was still the same from when she saw him in her dream and she did her best to suppress the blush threatening to paint her face. To her shock, she saw the large, black wings snuggled against his back.

"Oh geez, I must be fucking drunk to be seeing this..."

"Hush, it's the quickest way back to your hotel room."

"How do you know...you know what never mind. I'm obviously dreaming. I fell asleep in my room at the hotel and all of this is a dream. Might as well go with the crazy flying man to see what's next, huh!?"

The man rolls his eyes at her once again, not in the mood to try and convince her otherwise. Holding out his arms towards her, he motions for her to come to him.

"Come on. We shouldn't be out here."

Lorelei can only laugh at him. No amount of curiosity or vague sense of affinity towards him would make her lose all sanity and hop into this stranger's arms and *fly* off into the sky.

"Haha, no way buddy. I'm good. This night is already too much for me to handle, there is no way in hell I am doing tha-a..."

The man growls and finally goes to her, throwing a strong arm around her waist, and before she can fathom what is happening, they are zooming up into the sky at stomach-lurching speed.

'Holy shit, holy shit, holy shiittttt!"

Lorelei screams as he whips across the night sky back towards her hotel. She buries her head into his chest, just waiting and hoping it will end soon. She couldn't help but think she was going certifiably insane. None of this could actually be real, right? But as quickly as he soared her into the night sky, he was swiftly lowering her onto the balcony outside her room. She continued to cling onto him, her hair severely wind-blown and practically falling out of her ponytail. He let her gain her legs for a moment, and then recoiled his arm from around her, walking towards the glass door, and sliding it open. He pulled his wings back, letting them once again rest bundled up upon his back and put the hoodie back on. Surprisingly, the hoodie covered the wings quite nicely, with nothing more than a slight bump where they lay. If she didn't know they were there, she would never have known. He would've looked like any normal guy-although most men don't have this shoulder-length silver hair and looked a mix of a rockstar and a rugged biker.

Lorelei stood watching a moment and then walked inside, sitting down on the bed, her mind racing and spinning like a tornado. After some minutes in silence, Lorelei looked over at the man, who was now sitting in the chair by the desk in the room.

"Who are you? And...and what are you? You were in my dream earlier today and now you're here, why? You obviously know who I am? And why isn't it safe? And how did you know that Dean would be a no show?"

She was on the verge of hyperventilating with each question she asked, placing a hand on her chest, she tried to slow her breathing, and then her eyes met his once again. Sighing, he pressed a finger at his temple, applying pressure and then answered.

"Alright, slow down. I'll answer every question you have. My name is Daemon, I'm an angel...well, a Fallen angel. But that's a long story so we are going to skip that for now. I have zero clue how you saw me in a dream, so on that point, I can't help you. I know of you, yes, but only because I know what you are meant to do, and I want to help make it happen."

He looks at her for a reaction, but she remains speechless, her previously sarcastic attitude from before replaced entirely by shock.

"It's not safe because there are demons around trying to harm you. They are trying to get rid of you before you can even fulfill your destiny, Lorelei. And that prat, Dean? I knew he wouldn't show because I made sure of it." Daemon made a smirk with this last bit of information, leaning back in the chair and throwing a hand behind his head to prop himself up, a satisfied grin spreading across his face.

Shaking her head, Lorelei could feel a severe headache coming on from the amount of thinking she was doing over all of this new information. Furrowing her eyebrows, she returned her attention to him.

"What do you mean by you made sure of it?"

Daemon leaned forward, his elbows on his knees, his pupils widening like those of a satisfied predator.

"What I mean is that Dean was a demon. Do you remember when you passed out before leaving for your little date? I made that happen so that you would be delayed. Although, I mistimed the casting of the spell that put you under. I meant to cast it when you were closer to the bed-sorry about that. I did it though so that I could get to Dean before he could get to you. I took him out, to protect you. Otherwise, you would be dead right now. So, you're welcome by the way."

Blinking several times trying to grasp what he said, she shook her head once more in hopeless denial.

"Dean couldn't be a demon. He didn't look like a demon for one and he was so kind and generous."

Daemon rolled his eyes and gave a slight growl of frustration.

"What do you think demons look like, hm? Horns protruding from their heads? Big ol' bat-like wings and jagged, snarling smiles?" He laughed and proceeded to lean back in his chair again, folding his arms across his chest.

"Demons only look that way in Hell, and most of the time it's never that grotesque; besides the particularly nasty faction bred specifically for nefarious purposes. Most demons only have a horn or two, not much more than that. They are quite gifted in taking the form of humans though, as well as being deceptively charming when the need arises. It's no surprise really that you would be hoodwinked by him, he was even better than most; a master at manipulation. His real name was Erigos, and he was a high level demon, *with the sole mission of ending your life*."

"Okay hold on, you said I have some destiny or something, which is why Dean, I mean....Erigos was trying to kill me? But all I am is a writer for a small magazine. I'm just trying to get by in life. What kind of destiny could I possibly have?"

Daemon rubbed the back of his head and then answered her question, his eyes meeting hers, with a look of surety.

"You have to save humanity, Lorelei."

"What?!"

Lorelei looked at him pleadingly, exasperated by the evening's events. She couldn't believe what Daemon was telling her, or the fact he was a Fallen angel or the fact that supposedly she flirted with a demon today and narrowly escaped death at its own hands. But especially the fact that Daemon said her destiny was to save humanity somehow. And he just admitted to committing actual murder; with a smile on his face. Or, was it considered murder if it was a blood-thirsty demon out to kill her? She wasn't ever the religious type, her father instilling in her from a young age to appreciate more than the Christian ideologies, she often explored religions and spiritualities from around the world, especially favoring concepts from Buddhism. She often recounted her friends hurrying off to church on Sundays, while she sat researching in the museum religions and belief systems across the globe. Questions always formulating as she found countless ideologies that fascinated and calmed her. Although she believed there had to be truth in all religions to some capacity—but to actually be standing face to face with a fucking angel? Her mind was spinning uncontrollably, causing the headache that had been slowly approaching to hit her at full strength and making her close her eyes, resting her head in her hands.

"So there's Heaven and Hell? And what religion is this all from? Are you on the 'good' side or...the bad?"

She was exhausted and she knew she couldn't process another word. Daemon finally stood, making his way over to stand before her. Lorelei looked up from her hands and met his gaze. He was much closer to her than she anticipated and although it made her heart beat faster; she didn't mind it.

Daemon's eyes grew darker, a wave of concern taking over his features that before seemed haughty and sarcastic. He spoke with her in a softer tone, like he knew this was too much to understand all at once—like he knew she was overwhelmed to the point of tears with this new information and the questions whirled rapidly through her mind, getting wilder and more convoluted with each passing second.

"Aye..aye..it's okay. I'll answer more of your questions. But first you need rest."

Daemon knelt and placed a hand on her shoulder. A pulsing warmth emanated from his palm and into her, spreading throughout the rest of her body, making Lorelei instantly feel a little calmer. Her headache began to ease and her heartbeat slowed down to its normal pace. Standing back up, Daemon walked over to the sliding glass door leading to the balcony, opening it, he let the cold air leak into the room. He turned back to her and spoke again.

"It's been a long and trying night for you. I will keep watch over your room to make sure you're safe, so you won't need to worry about that. I will be back in the morning for you."

Lorelei only nodded, words unable to formulate in her mind to make a response. She knew she needed to sleep, as she was starting to have that aching feeling deep in her muscles that always happened when you were beyond exhaustion. The only thing she could think of was to thank him for his help tonight, so she looked back up to do so, but he was already gone. The sliding door was once again closed and she was alone. Closing her eyes, she gathered what strength she had left to wash her makeup off and throw on an oversized t-shirt to sleep in. Once finished, she crawled into the bed, which although wasn't the most comfortable bed, welcomed her happily. She thought she might have problems shutting off her mind from all that happened that day, but within minutes, she was fast asleep.

CHAPTER 3

DAEMON

DAEMON STAYED OUT ON the rooftop of the hotel all night, keeping a close watch on Lorelei's room. It didn't bother him having to stay awake, he didn't sleep much anyways. Angels were always able to conserve energy, and many didn't sleep at all. Daemon himself enjoyed a good cat nap now and again, human life sort of dictated him to change his routine these days.

Sitting on the edge of the building's ledge, feet kicking in the air, he stood up to stretch, his neck and shoulders popping vigorously. The sun was starting to rise, glowing orange and blues filled the morning skyline as the sun rose over the building tops. He knew Lorelei would be waking shortly, so he decided to smoke a cigarette before flying down to her balcony. Pulling out a pack from his jean pocket, he flicked his thumb against his middle finger and made a small flame appear, lighting the cigarette and then stuffing the pack back in his pocket. It was a bad habit, he knew; one he picked up in the early 1900s; but it was calming and helped settle his mind when it went on one of its racing tangents. Daemon rubbed the back of his neck as he took a long drag, his mind trying to plan what should happen next. He honestly didn't really know, which frustrated him tremendously.

Magnus. I'll take her to see Magnus.

Daemon couldn't believe that he had forgotten about the old oracle. He'd known Magnus for a long time and if Daemon remembered correctly,

35

Magnus owed him one. Last he heard, Magnus was working out of a small shop back in London. Finishing the cigarette, he dabbed it out on the ground. The sooner they were on their way, the better. There were sure to be more demons other than Erigos, once they realized that he would no longer be returning.

Within a few moments, he was rapping his knuckles on the glass door to her room, where a much more awake Lorelei than he thought he'd be seeing was opening the door.

"Good morning." His tone was a bit awkward, unsure how she might be feeling after last night.

She smiled and turned on her heels heading back inside. She was already showered and dressed, which made him wonder if she got any sleep at all. Her sandy blonde hair was pulled into a long braid down her back, a few wispy pieces lay by her cheeks, and she had some light makeup on, which really accentuated her bright, blue eyes. She was wearing a brown, knitted sweater and a pair of black jeans with some black tennis shoes. The jeans fit her frame nicely he noted, which he then shook his head, trying to rid the thought from his mind. Looking over at her suitcase on the bed, she was practically packed. Did she already know they would have to be leaving here?

"Um...how did you sleep?" he asked nonchalantly, hoping he masked the surprise in his voice at her seemingly casual, and unphased mood; like this was all such a normal thing.

"I knocked out thankfully. Did you do something to make that happen?" She was packing up a small bag of makeup and bathroom supplies when she turned to him, giving him a slight eyebrow raise.

"How did you guess?" He was impressed with how well she'd handled the recent events.

36

"I don't know...I felt a light tingling sensation when you touched my shoulder last night, and within 5 minutes of you leaving, I was out like a light. Is that one of your powers?"

She walked her small bag over and placed it in her suitcase, zipping it up before one last look in the mirror.

"Yeah, you could say that. I thought it might help considering the day you had."

Lorelei smiled at him again as she lifted the suitcase off the bed onto the floor.

"It did help, thank you. So I am absolutely starving...I didn't realize until this morning that I never ate at the pub last night. I found a small café down the road. I thought we could get some breakfast and talk."

Daemon couldn't help smiling in return, it had been a while since he had a good meal, and they did need to discuss what their next steps were. But they couldn't dally, he didn't know how quickly somebody else would be sent after her. He needed to be on his guard, but he'd forgotten the last real meal he had recently, and the reminder in his belly agreed with a rumble.

She probably has had some time now to think of a million questions too...don't blame her though.

"Sure, sounds good. We can come back for your stuff after we eat. I could use some coffee."

"Haha, I could probably drink an entire pot by myself right now!" Lorelei jokes, grabbing her jacket and glancing over at the balcony.

Turning to see where her eyes shifted, he laughed.

"I think we will be normal people today and just go out your room door. Can't just go off and pull my wings out in broad daylight often, yanno." Smirking, he followed her out the door and down the stairs into the main lobby, before stepping out into the sunshine. They walked in silence a few blocks down the road to the Rendezvous Café. When they walked inside, the overwhelming smell of bacon and coffee greeted them. Picking a small two seater table near the front windows away from the other diners, they both ordered coffee and what they wanted to eat. Daemon decided on an omelet while Lorelei got some French toast covered in strawberries, along with some eggs and bacon. Daemon couldn't help but chuckle to himself at the girl's appetite. They both let their first cups of coffee start working their magic before speaking again. What an odd thing to be doing, sitting in a café, enjoying a breakfast after last night, and especially knowing that precious time was ticking away for literally everybody in this room.

For having just been told that a demon was trying to kill her before she was meant to save the world, she seemed to be handling it all better than he could've thought.

Taking a sip of his coffee, he looked around the tiny café. Families, couples, groups of friends were all enjoying a carefree breakfast full of sweet and savory goodness. Picturesque and completely oblivious to the ways of the Universe or that they were in any danger at all. Which equally awed and infuriated him—it was a burden to be the only blasted person around who knew the gravity of the situation they were in. He tempered his anxiety and brooding by returning his attention back to Lorelei; he saw she had already finished her coffee and was looking directly at him.

"Looks like you're ready to ask your questions now." Waving a hand flippantly in the air, a shimmery cloak-like bubble enveloped them at the table, making the voices in the restaurant muted. Lorelei blinked several times and touched the bubble, it reverberated and instantly went back in place. As if knowing what she was going to ask, Daemon smiled and spoke.

"It only lets those I allow see it. It doesn't affect anything other than their ability to overhear our conversation, making it so we're not interesting enough to eavesdrop on."

He could see she wasn't at all surprised, merely curious about his magic now more than scared as she was the night before.

Resilient one, isn't she?

"Alright, what's your first question?"

Lorelei nodded, gathering her thoughts and then proceeded.

"I guess my first question is, why me? Why am I the one who is supposed to save humanity?"

"Ahh...yeah that one I can't really tell you..."

He'd forgotten how much he himself didn't actually know about the situation.

"What do you mean you can't tell me?" Her eyebrows furrowed on her forehead as she asked.

"I mean I don't know why you're the, uh, 'chosen one,' for lack of a better name. Look, it's just a known thing, between all in Heaven and Hell, that you are the person responsible for saving humans when it all goes down, *if* you are able. Well...that's a lie. Only a select few know who you are and your destiny. I am not one of those select few but I know my way around how to find things out. Let's just leave it at that. For the reason why you were chosen, I can't answer. All I know is that an oracle prophesied a long time ago that a human girl would be capable of stopping Armageddon, or triggering its start. And that girl is you, Lorelei."

Lorelei silently nodded, looking as if the cogs in her head were working in overdrive trying to grasp what he said. A flare of panic flickered behind her eyes. He felt for her, but letting her have a moment to digest what he said, Daemon began looking around for the waitress, irritated that she hadn't come back around to refill their coffees. For a split second, he was tempted to use his powers to make her come back, as he saw she was chatting with another table across the café, but decided that keeping the barrier around them was more important than a caffeine fix; although Lorelei also looked like she could use a refill. Rolling his shoulders back, he tried to unkink the knots building in them. Keeping his wings bunched up was uncomfortable, despite the necessity to do so. Most humans; although believing in some higher power or magical entities; would still be incredibly shocked to see an angel walking around.

A Fallen angel actually....

The thought was always in the forefront of his mind. Like it was branded on his forehead permanently. Swirling memories of the day he fell from grace started to overtake him once again.

Frustratingly to himself, he chided, *"Now is NOT the time, Daemon."* As he finished the thought, Lorelei finally spoke again.

"So, Daemon, where do you come into all of this? I'm assuming you're an...angel? But I thought angels had white wings. Are you like my guardian angel or..?"

Her voice trailed off. He could tell she sort of hoped he might be her guardian angel, considering the danger she has found herself in. He was sure she hoped someone was looking out for her. Daemon was, in a sense, but really his intent was larger than that.

Since Daemon fell, he has lived among humans all around the world. After defying orders on one mission that changed his life forever, he decided to settle down in the UK, which had always been a favorite place of his since his touring days all those centuries ago. Until his fall, Daemon was a one of the angels who toured Earth, going between civilizations and keeping tabs on their progress, watching out for demons lurking about, who often interfered in human development. Sometimes he helped stage coups, battled in wars for one side or another, and took out demons disguised as higher authority when their rule became more of a bloodbath.

Daemon as a young angel, thought Earth was spectacular—and the power he wielded in the name of righteousness, was something that made him feel as though he was one of the trusted to carry out order in the name of God. He used to believe that it was for the greater good of humanity and for the agenda Heaven had for the future of mankind and the Universe, to commit some of the atrocities he did throughout his time touring. His duties were his life, the reason for his very existence, and he led them out with an iron fist-often sacrificing the few for the many. Typically, he was sent out to survey and keep tabs on certain areas on Earth, acting as a sort of guard against the henchmen of Hell, or even to make sure an event went as instructed. How one seemingly small event affected something larger later—it was his honor to make sure they saw the exact end needed for a future, greater purpose. Upon spending time with humans, despite the bad eggs in humanity, most were genuinely good. Just trying to get by with the day to day struggles of life.

It never occurred to him that Armageddon would ever come—to be honest—it felt more of a long-drawn-out taunting escapade between the two sides; one that most angels after centuries on Earth forgot about. Sounds ridiculous, but why make a race of beings only to be destroyed later? Especially when angels were tasked with keeping order, aiding humans' endeavors and even protecting them to certain extents. It was laughable really, and when or if war did come, everyone thought the humans would be protected in the end. *But how they were all wrong; **how Daemon was wrong.*** It was all a fantasy concocted in their heads the longer they were around the humans, the longer they got to know them and enjoy their company and intricacies. This was when he started seeing that their demise during the great battle, which was finally announced to happen within the next 50 years right before he fell, was cruel. Both Heaven and Hell were willing to completely decimate humanity to show off who was more powerful. Daemon saw that it was a vie for power, and it made him begin losing faith in his own work. In the very cause he was meant to uphold. The very reason he was made.

"Um, yeah. I am. As for my black wings, it's what happens when you fall from grace."

He gave a cavalier smile, holding his mug out as the waitress finally refilled their cups and left without even a word spoken. He hoped the response would satisfy her for the time being. Diving into that right now didn't sound too appealing at the moment. After a long sip of the hot beverage, he continued.

"And as for your last question, I am not your guardian angel. I am however an invested party. I am fond of humans. And I believe the war is pointless. I have come to offer what help I can. Things have been brewing quicker than expected...it seems that both sides are so ready to fight that there are rumors it could start even earlier. Which is why I came to you last night, and upon finding you, I found Erigos. This also means that Hell is playing their cards quietly and quickly, secretly sending out one of their best assassins to take you out of the equation, suggesting they want to begin the war as soon as possible. We have very little time."

While moving the strand of silver hair that always tended to fall over his face, he caught Lorelei's eyes. The gleaming pools of greyish-blue, unwavering and steady, flickered with determination that made a sharp pain ignite in his chest momentarily. Afraid that he had been staring for too long, he coughed and downed the rest of his coffee. Daemon couldn't help but look her way once more.

"You know, you're taking this incredibly well. In all honesty, with how you freaked last night, I thought you might have a hard time with all this."

The memory of her clutching to him as he flew into the night sky flickered across his mind. He forced himself to push it away.

"Well...my father used to tell me stories of the Bible and swore to me as a child that there was something more out there. He also shared a love of lots of different religions and ideologies, it wasn't like him to be pinned down to one thing, so I never really did either. I always sort of thought that there must be truth behind most of them, and although I never became a religious person, I always thought there was an explanation. A greater understanding of the way the Universe works and the way humanity fits in that equation. I always hoped I had a destiny that was bigger than me. One I could grow, one I could live up to—that meant something. Or, at least, I always hoped that's how it was. Which I guess is why believing that before now could be helping me deal with the fact some angel out of a fantasy action movie scooped me up in the night telling me I'm some kind of "Chosen One" who must save humanity from annihilation."

The playful sarcasm of her last sentence took Daemon by surprise. She laughed loudly and unapologetically, and despite himself, he couldn't help but laugh along with her. It radiated throughout the café, although the enchantment was still keeping them from being noticed too much. Only a couple of heads turned in their direction and were quickly deterred by an oncoming arrival of food or a switch in the conversation.

Keeping up an enchantment such as this for long periods of time always made Daemon feel strained—like a piece of him was detached or missing while casting it. This wasn't uncommon; most all magic had its small effects. For instance, actually commanding someone to do something can cause severe headaches and sometimes even nausea for him.

Celestial speak, or the Enochian language, is the original language of the angels. When humanity was created however, many angels who lived among humans, began lessening their usage of it and speaking human languages instead. After so many centuries, only the most elder angels use it commonly. But most others never used it anymore. Daemon continued to speak it, unable to fully let go of that connection he once had to the place of his people. The only time it was used these days was when using a very potent form of magic that required the ancient language's power. And one of the most powerful spells in which to serve a final killing blow to a demon was *"Fvue Finiethal Spem."* The Finishing Spell. The one he just performed last night. Which explained why he was over-straining a bit from using his magic today.

Typically it was spoken with a chant-like quality to enhance its influence. Within moments, it incinerates the demons, and it was the only method in ridding them that angels had. That was an angel's death wish, overexertion of energy. If you're not careful enough, you suck yourself dry, quite literally. It is one of the only ways an angel dies—if not killed in battle—for no being is ever fully immortal. Daemon reminded himself of this as he lowered his energy output to their little shield, it was a quiet café. Perhaps they were safe for the time being.

Lorelei looked at him, seeing if he was planning on saying anything, but when he didn't, she continued.

"So, what's next? You said I am supposed to figure it out for myself what it is I have to know, but I have no clue how to go about doing that."

Daemon finished the last couple of bites of his omelet that he had all together forgotten about since it was brought out, and sat back feeling a little lighter, the food replenishing him. He felt a surge of power and the enchantment's load became easier on him once again. Looking up to see that Lorelei had also finished her meal, he scooted his seat back and stood, stretching before answering her.

"I have a friend of mine who I think can help us. He owes me for a bit of trouble I got him out of years back, so I think it's time he pays me back with a little information."

Lorelei merely nodded, "Where are we off to then?"

"Back to London, that's where he is set up these days. I'll go pay the check and then we can head back to your hotel to grab your things before setting off to the airport.

With a raise of her eyebrow, she gave a smirk. "Do angels pay tabs?"

Daemon purposely rolled his eyes.

"*Cheeky*. I can't go around breaking all of society's rules, especially when the waitress will call the police and draw attention to us, including the attention of possible demons nearby about a strangely, overly handsome man.." he paused, raising his eyebrow at her for effect, "leaving a Scottish cafe right after they sent an agent here to dispatch you. Yes, I will pay the tab and we will be quietly on our way like good little tourists. Fair enough?"

"You're not going to fly us back yourself?" She said teasingly.

He paused momentarily while grabbing a toothpick from the dispenser on the table.

"You're heavy enough as is. And with your luggage, it'd take us far longer than we can allow to get back to London from here."

Sticking the toothpick in his mouth, he sauntered off towards the front counter to pay. He let his enchantment wear off entirely as he walked, watching the once muted tones of the other people in the café resume their normal volume level. Out of the corner of his eye, he watched as Lorelei walked into the ladies restroom. Figuring he didn't need to wait outside the bathroom door for her, he walked outside. The sun was warming the day, even though there was still a cool breeze that made the leaves on the trees in the courtyard across the street rustle. Pulling out the pack of cigarettes from his jeans, he looked around to ensure no prying eyes would see him once again snap his fingers and secretively light it.

Suddenly the hairs on the back of his neck stood up and he rolled his eyes, taking a longer drag than usual, and turned to his right where a man dressed in an all white suit, his short golden hair in wistful waves upon his sleek, slender face whipping in the wind. He stepped out of the shadow of the awning above the restaurant. Daemon took the cigarette from his lips slowly, sizing the man up warily. A familiar humming sensation—the one that told him that it was an old friend in particular. A feeling that used to bring comfort, now only brought pain.

For it was an indication that Daemon was once again in the presence of the angel who betrayed him.

Holding the cigarette between his fingers, Daemon crossed his arms and finally looked up to meet the figure's gaze, shoulders tensing, ready for whatever might come next; his words laced with unease as he spoke.

"Hello, Raphael. Long time, no see."

Chapter 4

Lorelei

STANDING IN FRONT OF the mirror in the café bathroom, Lorelei finished washing her hands and then took a moment to look at herself. Although she still looked tired, she still looked the same as she always had, even though now—everything was drastically changed. Thoughts of her and Daemon's conversation during breakfast were swimming through her head.

I don't look like somebody who could save the world.

But from the moment she met Daemon and from all that he has told her so far, it was almost just as impossible to deny. First, Daemon could fly. Really, fucking fly. If he hadn't scooped her in his arms and she had not experienced that first hand; Lorelei knew the rest of what he said to her would be far harder to believe. *Yet* she had experienced it. Although absolutely terrifying, it was exhilarating, too. And, most importantly, she can't whisk that truth away easily no matter how many pints she had that evening.

At the same time, something inside her felt the words he spoke to be true. A deep longing in the pit of her chest, a whisper of some kind, her intuition possibly? She couldn't be sure, but despite her not understanding the reasons and despite the nagging feeling in the back of her mind attempting to convince her otherwise, her curiosity was getting the best of her. Wasn't every human's desire to know what their purpose was? To know why they were created? Lorelei couldn't help but want to know more about who she is, and why she is the one who was chosen to do this. What could this mean for her? *About* her? It was long since that she felt out of sorts, out of the loop since her father's passing. This experience, although incredibly new and outstandingly difficult to process, was feeling more right to her with each passing second, than her day-to-day life had in almost a year. Something about Daemon, about what he explained to her about the workings of Heaven and Hell; it reminded Lorelei of her father. The way he used to speak of these things, the way he used to hold her in his lap and tell her that there was no sure answer, but that when something came calling, something monumental, it was time to answer the call of the Universe; because it was taking you someplace better, *somewhere you needed to go.*

It was the closest she'd felt to her father since that awful day a year ago—and she couldn't stop herself from chasing his words, to find out if this indeed was a calling for her to find herself again. The darkness that slowly crept up on her in the last year was overbearing, and even with her days typically being alright, she felt a hole in her heart she couldn't ignore. A displacement in the city she adored. An echo in her mind of an endless unknown—an unknown of what would become of her if she stayed stuck in that pit. The work kept her busy, sure. But she found herself more and more drawn to the idea that there must be something more for her than this, if she could only find a sign.

This was her sign.

It came in a bonus package of black wings and snarky attitude—but she was taking it as a sign nonetheless. Could it end in hellfire and damnation? Yes. But could it also end in something more? Something fulfilling? Enlightening? She only hoped it was the latter, because she had no clue what to do, and the thought of failing made her insides ball into a million knots. Bile threatened to come up the back of her throat, and she steadied herself on the sink with her hand, the surge of denial plaguing her thoughts, the headache she felt the night before beginning to resurface. Lorelei gripped the sink harder, closing her eyes and forcing herself to breathe.

Deep breathes, come on, Lorelei. You can't falter now. Remember the little voice...the one that has always guided you. Breathe and listen.

After a moment, Lorelei's heartbeat finally relinquished to a steadier pace, allowing the pain in her head to dissipate—she was incredibly affected physically by her emotions, it was always that way. A crying episode could result in being in bed for the whole day afterwards from the headache and racking pains her body often got. Once the headache died down, she willed herself to clear her mind. Finding the small, lit pathway she envisioned whenever she needed to connect with that guiding voice. She called it her intuition, but wasn't sure if it was that or something she made up—but it never steered her wrong if she only let herself hear it. Reaching the end of the path in her mind, a clearing of blue and violet light came to her vision and she breathed. There were no warning bells, no sirens of distress coming from her. She didn't need to listen to those negative, harmful voices now. What she needed now, was to stay calm. She had to take the leap into whatever this journey might become, her father would've said so. Opening her eyes, she unclenched her hands and released the sink. She splashed a bit of water on her face, and whispered to herself.

"You can do this. Whatever happens, seek the truth, like Dad always said. It's better than staying in the dark.."

Which is where she has been. Determined it was time to seek whatever came before her, she nodded to herself once more, slinging her bag over her shoulder, leaving the bathroom, and making her way back to the table where she thought Daemon would be waiting for her. But when she saw that he wasn't there, she looked out the window and saw Daemon's well-built back facing her. Finding her way outside, she thanked the hostess before hearing the tinkle of the bell above the door as she exited the café.

Before her was Daemon. And beyond him, standing nearby, was another man. She stepped closer to Daemon and stood beside his shoulder. He seemed tense, but not in the same way he did last night when they were leaving the pub. Daemon's eyes didn't once turn to her, instead, they remained locked on the individual before them.

The man was tall, with a smaller frame than Daemon, but didn't lack any of the strength. Lorelei noted he sort of looked like one of those K-pop stars she used to listen to a few years back. The suit he wore made him stand out from any other person around, which Lorelei thought might've been the point. He had dark, almond-colored eyes and perfectly placed, blonde hair that flipped out in an intentionally haphazard manner. There was tension in the air between them all, and Lorelei could tell Daemon had no intention of speaking first. Lorelei caught the man's eyes and they gleamed with realization. He gives a fierce look to Daemon, a mixture of surprise, and disappointment.

"So, the rumors are true. You are helping her."

His voice was similar to Daemon's, but it had more of a regal sounding nature about it. A lovely combination of poise and intensity. Whoever this was, Lorelei could tell he was important. The way he carried himself, the outlandish outfit, and the way Daemon's shoulders shifted uncomfortably, spoke volumes. She hadn't thought that anything could catch Daemon off guard.

"Yeah. What's it to you?"

Daemon's tone was harsher than she had heard it yet. But there was an underlying nervousness that made even Lorelei herself worried.

Who could this possibly be to make Daemon so nervous?

The man just shook his head as Daemon took another drag of the cigarette he was holding.

"Let's walk. That courtyard over there, seems quiet enough for a little chat."

Daemon didn't say anything in response, merely followed reluctantly behind as the man in white walked across the street and into the courtyard. Clearly, Daemon didn't find being in the man's presence enjoyable, but at the same time, didn't offer any type of sarcastic remark or refusal to follow. Daemon obeyed, and for some reason, this lack of fight, made Lorelei all the more hesitant—and frightened.

Who could possibly make Daemon so uncomfortable, at the same time, command such authority that Daemon didn't even try to say no?

Lorelei silently followed the two men. There were a few benches around a large water fountain. Shrubbery in different shapes and sizes lay in a semi-circular formation around it, although no flowers were blooming, it was a lovely spot. The fountain had the image of a figure in a leaping position, its features were striking, its body built for the intricate movement it was performing, the eyes glaring down at them as they stood before it. Much like the man's eyes when he turned to face them, an eerily similar gaze that made Lorelei's heart race again. Nobody else was around, they were totally alone. She wondered if this acquaintance of Daemon's was making that the case. Daemon was able to keep a barrier around them at breakfast so nobody heard their conversation; there must be other magic that allowed the vacancy they were experiencing. Waiting a few moments, she was relieved when Daemon spoke.

"Have you come here to stop me, Raphael? Because the fact that you're even speaking to me, could cost you."

Raphael?

The name sounded familiar but she couldn't explain the reason why. Raphael sighed before responding.

"Mind if I grab a cigarette from you?"

51

Daemon glared at him, but slid the pack out of his pocket, throwing it to him.

"I thought you kicked the habit?"

"Well, considering that I am violating the "no contact" policy with you, a smoke feels necessary."

Catching the pack, he pulled one out, tossing it back to Daemon before snapping his fingers. To Lorelei's surprise, a flame flickered on his fingertips as he dipped the cigarette into it and shook his hand, the flame disappearing like it had never been. He took a drag and then shifted his weight, eyeing them both.

"You know that what you're doing is pointless, right?"

Daemon shrugged his shoulders at this and having finished his own cigarette, flicked it into a nearby trash can.

"Wasn't it you who told me that nothing in this world was pointless?"

"This is different. It's not just Lucifer who wants you dead, Daemon. The other ArchAngels are thinking you have become too much of a problem to allow it to continue, too."

"Oh? Well how thoughtful of them to think about me. I would've thought that I was too beneath you all to even be on your radar any longer."

"You're not if you're interfering in what is meant to be."

ArchAngel? Could this really be the ArchAngel Raphael? From the Bible!?

Lorelei tried to remember what she knew about him but she could hardly think due to the shiver that ran up her spine, her focus on the being before her changing first from admiration, to panic. They were pissing off all the wrong people-and they had hardly begun their little crusade. This couldn't be good.

When Daemon didn't respond again, Raphael looked at him, with a slight desperation behind his eyes. Daemon at last acknowledged Lorelei, and gestured a hand towards Raphael.

"Lorelei, love, I'd be honored to introduce you to ArchAngel Raphael. My old, best friend who so happens to be the one who carried out the ceremony to condemn me as a Fallen. Surprised? Yes, as am I. He hasn't dared return to Earth since that fateful day." Daemon's mocking tone changed to pure venom in his next words. "So tell me, Raph. What are you fucking doing here?"

Lorelei's mouth dropped open. No wonder Daemon hated being in Raphael's presence so much. It made far more sense the discomfort he was displaying, and it made Lorelei's heart clench at the recognition of suffering she saw flicker in Daemon's eyes while he looked at Raphael.

"I never wanted to have to condemn you, Daemon. You know that. But it had to be done. You disobeyed orders. The fact that I am here shows I still care for you like a brother. Please, don't be a fool. This isn't worth dying over."

This sparked something in Daemon and he finally turned back around to face him, an anger seeped out of him which made Lorelei catch her breath.

"And what, Raph?! It's worth the entire human race to die over some pricks who just want to show off how powerful they are? How can you stand by as humanity is slaughtered during a war that's not really about them!?"

He was breathing harder, the anger in his words shook Lorelei to her core. It wasn't just the anger she felt, it was compassion. For a moment, she thought of going to him. To comfort him. But she merely watched as the two men stared each other down.

"It's how it is, Daemon! Only God knows the true meaning behind it, but we angels are ones tasked to carry out his will. Like **YOU** were supposed to do 16 years ago. Or did you forget?"

With those words Raphael turned and looked at Lorelei again. She shifted nervously under his gaze, like he was judging her. Inspecting her in some way. And he didn't look happy with what he was seeing.

"It's wrong. And since I am no longer one of your lackeys—which if you recall was orchestrated by your own hands—I have no affiliation with your agenda anymore. Therefore, you are free to go fuck right off. Because you and I both know that unless you have direct orders, you have no authority to end my life."

Raphael looked like he might give a similarly angry retort, but Lorelei saw he stopped himself. She watched as he sighed, and took another drag of his cigarette.

"I came to give you a friendly warning. The rumors of what you are attempting to do has spread. Lucifer is more enraged than ever and is sending more demons your way. Not to mention if the other ArchAngels decide you need to be eliminated as well. The deliberations are ongoing, but I fear a decision will be made soon. I am risking everything by coming to tell you this, and you know that. So, please...hear me when I say you may want to rethink this plan of yours...before it's too late. I don't want to lose a friend."

With a huff, Daemon walks slowly over to Lorelei and gives her a look. They were leaving now. Fixing the strap of her bag that had fallen off her shoulder, Daemon being nearer to her made her feel safer. They were not going to die this moment. At least that was a little comforting to know. Turning back to Raphael, he ran a hand through his hair and once again put back on the blasé persona, shooting Raphael a coy smile.

"Well thanks, *friend*. But you and I both know I lost that friend the day you cast me out. You better be getting back to your cohorts, before you end up like me."

Daemon's tone was airy, but a sense of intensified concern laced it. It hit Lorelei for the first time how much danger they were both in. Not only did Hell wish to see their mission fail, but Heaven wasn't on board with it either. And from what she could tell, Raphael had something to do with Daemon becoming a disgraced angel. Before he allowed Raphael to respond again, Daemon took Lorelei by her arm and started leading her back towards her hotel. Taking one last look over her shoulder, she saw Raphael's eyes pleadingly watching her. Regret and sadness tinged his caramel irises, until he turned on his heels, walking in the opposite direction. The fading, white silhouette disappearing beyond the descending sidewalk.

They didn't speak for what felt like an eternity, and Lorelei found it hard not to turn around and look back at Raphael. She thought perhaps Daemon was on edge from the unexpected visit from his old friend, seeing as he still had a gentle grip on her arm. But he appeared to be in deep thought, and she didn't want to disturb him yet. She couldn't help but find his touch soothing. It made her feel less alone in this crazy, up-side-down situation she found herself in. She had so many questions about the interaction that happened, so when they were nearly back at the hotel, she broke the silence.

"Are you alright?"

She was getting concerned. Daemon looked panicked, which didn't reassure her. Upon hearing her voice, he blinked and finally released the soft hold on her. He placed the hand he just had on her arm on the back of his neck and rubbed it, looking a little embarrassed for forgetting to let go of her.

"Yeah, I'm fine."

She could tell it was a sensitive subject to him, so she waited a moment until he continued.

"I haven't seen him since...well, you know. I was never allowed to return to Heaven after that, so I haven't seen Raphael since that day. And since I also wasn't affiliated with Hell, I was left to my own devices on Earth by both sides."

His green eyes flashed with memory, like he could relive that day he fell from God's grace in his head over and over. He sighed and once again pulled his cigarettes out, a habit of years of tormented loneliness. It was another few minutes before he spoke again.

"It's a huge deal that he came to warn me of what was going on. If the other ArchAngels found out...he could end up like me; or worse."

Lorelei could only imagine what "worse" meant. The last image of Raphael remained in her mind, the way it seemed Raphael felt badly for what happened with Daemon. How much it looked like Raphael wanted to say more, but thought better of it. It honestly broke her heart, but it was Daemon she felt worse for. Shoving her hands in her coat pockets, the warmth of the soft material inside, slowly warming her increasingly cold fingers, she watched Daemon's face carefully as they continued on their walk back to the inn. Worry and sorrow imprinted on each, handsome feature. Clearing her throat, she let her gaze fall to the sidewalk ahead of them.

"He mentioned that there was a mission you were ordered to do that you didn't and that's why you became a Fallen angel. What was it you didn't do?"

The worried, and haggard Daemon suddenly vanished, like a window into his true feelings was promptly shut between them. The collected, nonchalant Daemon returned. Turning his head towards her, he put on a casual smile.

"That's not important right now...What is important is getting to Magnus as quickly as possible. Bright side, have you ever flown in First Class?" Daemon's smile broadened as he picked up his pace—his mind already on preparations for the next phase of their trek.

"No, but is it absolutely necessary to fly in First Class? Won't that draw more attention to us?"

When they finally reached the inn, Daemon opened the door for her to walk through and shrugged his shoulders as he spoke, a haughty tone now fully replacing the saddened one from before, a mischievous glint in his jade-inspired eyes.

"Who says we can't have a little fun before the end of the world, hm?"

CHAPTER 5

LORELEI

LORELEI LOOKED AROUND HERSELF, still impressed with *how* exactly Daemon got them First Class seats on a plane back to London; he tended to brush over the part of his well-off means or methods, which she felt, if a being has been around long enough on Earth, one could suspect he's got investments and ways to acquire wealth. Lorelei had never flown first class before, and she was not used to the large comfortable seats that allowed her to turn to face Daemon's, or the impeccable service of the cabin crew that delivered a large plate of meats and cheeses for them to snack on. Not to mention the Bellini she was contentedly sipping. They were the only ones in First Class, which she mentioned to Daemon who reservedly muttered a bunch of nonsense to the effect of "*Must've not been a busy flight, love.*"

When the flight was announcing its takeoff and no one else joined them in first class, she watched as he downed the remainder of the bourbon he was drinking before he answered her most recent question about who Magnus was.

"Magnus is an oracle I've known for many centuries. We met back in ancient Greece when I was doing some work out in Delphi. He was studying under Pythia, who was the Oracle of Apollo—The Greek god of the Sun. When in reality, Apollo was actually ArchAngel Michael, who was acting as Apollo, relaying messages to the Oracle Pythia. This was common at the time, many of the stories behind Gods or Goddesses were angels. That was before the ArchAngels started pulling back on their influence over humanity in such a manner. Early human civilization needed a lot of help back, it was frequently a nasty business."

"What were you doing there?"

"I was on a guarding tour. A lot of the major ancient cities were hubs for demons hiding in disguise trying to upset the balance, which was easy to do back then. My mission was to keep an eye on the city and eradicate any demons who happened to pass through in hopes of causing trouble. Anyways, I met Magnus there and stayed in touch after I left the city. It wasn't until many, many years later that the little worm came asking for my help."

To hear Daemon speak in such a demeaning way about an oracle made Lorelei raise her eyebrow at him. He chuckled as he saw her look of confusion.

"Magnus is a pretty good oracle, as oracles go. But he was never like Pythia who was getting direct messages from an angel. Magnus is more like a knock-off in that arena. Easily manipulated and not good enough to discern whether his messages are coming from the good side, or the bad."

He paused for a moment, trying to think of how to explain it to her.

"Not all oracles are powerful ones or have the Sight as well as others might. Some, like Pythia, were in good graces with Heaven and therefore her Sight was enhanced and was in direct contact with who she thought was Apollo. Pythia was also a powerful meditator, often going into trances for hours at a time to Divine her prophecies. Having the power to see the future as a human isn't common, but it is common for those who do, to be in such a fair standing with Heaven for angels to feel the need to enhance the oracles to see what is truly meant to occur. In other words, as I mentioned to you before, demons are deceptively good at taking on the form of not only humans, but giving off the notion that they are other-worldly or in this case, angels themselves. They know the lingo, they know what humans wish to hear, and they know that even a low-level oracle can be steered in the wrong direction if they don't catch on to where their visions are coming from."

"If that's the case, I can only guess that Magnus is not one of those highly gifted oracles and he was led astray by a demon."

"Bingo! Magnus for the most part is a shit "Seer" and has never used his abilities for the greater good; he only ever used them to get ahead in life. And being that way on top of being a terrible oracle, is a one way ticket to getting yourself into some serious trouble."

Lorelei mulled over what she was learning about Magnus and was starting to question why Daemon had picked him to go to. It wasn't looking like he was going to be much help to them.

"What was it that you helped him with?"

"It's a pretty humorous story, in my opinion. Magnus hopped around after training under Pythia and began working as an oracle for all sorts of historical figures...I was over in Belgium, which in the grand scheme of things, was a shit place to be at the time. I still don't understand why we didn't take the bastard out entirely to begin with, but those weren't my orders. So much loss... "

He didn't have to say what was going on at the time for her to guess where he was going with his story. With her extensive history backlog, within seconds she recalled what historical event was happening in Belgium over 200 hundred years ago. Meaning if her calculations were right, that would be near the year 1815. And what big thing happened in Belgium around that time? The Battle of Waterloo.

"The Battle of Waterloo was around that time, huh?"

She watched as Daemon's face filled with surprise.

"Yeah, it was. Man, you are full of surprises, how did you guess that?"

Lorelei felt a flush threatening to turn her cheeks a bright red at his semi-compliment.

"My father worked in a museum. He was the one who gave me a love for history and I used to read book after book on various topics. So I put two and two together."

Lorelei saw that Daemon was making an effort to refrain from smiling at her, seeing his eyes shift over her momentarily before he responded again.

"Well, Magnus was working as Napoleon Bonaparte's oracle. A lot of Historians say that his oracle was some manuscript found; a book actually; but in reality, it was a person. Anyways, Napoleon was a superstitious man and seeing as Magnus was...well the slimy little git he is, I wasn't surprised to hear he took that position. Magnus aided Napoleon by telling him the outcomes of his battles, and up until Waterloo, he divined correctly and was seen in high regard by Napoleon. But, he wasn't clever enough to see past the lie of the vision about the Waterloo outcome. A demon named Charun was the one behind the false vision. By the time Magnus realized his mistake, he knew he would be killed by Napoleon if he stuck around. He came to me, knowing I was in Belgium and begged for me to help him get away and start a new life somewhere else. He wanted me to use my thrall to make Napoleon forget Magnus was ever his oracle, to concoct the tale of the oracle book that everyone knows of today, so that he wouldn't come looking for him."

Lorelei furrowed her brows, confused. "Why did you help him? If he was doing bad things, why help someone like that?"

Daemon rubbed the back of his neck, "I didn't do it without cause, the higher angels already knew the war was coming to an end—but Magnus would be killed if the ArchAngels found out. I guess I didn't see a bother, I felt for the bugger—he was wrong, absolutely, but he was also an idiot, and not all idiots deserve immediate death. Especially since Napoleon was being dealt with. I told him if he ever divined for another person with that much power and authority again, I'd hand him over to the ArchAngels myself. He happily accepted my conditions. Now, he only does minor divining for lowlifes and people concerned that their boyfriend or girlfriend isn't their soulmate. That kind of thing. He isn't much harm to anyone anymore, trust me, I keep tabs on him."

Lorelei finished off the last bit of her Bellini and set the empty glass down. She still was finding it difficult to wrap her head around the fact that Daemon had been around for thousands of years, even though he only looked to be in his mid 20s. His silver hair lightly brushed the top of his shoulders, falling over his left eye again, and she got a little lost in watching him. Not realizing that she was doing so until he made eye contact with her again and a tiny hitch in her heartbeat brought her back to reality. His gaze into her own was piercing, and familiar. Ever since she first met him, Lorelei had this persistent inkling inside of her that she wasn't able to shake. It was as if she knew him before; in another time. Yet, she was positive that couldn't be the case. They had never met before.

Lorelei pretended to shuffle around something in her bag afterwards, afraid he knew she had been staring at him. But out of the corner of her eye, as she grabbed her lipgloss from her bag, she saw that he, too, continued to watch her. And it made her heart race for what felt like unknown reasons. After applying it, she cleared her throat and tried to carry on with the conversation.

"If he isn't that great of an oracle then, why are we going to him? I'm sure you know of..." She paused to think of the right way to phrase her next thought, "More qualified ones who might be a better chance at helping us."

A look of defeat washed over his face, and even though it was only for a split second, only a breath's worth of time, Lorelei still caught it before he put on his signature carefree charm once again.

"You see, as a Fallen, many oracles are too scared to interact with me. They think if they do so, their abilities will start to become tainted and they will end up being less useful to those they serve or divine for. But Magnus has always been a bit slimy, so I know he will be unwilling to keep his curiosity to himself when it comes to our situation. He's also the only one scared enough of me to actually sit down and chat with us. Plus, he knows he owes me."

He finished by giving a smug smile that made Lorelei wonder just how powerful he was before he fell...and how powerful he still was today.

As the thought formulated in her mind, the flight attendant came over the intercom to announce their arrival to Heathrow Airport. The next phase of their journey was now setting in motion. They had to get to Magnus, so he could hopefully tell them how Lorelei can unlock the secret to saving humankind. From what Daemon said, getting some answers from him looked promising. Lorelei's mind was someplace else entirely as they grabbed her luggage and made their way off the plane. Talking to Magnus was the easy part. But what of the rest of the mission? With both Hell's and Heaven's eyes upon them at full force, who's to say they would even make it to Magnus' alive?

CHAPTER 6

DAEMON

DURING THE FLIGHT, LORELEI and Daemon mostly spoke of different historical events or how Lorelei got a job with the magazine, which Daemon chuckled upon hearing she actually spilt her coffee on Mr. Fletcher the day of her interview. The conversation was easy and enjoyable with her, but a constant nagging about the surprise meeting with Raphael tugged at the back of his mind, having rattled him more than he originally thought. His mind couldn't stop thinking over what Raph said.

"It's not just Lucifer who wants you dead, Daemon. The other ArchAngels are thinking you have become too much of a problem to allow it to continue, too."

These words were haunting him.

Not only do we have to fend off Lucifer's assault...The other ArchAngels are thinking of getting involved. And if that's the case, we are in deeper shit than I thought.

Daemon wasn't sure he was strong enough to fend off both sides at once. It's difficult enough that Lucifer more than likely sends his best demons after them to keep Armageddon on track. Although strong, in comparison to Raphael, Daemon wasn't as capable as he used to be. With the last thought fluttering across his mind, a feeling of guilt bubbled inside of him. Turning to watch Lorelei, who was looking out of the window of the cab they got outside the airport, his heart twisted; and her question popped into his mind as well.

"He mentioned that there was a mission you were ordered to do that you didn't, that's why you became a Fallen angel. What was it you didn't do?"

There was no way he could tell her that, but it made his insides churn at the thought of keeping something from her.

Suddenly Lorelei turned back to him, and gave a small, reassuring smile. Which only made it hurt more to be keeping such a secret. When she finally turned away, he felt a sense of relief.

She is so strong. Stronger than I could've imagined. How she's handling this, even with so much at stake, is admirable.

He recalled her staring at him back on the plane, and his heart gave a lurch. Frustrated with himself because of this; he was grateful to see they'd finally gotten to their next destination. Camden Markets; where Magnus' shop was set up.

When the car came to a stop, he saw Lorelei looked confused, but he simply got out of the car and purveyed the crowd that was scuttling about the market. When he sensed Lorelei made her way to his side, he felt a little better. The closer she was, the easier for him to protect her if something went down.

And the closer she is, the more it soothes you....

He let out a huff. Of course he knew this was also true. Ever since the night he decided to get involved, her presence, her sense of calm about the situation, about the sheer absurd danger they were both in—made something inside of him relax when she was near. She was only human, and yet she had the tenacity and courage of somebody he had never seen prior. Daemon always felt humans had a knack for standing brave in situations of difficulty, but Lorelei was on another level.

Making an effort to shake these thoughts away, he nodded to Lorelei; a signal to stay close. There was no point to cast the enchantment to keep eyes off of them, there were so many people; they blended right into the crowd. When it seemed difficult for Lorelei to keep up, he turned silently to see her attempting to shove her way past a rowdy group of teens, and as she finally approached him, she smiled brightly.

"Busiest day in Camden Markets I have ever seen! I haven't seen a sunny day like this in London for quite some time. How lovely! Oh, and look—sunflowers!"

She chuckled, pointing to a flower stand they passed. He rolled his eyes at her playfully.

"Let me guess, they're your favorite, hm?"

Lorelei nodded vigorously, and Daemon couldn't help but find her excitement incredibly refreshing.

How does this girl act so unaware of the danger she's in? It's impossibly enchanting.

"Ah, of course they are. Well, now I have new ammo to use against you. I will forever call you Sunflower, now. My own personal nickname to torment you relentlessly. You should tire of sunflowers soon enough if I have something to do with it."

Lorelei raised her eyebrow at him in the way that confirmed he knew was succeeding in he quest to tease her; they may be in the middle of a deadly mission; but the expressions he elicited from her made his chest tighten, it was worth it a million times over.

"Ha ha, you're very clever, Daemon."

Rolling his shoulders back, he flashed her his most devilish smile.

"Now, dear Sunflower, would you mind happily moving your *arse* a bit quicker? Or are all flowers slow as molasses?"

Lorelei returned the eye roll and continued to look about the colorful array of shops and food stalls. The busied shoppers and their totes full of delectable treats and parcels. Daemon thought if this were any other day, how nice it would be. It was a perfect day for an outing, he too, couldn't remember when the day shone so brightly over London. It felt ominous, however—like it might be the last sunny day they have left. With Raphael's warning ringing in his mind, her getting picked off by demons in a crowd like this would be far too easy, which was increasingly becoming more likely; every few minutes he was finding her stuck behind groups of people struggling to make her way through. He couldn't risk her falling behind, or letting his thoughts wander to places that are meaningless unless they succeed. Before, it was just a joke to keep up, now the playfulness was replaced with urgency and fear; he couldn't let her get further behind.

When she made her way past another group of shoppers, he hooked a finger in her beltloop—the quickest thing he could grab to pull her near him, which forced a severe blush along her cheeks.

"Sunflower, I swear you are a *hazard*." He whispered roughly, his words more seductive than he anticipated and he immediately regretted his choice to grab her this way. Something about this woman made him react uncharacteristically instinctive—she literally pulled it out of him without even trying, and how natural it was worried him. Hurrying to release his finger from her pants, he cleared his throat.

"We need to make sure we don't get separated again. Here, I'll lead you." As he finished his sentence, he sent out a hand towards her. She blinked a couple of times, obviously still surprised by the previous gesture. He slapped on his signature attitude as he saw her hesitate.

"It's the easiest way to make it through the crowd without losing ya. I know how exciting it must be, don't get used to it."

She raised her eyebrow at him, making Daemon wonder if he offended her, afraid his remark came out too rude; after the moment of panic he felt from his instinct to grab her the way he did mere moments ago, he worried. Then she finally clasped her hand with his, rolling her eyes. He tried to hide the smile she incited in him; she was damn cute. He gripped her hand tightly and began leading her through the market. Holding her hand felt right; shockingly, it wasn't awkward at all. It felt like something he'd been missing in his life until this moment. A calm washed over him, and for the first time since meeting Raph, he let a sigh release. Her presence was increasingly becoming a comfort to him in a way he never experienced before. Over the centuries, he had been with women, obviously. But he'd never fallen in love. Never felt the instant connection like he did with Lorelei.

The only reason you feel that way is because of…Shut up! I know.

It was so hard to focus and stay on guard when he was having this constant duel in his head, but was happy with the distraction from himself when he finally saw the alley where he last heard Magnus was working from. It wasn't on the main strip of the market, but tucked away down what looked to be a deserted alleyway. The noise of the crowd was beginning to dissipate as they made their way further and further until he saw a small, dingey-looking door.

Before entering, he looked at Lorelei.

"Let me do most of the talking, alright?"

"Sure. Okay."

Her voice held back nerves but she remained firm. Was she going to keep surprising him like this? Releasing her hand, an instant cavity filled the space where their hands had been joined. Ignoring the feeling, he turned and made his way inside.

Daemon slowly opened the door which led into the dimly lit shop. The walls were covered in shelves that held all sorts of strange looking bobbles and questionable food in various sized jars. Glass cabinets displayed mixtures of tonics, salves, and medicinal herbs. On small tables lay curious objects from miniature statues, tarot decks, sage and essential oils. Business in divining must be slow these days for the man, as it looks like he's turned his shop into a knock-off spiritual commodity store—carrying things for personal divination, at-home remedies, and items of that nature. No doubt a way to keep up the front of his true intent and business.

Many oracles did similarly, as it wasn't the easiest service to get the word out about, considering the critics of the practice in modern-day culture versus how accepted and notable it was in the past. Today, many saw it as more of a hack-show, rather than a true, relied practice. Either way, typically you needed another business venture to maintain in today's world; it wasn't like in ancient Rome when being an oracle was a sought after affair, one that came with prestige and power. Oracles in the past were often treated like royalty, seeing they possessed a skill that held grave consequences and greater opportunity for reward if divined correctly. Kings and nobles favored oracles in their court—believing they brought about good fortune or dictated when bad fortune was on the way for them personally, or for their reign. It wasn't until the rise of "witch hunts" between the 15th to 18th centuries particularly, when being an oracle took a sour turn—more often than not, brandishing you as a demon worshiper or an incarnation of the Devil.

Despite the false blame and ensuing paranoia from humans, most true oracles were rarely detected, and merely staged deaths, moved kingdoms, or took backdoor dealings rather than remain in the public eye. Although not as many as there were before, many oracles still use their abilities throughout the world-but it's a much more secretive practice. The ones who couldn't adapt to the change from near-celebrity status to hidden transactions, or be able to find a modern-day equivalent to a notable figure, either stopped practicing or committed suicide—unable to cope with contemporary notions in today's society.

Daemon's eyes narrowed in the direction of a pudgy man standing behind a dusty countertop. Upon hearing the door open, the man looked up cheerily from what he was working on, expecting a customer. His eyes showed fear the moment he realized who it was.

"Daemon! Gosh it's been awhile, eh? How honored I am to be in your presence again, old friend."

The man's voice trembled and he quickly stowed whatever it was he'd been tinkering with. He had a large, round face with eyes that were much too small for him, and a bulbous nose atop a smile with several crooked teeth. He wore a black robe that had silver etching in it in strange letters and markings. Magnus changed so much since the time he helped him escape Belgium. Then, he was wearing regalia that shone brightly in the sun. And was at least 50 pounds lighter. Daemon was glad to see that all the time hadn't changed his fear from him, at least.

"Yes, it's been awhile, Magnus. But I'm not here to play catch up with you. I need to get some answers."

Magnus nervously wiped his hands on his robe and scurried around the counter to stand before them.

"Answers, huh? Well you know I have never been much good at uh...getting answers. I don't know how much help I could be to you!"

Daemon glared at the man, who was a good foot shorter than him, as Daemon walked towards the nearest shelf on his right, picking up an odd looking figurine and inspecting it before setting it back down. Putting a hand in his pocket, he turned and faced him.

"I am not sure how much help you'll be either. You know my situation, and therefore, you're my best shot at getting some insight. Why don't you take us some place more private, and start paying me back on that debt you owe me, hm?"

Magnus reluctantly nodded and quietly walked them through a secret door that was covered by vines that hung along the wall behind the counter, to a small den area beyond the main storefront. There were pillows and rugs that didn't match lining the floor. Tattered drapes hung from the ceiling, and the overwhelming aroma of recently lit incense filled the air with a sweet, almost suffocating scent. Magnus fumbles with a few of the pillows, pretending to clean up briefly before Daemon gives him a forceful look, finally settling himself on one of the cushions, holding his arms out to invite them to do the same.

"Can...I interest you in some tea?"

Magnus for the first time noticed Lorelei, and his gaze lingered on her for longer than Daemon was comfortable with.

"No. We don't have time for that. What do you know of Armageddon, Magnus?"

Magnus' eyes went big as he finally understood why they'd come. His eyes darted back to Lorelei and he was quick on his feet.

"I...I know what you're doing, Daemon. There's been a lot of talk the last few days. If I get caught helping you, they could kill me."

Daemon's patience was now wearing thin. Of course he heard what was happening. This wasn't, however, a good sign. If rumors of what Daemon and Lorelei were attempting to do were reaching people such as Magnus, they needed to move fast. The danger was rising with every moment they spent figuring out their next move.

Daemon spoke next, a growl underlying his words, "And *I* will kill you if you don't."

He felt Lorelei look at him, but he didn't want to look at her face. He knew if he did, he may lose his edge, and now was not the time for that.

They had to get answers. He waited momentarily for his threat to sink in and watched Magnus thinking through what he should do, before settling back down on the cushion.

"Alright. Fine. But there isn't much I can tell you."

With this, he looked directly at Lorelei.

"It is true, you are the only one who can stop humans from dying in this war. But it has always been known that only you can reveal how to do so."

Frustrated, before Lorelei has a chance to respond, Daemon nearly growls at Magnus.

"We already know that part. That's really all you can give us? There's got to be more you can tell."

Magnus hesitated and returned his attention to Daemon. He sighed and closed his eyes; he was divining. After several minutes, Magnus opened his eyes and spoke.

"The future is unclear right now. And I honestly don't know how Lorelei is meant to learn what she must. Is there something you've noticed, my dear? Anything you can think of that lingers in your mind's eye?"

Lorelei scrunched her nose in thought, he'd noticed it was a go-to reaction when she was struggling with something—something she couldn't quite place in her thoughts. He watched her features curiously, wondering what might be going through her mind, and reflected how absolutely adorable the expression was.

Tentatively, Lorelei answered.

"Actually...I mentioned a dream to Daemon when we first met. I didn't go into detail, but he wondered if...if my dreams were somehow prophetic. Is that something that could be helpful to me?"

Magnus looks at her with excitement, rather than hinting at any facet that what she said was crazy.

"Dreams! Yes, my dear, yes! Dreams are far more powerful than we really know-most humans are able to recall dreams like a past memory, or even a future event. Yet, many humans do not have the in depth connection with their Higher Self, the part of you that is beyond the human ego-the one that connects you directly to your soul's greater knowledge. It's the one most closely connected to the source of the Universe and the connection we all share. Oh my dear, please tell me this dream so I may see to decipher it."

Lorelei's breath hitched, but she recounted the recurring dream she had throughout her life. Told of the pyramids, how she needed to open them, how she never got to the part where she saw what happened next, and that the last time she had this dream, Daemon appeared in it-although she wasn't sure who he was until they met that night in the pub. Magnus listened fervently, and Daemon watched the excitement on Magnus' face turn to concern. He paused only a moment after Lorelei finished, Daemon could feel the sudden silence that sat in the room around them. When Magnus eventually spoke, the look in his eyes that previously filled with delight, was now replaced with dread.

"It seems to me...that you are the makings of a proper Seer. You, although completely unaware, have an adept connection to your Higher Self; your intuition is nearly so engrossed in your very being, it's practically palpable in the air around us. When you were speaking, the energy around you shifted. I am quite sure even Daemon felt the energy fluctuation..."

Daemon nodded; he had felt the shift. Energy in the Universe can be changed and adapted and it can elevate or lower in relativity to each individual, or to the cosmic energy that all life shares. Each person's energy level or their ability to handle energy, varies from person to person. Some are more keen and aware of it. Highly empathic people especially, are incredibly affected by the energy of others and the environment of the world around them. You might be sitting there and out of nowhere, a wave of sadness hits you, and you call your friend to ask if they are alright. They tell you their spouse has left them but they hadn't told anyone yet—that's to this effect and also encapsulates how in tune some are with their intuition. When Lorelei finished her dream description, something about it triggered a sense of power that radiated throughout the room. It made Daemon's heart rate escalate, he'd never been around a human who caused such elevation in energy, even with a common discussion of a dream. Eyeing Lorelei, the curiosity mixed with distress made Daemon yearn to hold her hand again, to give her a reassuring squeeze, but he dared not. They didn't know each other that way. He wouldn't cross that boundary. He couldn't.

Magnus continued on with his explanation.

"There was only ever one person I knew with this much intuitive and prophetic power—because yes, Daemon is correct in assuming this dream of yours is prophetic. I have never met another human with such a tenacity for connection to the spiritual and divine. The last to have such a deep connection to their intuition and ability to reach enlightenment in this way—who was a human—is who you now know as ArchAngel Metatron. He is the only known human who ascended to angel status by way of living a righteous life on Earth. In the book of the Bible, you can find him referenced as the so-called prophet Enoch....Not sure how accurate that tale is; humans always exaggerate tales of this grandeur, you know. Anyways, he was made the sole keeper of the place of infinite knowledge of the Universe because of this very gift of intuition you also have, Lorelei. You are a wonder, my dear. There is no telling what you would've been able to accomplish as an oracle or Seer if you were to have known about this ability long ago. It's untapped potential, but there is room for growth to enhance this ability. My...I am awestruck, to say the least. Other than the Great Pathea, I once served, you are gifted with intuitive abilities beyond reproach."

Lorelei's voice shoots through the room quickly, passionate curiosity ringing in her tone, along with desperation.

"Okay...I hear you when you say I have this ability that isn't common. It springs to mind the few times I knew something bad happened to a friend...or more recently, my father before his death...that I didn't have true logical awareness of how I knew it. But what does the dream actually mean? Is there a sign in it that could help us now?"

Magnus frowned, taking the tea he made for himself and holding it in his hand, sighing.

"As for that, I have no idea. "Opening" the pyramids is most likely metaphorical, a symbol for something else. I highly doubt it would be literal. Have you tried meditation? Meditation for people with prophetic dreams is a renowned way to channel that energy and perhaps receive insight into the meanings behind the dreams."

After staying quiet for long enough, despite confirming the suspicion he felt about Lorelei's abilities, Magnus has done nothing to actually help them with their current predicament. The knowledge they learned, or lack thereof, was starting to eat away at him. The anxiety of not knowing if their task was achievable—posed too great a threat. This didn't help them, and only wasted more of their time. Daemon couldn't help but snap in frustration.

"We don't have bloody time to meditate, Magnus. Tell us something that will actually help us now. Do you know anything? Any place to start looking for some answers?"

Magnus swallowed fearfully nDaemon felt a tinge of regret. It wasn't necessarily Magnus' fault they were in such a rush, nor was it his fault he didn't have more answers for them. Coming here was a long-shot as is, there was no guarantee there would be some great epiphany that handed them a detailed map on what to do or where to go next.

Magnus finally sets his teacup down, taking a moment in silence, eyes closed to divine again. When he opened his eyes, he nodded solemnly.

"There is a place that appears above anything else. But I have no idea what awaits you there or what you might find; if anything."

Lorelei's face turned serious, a glimmer of hope peeking behind the mask of uncertainty and fear.

"Where?" Lorelei asked eagerly.

Magnus looked between the two of them, "Stonehenge, my dear."

Daemon stood.

If that is all he can give us, we need to get a move on.

As he begins to stand, he stops and gives thanks to Magnus the only way he knew how.

"If they come looking for you wondering if we were here, you can tell them I forced it out of you. Considering the circumstances, they'll believe you. You should be safe. Take care, Magnus."

Daemon waited for Lorelei to stand and they made their way back out the shop door and into the alleyway. It was shifting into late afternoon now and the alley was getting darker.

"I know he didn't say a lot but at least we know where to go nex-"

Before Lorelei could finish her sentence, Daemon was pulling her back against his chest, one hand over her mouth and the other wrapped tightly around her torso. Further down the alley, two dark figures were turning around the corner in search of something. *In search of them.* He felt Lorelei's heart beating fast as she too, saw the figures. Her hands were now over top of his and he knew they had to get out of there. But in the middle of broad daylight, a busy market nearby filled with people, he couldn't whip out his wings and fly them to safety. They'd have to make a run for it. When the figures were around the corner, without a word, he unraveled himself from Lorelei and grabbed her hand, whispering.

"We need to go. Can you keep up?"

Lorelei nodded silently, and he tightened his grip on her hand, sprinting off toward the market crowd, weaving and bobbing between bodies. Daemon's mind was racing uncontrollably, he had to get them out-but already, they were drawing attention. The situation was becoming dicey, but all he could do was put one foot in front of the other, hold onto Lorelei, and *run.*

I didn't think they'd find us so soon.

He could smell them coming. Demons. Their scent saturated the air outside the shop. They must've come in the shop after them, but didn't know about the hidden door Magnus had to the other room.

I guess you came in more handy than I thought, Magnus.

Yes, their initial run in with the demons was postponed. Still, it was only a matter of time before they caught up. As he finally got them through the hardest part of the crowd, he looks around for a car to take. Just as he spots one parked nearby, he smells them again.

Spinning around, he sees two demons standing about 100 metres away. He recognized one of them as Zanul; one of Lucifer's personal guards. The other was one he had also seen before but didn't know his name. They each had eyes the color of red wine and black smokey rings around their eyes that made them look like they were wearing eyeshadow. Maybe they were. Zanul had pitch black hair in braids plunging down his back. Battle ready hair. The other was dressed head to toe in punk-inspired attire that only added to his menacing demeanor. Zanul was crueler than most, and often enjoyed toying with his victims before releasing them from their suffering.

"Come on!"

He tugged at Lorelei and headed straight for the range rover he spotted, his sense of urgency demanding every fiber of his training to take over; he needed to remain calm; but damned if he didn't panic more about Lorelei's safety in a way that forced him to react uncharacteristically in the company of danger. Daemon felt badly for having to stoop to such methods as stealing a car, but this was life or death. The quicker they got away from the market, the safer it was for everyone there. Demons were not often known to create spectacles of themselves in a public space like this-but with the stakes as high as they were for success, they would do just about anything. Daemon couldn't risk the humans there, he needed to get them to a safer location to regroup; if only to lead the demons away from the humans in the area. If he didn't, mass death and destruction would very likely occur.

When they reached the car, he looked back to see the demons racing towards them. Light on their feet, Daemon heard several humans chastising the demons as they knocked into them, even a small child cried. People were already starting to notice too much. He had to act fast—get them out of here. He focused hard, trying not to panic in front of Lorelei and within another moment, commanded the door to the car to open. Sitting in the seat and doing the same to start the engine, he was shocked to see Lorelei still hadn't gotten in the car. Breathing heavy, he yelled out of the passenger window to her.

"Lorelei! Get in the car!"

She looked back at him pleadingly.

"But we're stealing this from someone...and..."

"Better to steal a car to hopefully save whoever owns it from desolation than give up by being killed by a bunch of demons because you feel too bad to do so. Now get in!"

The harshness in his voice finally forced Lorelei into the car. Daemon slammed his foot onto the gas pedal and floored it. Checking the rearview mirror, he watched as the demons came to a halt. They wouldn't risk exposure by running at full speed in front of so many humans, not yet.

Neither spoke for at least half an hour. He knew he was going way past the speed limit, but he couldn't take the risk. He had to make sure they were far enough away so the demons wouldn't be able to get to them, at least for a little while. When it felt like the coast was clear, he slowed down a bit, and looked over at Lorelei who was visibly upset.

"Lorelei, I'm sorry we had to steal the car. It was the only way I could keep you safe."

When she didn't answer immediately, he felt that lurch in his chest again. But it faded quickly as he heard her voice at last.

"I...I know. I know it had to be done. Thank you for getting me out of there."

He felt her looking at him, but he remained stoic and focused on the road ahead. The sweetness of her voice made it hard to not look into those bright, blue eyes of hers.

"Do you think Magnus was much help?"

Thankful for the shift in conversation, Daemon relaxed into the seat and nodded.

"Actually, yes. I know he was going out on a limb even telling us that much."

"What do you think is going to happen when we get to Stonehenge?"

This question stumped him. He had no idea. If it was really true that only Lorelei could unlock the answers, he wasn't sure how she would.

"I don't know. You're always surprising me though. Maybe something at Stonehenge will call out to you. I'm not sure...but it's our best start. Which is better than nothing to go off at all."

Lorelei sighed, and Daemon's heart ached while hearing it.

Lorelei leaned on her arm, looking out the window. So much had changed for her in such a short time, and Daemon worried for her, worried for how the weight of the literal world might affect her. They may know where to go next, but that didn't mean she would be able to do anything once they arrived. Daemon's eyes darted over to her several times, her silence became unsettling, forcing his brows to scrunch uncomfortably. He cleared his throat.

"Lorelei, are you...alright?"

Upon his question, a flooding of emotions gushed out of her unexpectedly. The fears and doubt that she'd successfully kept at bay, now had no other recourse but to release.

"Daemon, I don't see what there is that I can do. I..I am only human. I have nothing that screams hero. What...what if I fail? What if I can't figure out what to do and I am the reason humanity dies?"

She tried to keep the wavering in her voice to a minimum as she spoke, but it was hard when Daemon opened and closed his mouth several times, as if to say something that might comfort or reject her statement. When at last his mouth remained closed, and that hardened expression remained, Daemon felt totally defeated, unable to think of anything encouraging to say.

He looked at Lorelei and felt his heart might break. Tears started to stream down her face, falling like rain droplets on a windowpane. And despite stopping being risky, as the colors of purple and orange of the sun setting began filling the car, he pulled the car over on the side of the small country road they were on. Putting the car in park, he pivoted to face Lorelei better. Tears were dripping from her chin onto her lap, and although she made no noise while she cried, he could hear the sound of her own doubt and fear rushing through her body, leaving her untethered. Another energy shift was felt, but it was different than prior. This energy shift was heavy, suffocating, and incredibly dark. It shook him to his core, seeing that she was starting to crumble in on herself emotionally. The first major breakdown since he found her a couple of days ago. She was staring down at her feet and as her body began to shake, he huffed loudly and with his hand, placed it on her cheek and forced her to face him.

"Look. You're not alone. I know that the odds are against us, but look at how you have handled everything so far. You have held up when most humans wouldn't."

Lorelei only gazed back into his eyes. Her own shifting into a dark, cloudy grey as tears continued to fall from them. This entire time, she had not shed a single tear. Hadn't let the stakes stacked against her take her down. And now, seeing her look like she might collapse from the pressure, killed him. Because he wasn't sure how to comfort her. He didn't know if their mission was going to succeed. He didn't know how she was going to save humans. But he knew she was stronger than any human he'd ever met and he knew that even though he was terrified that saying it might open a door he may never be able to shut again, a door leading to his own heart—he had to tell her that.

Tilting her chin up for her eyes to lock with his, he melted. That cold, outward demeanor fading with one look into those captivating eyes. There was no sarcasm he could conjure, no desire to shift the moment to something more lighthearted. He wanted to be there with her, to pull her from this darkness he saw rupturing her. He needed her to feel he was there, fully with her. His guard lowered, and when their eyes met, lip quivering, he thought his heart might explode out of his chest altogether. Continuing to gently hold her chin to look at him, he mustered up all the encouragement he could.

"Lorelei...from the moment we met, you have surprised me at every turn. You have been *so strong...*"

His voice trailed off as he wiped a tear from her cheek with his thumb, the gesture igniting a desire to pull her even closer, but he kept his current stance and continued.

"If anybody can figure it out, it's you. This is your destiny. You have the power within you, Magnus told us as much."

As she looked into his eyes, and as the tears began to recede, she blinked several times. A faint smile started forming, her eyes changing from doubt, to longing. Her lips parted and Daemon's heart quickened—rattling beneath his chest. Temperature rose within him and he hesitated, unsure if words indeed comforted her and she was relieved, or if her gaze suggested something more. Abruptly, Lorelei's facial expression turned to shock, and she quickly pulled away from his hold on her. Lorelei merely continued to stare at him. He was afraid he'd said something wrong.

"*You.* I saw...a memory flash through my head. It can't be true...You were there that day. You were doing the same thing, holding my face like this, checking into my eyes to see if I was responsive. You saved me when I was 6 years old. Didn't you? The mission Raphael mentioned, the one you didn't follow through with. You stopped me from dying."

When Daemon couldn't find the words to respond, Lorelei's voice no longer held back, and its intensity shook the car; anger radiated from her, ricocheting like a boomerang in the energy around them. Daemon could do nothing but stare at her as she shouted.

"Didn't you!"

CHAPTER 7

LORELEI

16 YEARS EARLIER...

It was a cold, rainy afternoon and Lorelei was walking with a few of her friends back home from their elementary school that was down the street from her house. Having her school only a short distance from her home was so much fun,; she loved meeting her friends in the mornings and walking home with them in the afternoons. After her friends finally hugged her goodbye, they headed down the road before her to their own homes; all she had to do now was cross the street and she'd be walking into her humble little house, to find her father cooking her favorite meal; sausage and potato soup. He told her before she left for school that morning that he would because it's what she'd been begging him to make for a couple of weeks now. When he told her it would be ready by the time she got home that afternoon, she jumped up and down and clung to his neck, kissing his cheek, before running off down the road to school.

Usually Lorelei looked both ways, just as her father taught her; but her mind was so preoccupied with dinner and how delicious it was going to be, that she stepped out into the street without doing so. She only noticed what was happening seconds before it did; screeching noises and a horn blowing hard finally alerted her. But it was too late.

Headlights of a car were barreling toward her, and all she could hear was the sound of her own screaming. Closing her eyes tightly, she waited for the impact, her sweet father's face flashing before her eyes.

Opening her eyes, she found herself lying on the asphalt. The rain had intensified and a crack of lightning illuminated the sky above her, as well as the figure who kneeled beside her body.

"Don't move."

The voice was low, but she feared to disobey it. She turned her head to the side and even the slightest movement made her cry out in pain.

"I said not to move. Your spine is broken."

Another strike of lightning above them finally allowed Lorelei to see the figure beside her. His silvery hair fell over most of his face, but as he wiped it away, the shine of his mesmerizing green eyes caught hers.

She was finding it tough to breathe, like she was working overtime for each breath, and yet no matter how deep of one she took, it didn't feel like enough. She was dying, and although she was too young to understand that concept in its entirety, she felt panic rise in her throat. Tears fell from her eyes, her vision blurring in and out.

"Lorelei, you're going to be alright. You're not going to die. I have a way I can save you."

Die? Am I really going to die? How does he know my name?

There was only one thing she could muster up enough of a breath to respond with.

"How can you do that?" Lorelei spoke feebly, words were hard to get out. Getting any amount of breath was becoming increasingly difficult. It felt like her chest was on fire, her throat swollen, hardly able to swallow; a single strained breath caused her body to convulse in pain.

Her vision was beginning to fade. Black spots flickered across her vision and she barely saw the man standing before her. Her body became colder with each passing second.

"I can give you a piece of my soul. It will heal you enough to keep you from dying. The only catch is you have to give me permission to do so."

Lorelei managed to blink enough times to set her vision back to normal momentarily and look at the man who was hunched over her body. His eyes shone brightly and through them, she saw his desperation for her to give him permission.

"I don't understand...I need my dad.. please will you get my dad? It hurts so much.."

The man shook his head.

"I promise, your dad will be with you soon and you will be okay. Will you give me permission to help the hurt go away?"

He paused, the look in his eyes confirmed to Lorelei that it was the only way, but she couldn't form another word, only nodded in response. Lorelei needed him, desperately. It was always just the two of them, and she needed to tell him she loved him more than anything. She'd do anything to get back to her sweet dad's arms, she didn't want to die

The pain in her back now overwhelmed her. She only saw out of the corner of her eye the man beside her, lifting his hands in the air inches from her chest, as a glowing white light was pouring out of them; she watched the light begin funneling through her chest. She felt it instantly. The sensation was warm and comforting. She looked back to the face of the man, and he met her eyes once more with a wary look, and began to sing.

His voice was beautiful, the most beautiful thing in all the world. But he sang no words she knew. They were odd and dream-like. She couldn't keep consciousness any longer, his words forcing her to drift off into darkness, carrying her away to a slumber unlike any she experienced before. Unlike the fear she felt earlier, she felt nothing but peace and protection. The darkness no longer frightened her. The man's words turned into the most tranquil lullaby. She swore, as she fell away, that she would never forget. She would never forget the kind, mysterious man who saved her life that day. But when she woke again, she lay in the hospital bed with doctors surrounding her, her father kneeling beside her, his hand clutching hers tightly; she only remembered being told she was hit by a car, and the fact she was alive was *a miracle.*

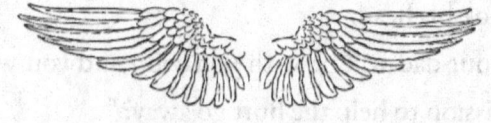

When Lorelei came out of the vision, she felt a surge toward Daemon she hadn't felt before.

Anger.

She was furious that he'd indeed met her before now and continued to keep that fact from her. Before Daemon could say a word, she was slinging the car door open and jumping out. Not only did they meet before, but he gave her a piece of his soul to save her. This must be the reason she felt the way she did around him; lost in his words, his subtleties, the way he looked at her and the aching, longing to be nearer to him. It was this, and only this. There was no truth to the feelings other than that she owed him her life. Nothing more.

Lorelei started pacing along the grass that flickered, a breeze forming. Hearing Daemon's own car door close, she knew he was standing there watching her, but her mind was reeling too much with every emotion imaginable, so she ignored him. She was battling herself internally now more than ever.

One side of her was saying: *How could he keep this from me? So this is the real reason I have felt such a pull towards him. Not because he actually cared for me. Not because I actually cared for HIM. It's this damn soul bond thing that is the culprit. None of what I thought I was seeing and feeling with him has been real.*

While the other half was saying: *He also saved my life. He sacrificed his entire existence to save mine. He saw something in me worth saving. He cared for me before I even knew who he was.*

This second voice was far too irritating in her heightened state, so she did her best to try to shut out this second voice. She was too angry, and too hurt to listen to its logic now. She only came out of her own thoughts when she heard Daemon's voice. Lorelei knew that the energy around her was starting to feel too heavy, too much fear vibrated her body and she shook her head—it was starting to feel like that dark, lonely place she'd been in for the last year.

The place that held no solace for her, no peace of mind. The way her thoughts seemed to manifest themselves in the very air surrounding her made it all the more dizzying, and all the harder to think properly. A ringing sensation echoed in her ears, and she covered them; a panic attack began to overtake her. Breaths became haggard, and she gripped her head, willing the emotions to subside, to break the tension that settled deeply rooted in her core. The way it nearly took her before—the drowning effect of her own tumultuous thoughts.

The one person she trusted out of this insane endeavor, also lied. He held back. The person who made her feel more at ease and more herself in so long, she now didn't know if she could trust. Didn't know if the feelings blossoming slowly within her could ever be real, or if they were merely a bi-product of the connection forged for the purpose of saving her life. How could she know if he felt the same? Was he doing it out of obligation? Were his feelings only ever out of some righteous pride that he saved her, and Daemon returned out of that same instinct as before? A guilt that never resolved? Could the growing fondness between them be nothing other than a cruel, sick joke of the Universe? Daemon's voice barely made its way through the chaos of her mind.

"I know I should've told you, but I was scared to. I was afraid of what you'd think."

This riled her up even more.

"What do I think? Really, Daemon. Well you know what I think, I think that I can't trust you. I think that you kept something majorly important from me, and I think you're a massive dick!"

The words were out before she could stop them and as she turned, she saw they made their mark. Daemon's shoulders dropped and pain washed over his face.

"Lorelei, I'm sorry. Really."

"Sorry? You're sorry Daemon? Well that's rich. You know, this whole time, I thought there was something familiar about you. Something I couldn't place. I couldn't help but feel connected to you. I thought maybe it was because they were genuine feelings, but now I see that they aren't. Because they are only there because you had to give me a piece of your fucking soul!"

Those words struck Daemon, hesitating his movements a moment until she felt him walking towards her with urgency. He only stopped himself a few paces from her, trying to keep a respectful distance, his eyes acknowledged the air that now made the hair on his arms stand up straight like static; it undulated around them and it was like he was scared to disturb it, for fear it might erupt.

"Look. I thought that's how it was when I came to you the other night, too. I've been pushing away the idea because I believed I was only feeling this way about you because of the soul bond, as well. But I know that's not true anymore. Yes, there is this connection between us because of what I did to save you all those years ago, but it's not the only reason. I hoped.. you of all people would've understood and seen that."

Daemon's words surprised her. He wasn't denying the connection she felt with him; and he was even admitting he felt the same way. Yet, something about the entire situation still stirred up resentment towards him.

"Lorelei. Do you want to know why I saved you that night? Why I decided to go against my orders, instead of making sure you did die from getting hit by that car?"

Lorelei continued to ignore him. Turning her back to him as she watched the sun inch its way further behind the hills in the distance. Daemon's voice softened to a near whisper behind her as he at last, closed the gap between them. He stood so close, perhaps a thin sheet of paper could barely penetrate the space between their forms. But he didn't touch her, he didn't dare. She could feel his warm breath against her head which could've easily pressed upon his chest. A part of her screamed to close that gap further. To let her body rest against his, to turn and face him, look into those emerald eyes that made her swear she could see the whole of the Universe within them, like galaxies swirled just beneath the surface, a pool of endless cosmic night—one she wished to explore in its entirety and become one with. Lorelei stubbornly stood her ground, her heart twinging at the fact he kept this secret from her, a hurt she wasn't sure she'd experience from Daemon.

The air around them, even her own emotions, stilled at the sudden closeness. The energy between them, *his energy*—calmed her own. A sweetening, intermingling that soothed the raging sea of emotions that moments before, were seconds away from drowning her. Her breath altogether stopped, and although she wasn't looking at him, it felt like the world stood still, and he was holding her in a breach of frozen time.

"I did it because of what I saw in you. I was tasked to watch you all day, to make sure that your death went as planned. I watched you at school, with your friends, with your teachers, I couldn't help but see the bright light you were in this world. You were so kind and caring to everyone around you. Your soul shone brighter than any other's I'd experienced in all the thousands of years I've been on Earth. Even at such a young age, you saw those around you as more important than yourself. You did all you could to make everyone smile and feel better when they needed a helping hand. So when the car hit you, I didn't think twice about my decision to save you. You are the kind of person this world needs. That's when I truly saw the cruelty of Heaven ending your life, just to play out their idiotic fight. And when you gave me permission to attach a piece of my own soul to yours, I performed an ancient and forbidden spell that would give you enough of my strength to heal yourself and live. No angel is meant to do it, because it could kill us if we attempt it. By doing so, it changed your timeline. Or, so it seemed to. The spell created a false outcome of your destiny, which allowed the ArchAngels to believe you would no longer be capable of stopping Armageddon. In reality, it was merely a facade I placed over you; like a shield, so that they wouldn't feel the need to send anybody else to finish the task I was unwilling to carry out. It was a decision that would keep you safe until it was time to fulfill your destiny, while everyone else believed the incident changed the course of your destiny completely. I didn't know if it would work, and I didn't know if I would survive it once it was set in motion. But when your little blue eyes met mine, I too, saw a vision. A vision of a beautiful, intuitive girl who would one day grow to be the person who could save this world with your power of love and desire to help others, from those who seek to only fight for themselves."

Daemon paused one last time. She could tell he was wondering if he should say what he was going to say next.

"And...I also saw the girl who would end up being the one person I cared more for than any other in the entire universe."

Each word that fell from his lips, made her feel she saw into him, into his soul. *The soul she now shared; and savored.*

Lorelei finally faced him, tears once again running down her face. Even though part of her still wanted to be angry, to lash out, his words confirmed the same feelings that had been building up inside of herself. She watched silently as Daemon took her face into his hands, cupping her cheeks and wiping her tears away. The sun now completely disappearing over the hilltops and plunging them into the early commencement of night. Her lips trembling, begging to solidify the feelings that they both built up, the fear that could've swept them apart now only intensified the very sure connection she could no longer deny. He saved her, he protected her when the very Universe conspired against her. When destiny called for her demise, he sacrificed not only his grace, but his life; to save hers. He saw her fully, for what she was, and who she could be. It was the greatest gift to her the acknowledgement she needed that this was Divine. Their relationship transcended boundaries that shouldn't have been crossed—yet, here they were, falling into the depths of a connection she couldn't fathom with words or logic.

She leaned on her tip-toes, her hand finding its way up his chest. Daemon holding the back of her neck so delicately, and with so much care, she thought she could cry from the sheer tenderness of the act.

His lips brushed hers, sending her heartbeat into a free-fall, hurtling over the barrier she no longer wished to submit herself to. She craved for nothing more than what came next, what they could discover—together. But as she let her lips meet his, she gasped. Daemon was pulled backwards into the darkness behind him, and she watched in terror as he slammed hard into the side of the car and crumpled to the ground.

Chapter 8

Samuel

SAMUEL WAS STANDING IN front of his father who was raging; but when was he not?

"I don't understand why we have to go through this as many times as we do. You are a demon. Your purpose is to aid the movement against Heaven. The reason we do it is because *we must*. It's the way of things. If we do not show our hand, Heaven will win...and this war is a chance for us to tip that balance! To take our rightful place as the true rulers of Earth, and this Universe!"

The amount of times Samuel had to be reminded he was a demon, was only one of the reasons his father resented him so much. He wasn't the son he ever wanted. He was the screw up. The weak link. The one who didn't want to fight for the cause. The one who questioned the way things always were between Heaven and Hell. And he knew his father deep down, loathed him for that.

Ever since his birth, Samuel had never been like the rest of the demons in his classes. When they were learning about how to fight, how to hunt and destroy angels, and how to change forms or alter their voices to better manipulate humans—Samuel would be the only one who would raise his hand meekly asking why they had to fight back or harm anybody to begin with. Each time the teacher would call his father, one of these fun conversations would take place.

But no matter how much his father drilled into him that he was the son of Lucifer, so he better act like it, Samuel never understood him.

Samuel was fascinated by humans. Although he was never allowed to leave Hell to go and explore the human world, he read book after book on them. Their history and their way of life in places all over the globe. It was the only sanctuary he found in this life; the life of the 17-year-old son of Lucifer, was no cake walk, especially when you didn't want to take over Earth or kill angels.

The prodigal son, destined to be the Anti-Christ, wanted nothing more than explore the places humans dwelled, and be their friend. Figures, right?

In many ways, Hell wasn't so dissimilar to the Earth. Although it functioned in another realm or dimension. Realm geography is a complicated subject, and to be honest, one Samuel never did well in. So it was easier to think of Hell as not on Earth or *inside* Earth—as human religious texts suggest; they didn't need to be surrounded by molten lava and fire—it was more...*around*. And nowhere close to it at all. Portals are involved, and nobody could leave the realm without his father's permission. Heaven apparently, is similar—both of them functioned on a different plane of existence, and time ran differently here, which explains the lack of aging or slower aging.

Long story short, Samuel was inevitably stuck. Hell had schools, jobs, and demons had families and produced more minions for the cause. The biggest difference was that most of the inhabitants had the occasional horn or whip-like tail. In comparison, Samuel looked and acted more human than demon, so his father tended to remind him. He didn't have any distinguishing demon-ish marks. No horns. No tail. No wings. And, no desire to harm the humans or to fight against the angels. With only a mop of unruly, blazing red hair, and his inability to make a blow in their staged fights, Samuel never felt he belonged, which made him the disgrace of Hell.

Unlike the other students in his grade, Samuel was thin and lanky. Having always preferred to workout his brain rather than his body, he was never able to keep up with the other kid's ever-growing strength and appetite for battle. Samuel was never meant to be the soldier his father dreamt of.

Or the son he dreamt of in general...

Samuel was lost in thought until he heard his father's next words, which was a usual occurrence during one of his father's drawn-out tirades; but when Lucifer's voice boomed louder to get Samuel's attention, reverberating the walls around them, Samuel dared to look at him.

"This is your last chance, Samuel. To prove yourself to me. I need a warrior. A leader. Somebody I can entrust when it is time for another to take my place. You were born the fucking Anti-Christ, boy. I bedded your mother to create the strongest force in the war the Universe has ever known—I created you for a reason; you are meant to lead this war with me, Samuel. It's time you prove to me your worth."

Samuel's mother was rarely spoken of; growing up without her was part of his father's demands. She was apparently a high-level demon; one Lucifer scoped out for centuries before deeming appropriate enough to bring Samuel into the world. But after Samuel was born, Lucifer killed her. He wanted no competition in the raising of Samuel; her worthiness ran its course. As sad as it was to never know her, if she was anything like his father, he didn't think it was worth having two blazing assholes ruling Hell; or his life.

Samuel was no Anti-Christ. The efforts his father went through to enforce this idea, bring about some unnatural power strong enough to take down forces of angels and to bring about destruction of Earth, was the top of

Samuel's inabilities to tackle. From a young age, Samuel seemingly possessed no extraordinary abilities.

Lucifer's thought process on the powers that would pass to Samuel between the mixture of his own, and of his powerful mother's, was proposed to be enough to create such a force in Samuel. But Samuel was never able to conjure or manipulate Shadow and Darkness, turning it into a weapon. He was never able to control emotions or possess anything. Never able to fight or block or even so much as make a dent in the stuffed dummy used for practice training. Frustratingly, Samuel wasn't special, nor compelling in any way, shape or form. And once Lucifer realized the insufficiencies of his son, he all but left Samuel to his own devices; he gave up on him, finding it too much of a headache to even look at the child. Samuel all but hardly saw his father, but every random occasion.

Then last month, Lucifer began coming to watch Samuel's training sessions. Disappointment seeped from him as he watched Samuel take blow after blow, without a single retaliation. The only time Samuel was acknowledged by him during these random visits, was when Lucifer would come to him, bandaging himself on the bench in the training arena, scolding him on his inability to make a hit against his opponent, before silently walking away, not another word spoken.

Until today.

Samuel is about to give a snide retort when his chance to do so is stopped. Abruptly, footsteps began echoing off the walls of his father's office as four demons walked in and stood in formation behind him.

Lucifer made no remark to the men who entered, only turning his eyes to Samuel. "I am sending you on a mission. You will assist Zanul and his team tomorrow."

Zanul, his father's personal guard. No matter how long Zanul had worked under his father, Samuel would never get used to those unfeeling eyes that watched him menacingly. Samuel felt small beneath his leer. He heard of the missions his father usually sent Zanul on, and knew how vicious he was.

One night while his father and his friends were playing a game of poker while Samuel was doing some homework nearby, his father turned to Zanul and asked how his most recent mission went. Samuel saw Zanul's eyes flare with satisfaction as he recalled the full details; far more gruesome than anything Samuel heard before, causing him to immediately puke in the nearby trash can. Lucifer and his group laughed at him, and it took two full weeks to stop dreaming of the scenario Zanul described. After that night, Samuel was more frightened of Zanul than ever before and did his best to keep out of his way.

Samuel swallowed, returning to give attention to his father rather than Zanul. "What will I be helping with?"

His father looked at him and Samuel could tell it wasn't going to be something he wanted to participate in at all.

"You will be going on a hunt. Your mission will be to aid in the elimination of an angel and a human who are threatening the surety of the war. I expect you to fulfill any and all orders Zanul gives you; even if that order is to kill them both yourself. If I hear you have not complied, you will be destroyed."

Panic welled up inside of him; he watched as his father spun on his heels and started walking out of the office. He yelled out to him, in desperation or in search of some semblance of care for his only child—Samuel wasn't sure what he was searching for.

"How can you do that? I'm your son!"

Samuel couldn't hold back the tears, the tears that he kept buried inside himself until he was all alone. The tears he never allowed a soul to know the pain and torment his father put him through, the lack of guidance, the lack of nurturing, all of the diminishing comments, all the times Samuel was told he was useless—they all found their way to the forefront now, escaping in a turbulent flurry of erratic disbelief.

But this was Lucifer, Satan, the embodiment of Evil. And he was that embodiment's incompetent child meant to be the harbinger of that chaos—destined to forever be hated by his own father for the pure fact that he was nothing but a waste of space. These feelings tumbled out of him, along with an anger he never knew lived in the pit of all that sadness. Lucifer didn't notice his son crying in shock behind him when he spoke again, only pausing a moment in his steps towards the door.

"No true son of Lucifer would behave the way you have since you came into this world. If you are my son, then prove it."

And Samuel watched, falling to his knees in a ball of tears, as his father left him to begin his mission, without another word.

CHAPTER 9

DAEMON

DAEMON FELT THE PAIN erupt through his back as his body collided into the side of the car and dropped like dead weight to the ground. For a moment, he was afraid he wouldn't be able to move.

But when he heard Lorelei scream his name, a new kick of energy rushed through his body and his eyes shot open.

Lorelei was still on the side of the road, but was now surrounded by four demons. Zanul was directly in front of her, inching his way toward her while the other three flanked her from all sides. The fear that he felt, the fear of them harming Lorelei, fueled him to stand. Getting to his feet, he breathed through the pain from the impact and started putting into motion his self-healing to alleviate it enough to die down to a dull ache.

Lorelei turned to look at him and the relief on her face to see he was alright guided him through his next moves.

Quickly, he ripped off his sweatshirt that was concealing his wings in one swift motion, and let them unfurl to their fullest capacity behind him, spanning 6 feet in full width, which only enhanced his imposing frame. With the moon in full view above them shining brightly down on his now exposed chest, the muscles in his shoulders and arms tensed when seeing Zanul was a few steps away from Lorelei. Daemon sprinted at full speed, his wings helping him glide over the ground, and with one brutal kick to his side; Zanul was flying off and skidding across the dirt.

The other demons sprang into action, and Daemon's eyes burned brighter, channeling his power throughout his body to enhance his blows. Power and magic spilled from them as the gentle demeanor he had moments ago, vanished completely.

There's a lot of them. But if I can just weaken them enough to use the Finishing Spell, we can get out of this alive.

Suddenly, a demon from behind, a woman with dark purple hair that formed an overly-large mohawk on the top of her head, came running toward Lorelei. Daemon mumbled the words to ignite his full strength and flew toward her.

It happened so fast, mere inches from Lorelei's back; Daemon intercepted the demon woman and punched her square in the jaw so hard that it looked like he might have knocked her out cold. But he watched as she got back to her feet, her face now screwed up in pain and she hissed as she jolted back at him, her hands long and the claws she released from her fingertips like daggers, they sliced through the air around Daemon's head. He moved like a dancer-easily dodging each swing the demon woman attempted, waiting for her to make a mistake. And after a few more slices through the air, there it was. The demon woman had over-extended her slashing arm and was off balance, leaning forward a fraction of a hair too much—the perfect, seemingly innocent mistake.

A mistake that would cost her life.

It was these kinds of moments in battle, the smallest, minute overreaction or underreaction that determined the winner. One that Daemon was particularly skilled in noticing. One of Daemon's special abilities, one that used to earn him the title as one of the most skilled warriors in God's arsenal, was the ability to slow down time for himself, but keep others around him unchanged. It didn't slow it down by much, but enough to catch these fatal errors before the other party could see what hit them. Waiting one more second, he then spun around, his foot hitting her chest precisely; he heard the crack of her ribs collapsing over her lungs and she fell to the ground. Before she could regain her strength, he sang the words that ignited her in an instant. The power from the Finishing Spell surrounded Daemon like a bubble, it's green light building up, resembling a firework exploding—sending the light directly at the demon woman and setting her alight. In a swift pop, she was dead.

This was all done so quickly, Lorelei didn't even have time to react to Daemon speeding past her. Seconds was all it took for him to defeat one of the four demons. Although it looked easy, this one fight had already zapped a good portion of his magic away; seeing as he didn't have as much as he did before his fall and it being years since his last major battle, he was weaker than he imagined he'd be. And if this demon had been the weakest of the others by far, he desperately needed to be smarter to conserve what magic he had left. Whirling around, he caught Lorelei's eye and ran back to her. Grabbing her shoulders firmly he made her look at him.

"Lorelei, you need to run. Take the car and get out as fast as you can. Do you understand me?"

He watched as she thought to argue with him, but he shook his head and couldn't hold back the desperation in his tone.

"Please. I'm begging you."

She nodded without another word and ran toward the car that surprisingly hadn't collapsed completely at his body hitting it, watching her fumbling to open the driver's side door. The demon who he had seen with Zanul in the market, brandished a fiery whip and lassoed it, catching and wrapping itself around Lorelei's left arm. She screamed in agony while fire began burning away her skin. She was now being dragged along the ground, pulled by the demon and Daemon let out a growl that sounded animalistic as he lifted out his wings and soared through the air.

Stop holding back, you fool! You have to use your more powerful spells! If you don't, Lorelei will die!

Right before Daemon plunged into the demon, whose eyes were filled with satisfaction at Lorelei's screams of pain, Daemon cried out his next attack.

"BODVA POILP I OBZA!"

And without touching him, the demon's smile faded instantly as the top half of his body slid off from the bottom half. Not a killing spell by any means, as it was a type of slicing spell which would resemble the damage done by brandishing a real sword. But it was enough to slow down demons and typically injure them enough to then be terminated. The demon howled in agony while testing whether he could pull himself by his arms to get to his legs and somehow re-attach himself. But Daemon was on him again quickly, knowing that the demon could still recover from the blow if he had the time, and began singing the words that made the demon become nothing more than a pile of ash.

Daemon didn't have time to relish in this victory though, as the third, massive blonde-haired demon, who was probably twice the size as Daemon, knocked his large fist into the side of his head. Daemon soared through the air, landing with a thud and began rolling over on his side, trying to regain his breath as the demon now went for Lorelei, who was cradling her arm to her chest.

No..no...I can't..let him...get the fuck up, Daemon!

Before he could make himself move, a rough hand grabbed a fistful of his silver hair and was wrenching his head backwards. Zanul's face was above him and he smiled at Daemon.

"It's lovely to be running into you like this, Daemon. Although, I must say, the last time we crossed each other, you were much more fearsome than the sad sack that's before me now."

Zanul's grin grew larger; he was loving every second of this.

"What's all of this to you, anyways? Why help the pathetic girl?" Zanul narrowed his eyes, curiosity lingered in his question.

Daemon didn't respond, but sputtered out blood that dripped down his chin as he forced his head to swivel to where Lorelei was now knocked out in the large demon's arms.

His heart felt it could break into a thousand tiny pieces. Her slender frame, her dusty-blonde hair falling over her face, the arm that had been injured hung over the demon's own that was holding her up. Daemon's strength was practically gone. The pain from the blows he took were now creeping back up on him. It was difficult to keep healing himself while also performing such high level spells. It was draining him. He felt totally helpless.

"Why aren't you just killing us, then? If that's what you were tasked with doing, why haven't you already?"

Zanul licked his lips, and it made Daemon's stomach churn.

"You know me, Daemon. You know how much I love to play with my prey before finishing it off.."

Daemon didn't have to hear Zanul directly say it for him to know he was talking about Lorelei. Daemon knew all too well the rumors of what Zanul meant by "playing." Daemon's anger spurred him to grab the hand that latched to his hair, and chant the only spell he could think to use. The Finishing Spell. He'd never used it unless he knew the demon was already weak, but this time, he planned to use it to kill both demons off at once. It was something he didn't know had been done before; and one he wasn't sure he himself would survive from.

But it was the only chance he had to save Lorelei.

Using the last of his power, he focused all of his magic energy on this one spell. Looking once more at Lorelei, it renewed him enough to give it his best shot. The chant and song-like quality of the spell changed; it was pouring out of him in a way he hadn't heard before and yet, he knew that his instincts were kicking in to carry him through the rest of the way.

Daemon slowed time again, so that Zanul couldn't stop him from finishing it. In mere seconds, the entire area surrounding them glowed with intense green and white light that caused Zanul to release Daemon's hair long enough to sing the final word of the spell; he watched as both Zanul and the other demon screamed in anguish as the light flickered in the air like fire, consuming their bodies at the same time, causing the demon holding Lorelei to ignite instantaneously. Daemon sprung out of the way as fast as he could and caught Lorelei before she hit the ground just as Zanul burst into flame and was no more.

Lorelei was still unconscious and injured, but she was safe. She was alive. *Barely alive.*

The happiness at this one fact could've lit up the entire night sky around them. Daemon could no longer hold back the emotion that filled him to the brim. For the first time in centuries, he let the tears fall, and hugged Lorelei to his body, pulling her head to rest against his bare chest, his wings curling around them both like a blanket as the world around him started to fade in and out. He used so much of his power, he wasn't sure he could move. His insides felt like broken glass, but he continued to cradle Lorelei to him, swearing to himself then and there, that he would never let Lorelei's life hang in the balance like this ***ever again.***

CHAPTER 10

LORELEI

LORELEI FELT A WARMTH surrounding her; it brought with it a sense of peace. She thought she could stay in that place for all time; to luxuriate in this moment that made her feel safe and loved. But a searing pain originating from her arm evaporated that feeling of tranquility, pulling her away from the coziness she found herself in. She opened her eyes and found Daemon.

Her heart fluttered at the initial sight of him. He was holding her to him, cradling her gently while propping himself up against the car. His wings, which she hadn't seen up close before, engulfed her like a warm, living blanket of inky silk. The black feathers were soft against her skin and when light caught them, an iridescent green pulsed throughout. The feathers shifted and stirred with Daemon's breathing, like they were an entity all their own. She looked again at Daemon's face and he was smiling from ear to ear at her; but he was different than she'd seen him before—absolutely exhausted. He seemed on the verge of falling over if not for how tightly he clung to her. Dark bags were under his eyes and she could feel his heart beating furiously.

"Oh Lorelei, thank goodness!"

Exasperation lingered in his words as Daemon hugged Lorelei tighter to him and bent down to leave a gentle kiss on her forehead, one she could feel even after his lips pulled back.

She tried to sit up from his lap, placing her arm down to reinforce herself when she was reminded that this arm was still injured, and a wave of pain shot through her that was so intense, she yelped and lost her balance, falling back into his arms, sweat forming on her brow from the exertion. Daemon helped her sit up slowly, shushing her to not move much as he leaned her against the side of the car to sit upright beside him. He carefully held her arm out for him to inspect, and Lorelei did her best not to show on her face how much it hurt.

"I would usually be able to heal this for you, but under the circumstances..."

Lorelei saw that his eyes betrayed a feeling of guilt, and she did her best to buck up her strength and reassure him.

"It's okay, I know you need to rest and heal yourself. I can manage until then."

Although she didn't see the end of the battle, having been knocked out cold by the monstrously large demon, she only imagined how difficult it had to be for him to defeat all of those demons on his own. His eyes weren't glowing as brightly as usual, and she felt the tremble in his hand when it held her wrist to better see the lassoed burn marks encircling her forearm.

Even though they were both hurt, they were alive. They made it through their first major fight which was a victory in itself. But as she looked into his eyes again, she knew he was worried about how much trouble they were both in, and whether or not he was going to be able to protect them enough to see them make it to their end point.

The night turned severely quiet after what was such a tumultuous and near-death incident. It felt odd; like this was only the calm before the real storm, and that things were only going to get more difficult and more dangerous from here on out. Daemon stood up and rummaged through the car that was badly banged up, and pulled out her suitcase from the dented trunk.

"Is there something in here you don't care too much about for me to use as a bandage for your arm? We're going to have to do this the old fashioned way."

Lorelei nodded and was able to get herself up, bracing herself against the car for support caused more pain to radiate throughout her arm, making her feel a little dizzy. Breathing through it, she felt the dizziness subside and returned her attention to where Daemon stood. Worry etched his face and she put on a reassuring smile to ease his mind. Walking over to him, she unzipped the suitcase and pulled out an old t-shirt she usually slept in, quickly covering the lacy underwear that lay beneath it with a sweater, hopefully before Daemon had time to notice. She sat in the back seat while Daemon crouched by her knees and began ripping up the shirt into smaller pieces, before tying them tightly around her arm. His face was focused and when he finished, he stood again and let his wings stretch out; the look on his face suggesting doing so was more painful than he previously thought; letting them fold up once again against his back and finding the hoodie he'd thrown off him earlier laying in the grass, he brushed it off to put on, and stood quietly looking around at the carnage before them.

She wanted to say something to him; about the battle, about whether he was alright, about the conversation they were having just before the demons showed up; but she was afraid to. Afraid to disrupt the singular moment of peace that might vanish in a blink of an eye if she did. She got up from the seat and closed the door behind her. Daemon was standing a few feet away, staring up into the sky; the stars were blinking softly against the velvet black backdrop of night. She was almost to him, opening her mouth to finally speak, when she heard a rustling sound off to their right.

Daemon was immediately in front of her in a protective stance before either had the chance to see what or who it was. Lorelei peeked around his broad shoulders and watched as he scanned the grassy area on the side of the road in front of them. When a pair of red eyes meets her own, Daemon was zooming across the field before she has the chance to stop him. A shadowed body popped up from behind a tall patch of grass and raised its long arms into the air above its head.

"Wait! No, please! Don't hurt me!"

The voice wavered with fear and Lorelei took several steps forward in its direction. As she got closer, she finally saw him. It was a tall, slender boy who looked to be in his teens. His red eyes blinked, but before she could respond, Daemon rounded up on the boy and put him in a headlock. He was squirming under Daemon's hold, but impulsively Lorelei ran to stop him.

"Daemon! Don't hurt him! He's just a kid!"

Daemon looked at Lorelei in shock and furrowed his brows making no indication of any intention to loosen his grip on the boy.

"Lorelei, he's a demon. He must've been skulking around, hiding during the fight. We can't let him live. Not after what happened earlier. Not after what could have happe–"

Shame crippled Daemon's usually flawless features, the heart-wrenching reality that Daemon was unsuccessful in keeping Lorelei from being harmed, was written all over his face. She felt for him, and wanted nothing more than to reassure him that he saved her, but an unsettling feeling that doing so would bring about no comfort for him—not here when another demon was in his grasp and she was clutching her maimed arm close to her body.

Lorelei was only a couple of meters from them both and caught the eyes of the boy. He had curly, bright red hair that matched his eyes, and freckles splattered his face. His eyes were pleading; he was nothing more than a scared kid. She looked back to Daemon who tightened his lock on the boy.

"I don't think he's dangerous. Don't you think he would've tried to attack us by now if his goal was to do so? The fact that he's been hiding here the entire time and hasn't, should say something."

Daemon let out a huff, clearly frustrated.

"This isn't some normal kid, Lorelei. He's Lucifer's son, Samuel. I can smell it on him. The same scent of his father. He's literally the closest person to one of our enemies! There's no way we could trust this kid."

For the first time since he was spotted, Samuel spoke up.

"Please, yes...I am Lucifer's son. But I never wanted to come along on this mission. I never planned on hurting you two! I swear!"

Lorelei walked to Daemon and placed a hand on one of his arms.

"Daemon, please. Let's at least talk to him. He's young and obviously terrified. I think we will find he isn't a threat."

Daemon met her eyes and she watched as he wanted to fight her on this, but instead released the boy and walked to stand beside Lorelei, glaring at the boy in front of them. Samuel rubbed the back of his neck; Daemon's hold on him had obviously been uncomfortable. He kept looking at Daemon, clearly terrified of him. But Lorelei moved a little closer, which Daemon was not okay with. He quickly grabbed her arm, attempting to pull her back to him. Lorelei turned and raised her eyebrow at him, and he begrudgingly released.

Lorelei gave the boy a smile. He couldn't be older than 17, and from his demeanor and the fact he looked nothing like the rest of his demon buddies, being so much smaller in comparison, made Lorelei curious why they sent him on this mission in the first place. And if Daemon was right, and this was the son of Lucifer, why would he risk losing his child in case something had gone wrong?

"Samuel, was it? I'm Lorelei. Do you mind explaining to us why you didn't attack us?"

Samuel stood nervously, one arm holding onto the other.

"I...I am sure it will be difficult to believe me. But I am not like my comrades. I have never understood the fight between Heaven and Hell and humans. It all seems pointless to me, which is why my father sent me on this mission. In his eyes, I am a failure and a dishonor to all of my people. He told me I would be killed if I didn't go on this mission, that you had to die, and it was my duty to make sure of it. I couldn't do it though, the moment we arrived and the others were busy, I hid. I couldn't bring myself to do anything."

Samuel's voice caught in his throat, and Lorelei's heart wept for him. This boy grew up in a place he didn't choose to be; in a life he didn't choose to live, to a father who would willingly sacrifice him for his cause; cried out to her in that moment. It wasn't a cry she heard with her ears, but a cry she heard and felt with her heart. It ate away at her insides, a mixture of sadness and resentment. This war was destroying lives; even the life of Lucifer's own son. How could this be what was meant for them all?

Lorelei heard Daemon behind her, which irritated her greatly.

"He's probably making all this up. I bet you he was hiding there to attack when we were at our most vulnerable."

Lorelei spun around and she let her irritation show through her next words.

"If you truly think that, isn't it one of your powers to discern whether a demon is lying? Why not put that to the test. I think he will pass with flying colors."

She watched Daemon's look of astonishment at her tone, but she held firm as his eyes narrowed in the boy's direction and he began what she assumed was his method of seeing into him; of knowing whether his words were truth or if he indeed was deceiving them. After a moment, Daemon let out a gruff groan.

"His story checks out."

Lorelei was elated and smiled at Daemon, who in return attempted to give a small one back; but she could see he was still untrusting of the kid. Lorelei walked slowly towards Samuel, whose expression was full of relief now.

Lorelei gave a broad smile and reached out to pat Samuel on the shoulder.

"It's lovely to meet you, Samuel. Welcome aboard our crazy ride." Lorelei giggled and Samuel joined her. Daemon, however, was quick to interject.

"Welcome aboard? Lorelei, I have agreed there isn't a need to kill him. But we can't possibly bring him along with us."

"Why not? He said he never understood the fight or supported it, which suggests he is on our side. And, he also said if he returned from this mission without accomplishing it, he would be killed. We can't let that happen, Daemon. He cannot die because of me. Please...I can't have that over me...weighing on me. I can't, Daemon."

She swallowed; tears sat beneath the surface begging to come forward and take her all over again, her heart overwhelmed with the prospect that anyone being around her meant death for many, and the thought of another death—*a kid's death*—was too much to take; even if he was from the enemy side. Daemon sighed, finally turning his back to Samuel and walked to Lorelei, cupping her face, his thumb running along her cheek gently.

"Okay, Sunflower, okay." His voice was hushed in reluctant understanding.

The pet name sent a thrilling sensation throughout her. Before, back at Camden Market when she mentioned her love of sunflowers, he joked calling her that. Now, he spoke it with only affection and warmth, no sarcasm, no cheek—and it felt right; his velvet tone softened just for her, and it caused the flutter of her heart to intensify as his lips grazed her cheek ever so slightly. Lorelei saw this was hard for Daemon to let his guard down like this, so she grabbed his hand, intertwined their fingers and gave a reassuring squeeze. This seemed to lift him a little and he squeezed her hand back; Samuel would come with them.

Lorelei looked around at both of them, their strange crew against the end of the world, and couldn't help but smile at the absurdity. A human girl, a Fallen angel, and the son of the actual Devil against Armageddon? It sounded like some ridiculous comedy movie. Yet, here they were, climbing into a beat-up car after a fight scene from Hell, *literally,* off to face who knows what, as the most unlikely trio imaginable—it wasn't hard to find the comical effect it created. She strode behind them, a playful hint in her tone, shrugging her shoulders as she spoke.

If this was her destiny, she might as well embrace it head on—insane or not.

"Alright, boys. Let's save humanity, shall we?"

CHAPTER 11

SAMUEL

EVEN THOUGH DAEMON DID his best to fix the car and it was still running, Samuel still felt the bumpiness of the road beneath them and a creaking sound from the vehicle that left room for doubt at its abilities to get them safely to their next destination. Daemon said he'd make sure they got a better car before driving to Stonehenge tomorrow, seeing as it was near midnight now. Although Lorelei was being nothing but kind to Samuel as they drove to find a hotel nearby, Samuel could still feel Daemon was checking the rearview mirror on him while in the backseat of the car. Lorelei obviously noticed this too, and was doing her best to keep conversation going as they finished their trek toward Stonehenge.

Lorelei had done some research on her phone to find The George Hotel to stay at for the next couple of nights. Samuel listened contentedly as Daemon and Lorelei discussed how long they needed to stay—as they were unsure whether they would be able to get close enough to the boulders at Stonehenge to unlock whatever it was Lorelei needed to in daylight. Daemon suggested they go scope it out earlier in the day and then return when the crowds were gone so they could be alone, allowing Lorelei time to spend within the massive stones.

Samuel was so fascinated by their story of their adventure so far and felt relieved to know he was not the only one from one of the sides who didn't feel the necessity of the war. Even though Daemon hardly spoke to Samuel, he only hoped he would have the chance to continue to prove to the both of them that he meant no harm.

Lorelei trusted him from the moment their eyes locked in the field when he gave away his presence. She was so caring and Samuel perceived that despite her only being human, there had to be something extra special about her to make her be the only one capable of saving the world. It was so strange to finally be out of Hell and be around someone who was human. Sitting in the soft seats of the car, which they called a "Range Rover," and listening to interesting music that played from a little box in the front of the car was all so surreal to him. Music in Hell was only played live—the inventions were amazing here!

For his entire life, he spent hours upon hours with his nose in books learning all he could about human life; but actually being in it was more than he ever thought it'd be. In reality, it was so simplistic—if you ignore the fact that the three of them were endeavoring to stop the end of the world. If he ignored *that* portion of truth, and just sat there listening to the other two talk and Lorelei softly sing the words to the music, Samuel almost felt like this might've been what it was like to be with friends or even a family. Although there were similar things to what was around him in Hell, he never really had any friends or a family who cared for him. And his father was never one to be caring or to show affection. The only thing he cared for was the cause. Samuel was only ever in the way.

Samuel spent the majority of the car ride trying to explain to the two of them why he was sent on the mission after them in the first place; how his father believed him to be weak and needing to prove himself; how he always was in trouble for questioning the way of things; how he was fascinated by humans and couldn't possibly believe the only way to live was to manipulate or kill others. Lorelei was incredibly understanding, asking various questions about the way of life in Hell and then they even got lost in discussing several topics of human history they both were particularly fond of.

Daemon would chime in with the occasional question, mostly on Lucifer's plans Samuel might happen to know about, how agitated was Lucifer and how likely was it he might strike sooner than the arranged date, and how many did Lucifer have in his army so far and what methods were they procuring to aid their chances of winning. These questions were much harder for Samuel to answer because in all honesty, his father never felt him worthy of knowing his battle plans. He could only tell him the rumors that were going around about how the tension felt high, but that many beneath his father believed it was unwise to strike too soon. Daemon seemed annoyed at how little Samuel was able to tell them, probably assuming that if they were going to bring him along, he might as well be useful. Daemon kept these thoughts to himself though, clearly not wanting to upset Lorelei.

"So Samuel, do you believe your father will send others after you?"

Samuel swallowed; he hadn't thought about that.

"I don't think so...I think he will hear the mission failed and be sending others after you two, but that will take a little bit because no one successfully returned to report the error themselves. Most likely a recovery team will be sent in the next several hours to see why there hasn't been any communication, and then plans will be made on what to do next. So we may be in the clear for another day or two at least. I'm sure it won't be good when he finds out I tagged along with you either though. I'll be considered a traitor. But that doesn't matter to me. You guys are doing what is right and I don't want to be a coward and stand by while innocent people get hurt..."

He was surprised at himself for speaking so confidently. He had never been able to say these kinds of things outloud to anybody else before without getting punished or reprimanded or told he was being crazy for going against what has always been. But Lorelei smiled so brightly at him, and it eased the anxiety over what his father might do if he were caught.

Daemon finally spoke up for the first time in awhile.

"Alright, we're coming up to the hotel now. I'll go check us in. I'll get a room for me and the boy, and I'll get you a room by yourself."

His eyes shot to Lorelei and she nodded. Samuel felt a little uneasy about sleeping in the same room as Daemon, but Lorelei turned in her seat to give him a reassuring nod which did in fact make him feel better. Samuel knew Daemon wouldn't do anything to him as long as he didn't want to hurt or upset Lorelei. He only hoped that in time, Daemon might come around to accepting and trusting him.

Parking the car, Daemon got out to go secure their rooms and Lorelei went to the trunk to pull out her suitcase. Samuel quickly offered to help her with it when he noticed she was having a hard time lifting it, wincing in pain. Samuel noted the wrap around her arm—the same arm that was nearly ripped off her body by a deadly fire whip. If only he was brave enough to have stopped it, it must've hurt horribly. Her gaze followed his eyes and she shoved her long sleeve over the injury to hide it.

"Nothing to worry about, Samuel. Thanks for your help!"

Samuel rolled the suitcase to the front door of the hotel for her and when Daemon came back with room keys, Samuel followed him to the one they would be sharing. He hadn't realized how exhausted he was until he stepped foot into the small room with two twin beds. He mumbled a goodnight to Lorelei at the door and nodded at Daemon before picking the one nearest the wall, flopping onto the bed. He decided he would shower in the morning, but for now, the feeling of finally being accepted with people who felt the same as he did his entire life helped him drift into a deep, and restful sleep, for the first time in his existence.

CHAPTER 12

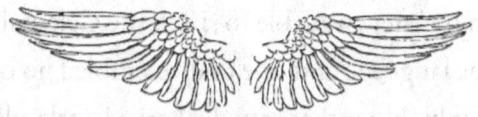

DAEMON

DAEMON WATCHED AS LORELEI said goodnight to the both of them and closed the door behind her. The lack of her presence seemed to make itself clearer to him more than usual now. When Daemon walked into his own room, only a few rooms away from Lorelei's, he saw that Samuel was already passed out on the bed nearest the opposite wall.

At least if he gets up in the night, I'll know if he's just going to the bathroom or snooping around...or worse; attempting to assassinate Lorelei in her sleep.

Thinking this made Daemon feel a little bad, but it was better for him to be on guard still rather than letting it down just yet when a threat could still be present. Maybe Lorelei was right; maybe his story was true, which he kept validating throughout the car ride to the hotel every so often just to make sure he wasn't lying. But it was hard to think that the son of Lucifer would be so drastically opposite to him. Daemon at least thought the kid would be useful as far as information on his father's plans or perhaps even fighting skills.

But from what his responses in the car would suggest, he was good for neither of those things. And to Daemon, this was concerning. After the showdown with the demons, it was very clear to Daemon that both Lorelei, and now Samuel, needed some training. If more were going to come after them, and it was sure that would be the case, then they needed to be better prepared. Something that crossed his mind more than once on the journey to the hotel was whether or not he should try to teach Lorelei some Enochian. It has never been said that a human was ever taught it before, but seeing how she's the one they all want to kill most, it might not hurt to give it a chance. No human he knew was able to speak the Celestial language. It was an ancient, complex language and one that resembled no other on Earth. It may be one of the only things that actually keeps Lorelei alive in a pinch.

The other thing that was bothering him was the fact they hadn't really had any closure about their conversation before the demons arrived. The look of Lorelei's deep, blue eyes turning a misty grey as tears streamed down her face because she felt a sense of betrayal at Daemon keeping the secret of the soul connection from her, still made his heart clench with guilt.

Not to mention her arm was concerning to him. Demon weapons were no joke, and a human who didn't have the healing capabilities of an angel—was far worse off. Breakfast at the little café in Inverness felt like a world away now; so much pain and suffering already happened since then. Daemon did his best to push these thoughts from his mind temporarily as he took a quick shower.

The water felt good against his aching body. Since the fight, he was healing steadily but it was definitely slower than it usually was. The image of the double Finishing Spell he performed flashed through his mind; it was miraculous that it worked in the first place. He'd never heard of an angel doing it before, and wondered how he had been able to when his power was already so low. He leaned his head against the shower wall, letting out a breath that felt like he might've been holding since the moment the group of demons showed up, and allowed the hot water to trickle down his wings which extended to the floor behind him. They took up most of the tiny shower and the black of the feathers glistened as the water bounced and shimmied their way down them. The hot water helped relieve the ache from keeping them bunched up so often. It was a necessary thing to do obviously, but being able to stretch them out at the end of the day was a welcome relief.

Breathing deeply, he tried to calm his racing mind but he was finding it difficult to do so. He was so close to losing Lorelei earlier that evening. The thought made him want to buckle over in shame. He had been able to protect her, but not nearly as well as he should've. She still got hurt, and if he hadn't performed that last spell, her life may have very well ended tonight. Knowing that only made him angrier at himself for his inability to do more. He only felt that scared years ago when he watched her small body get hit by the car and wondered if he might be too late to save her.

Shaking his head, a piece of his hair falling over his face, he sighed and turned the water off. Drying himself, he got dressed again. His clothes were dirty but he decided to find a change of clothes somewhere tomorrow. For now, he threw on his black jeans and sweatshirt again, before checking one last time to see Samuel still fast asleep, and then slipping out of the room quietly, he walked a few doors down to stand in front of Lorelei's.

Knocking softly, Daemon waited until he heard shuffling feet quickly coming to open the door. Seeing Lorelei's face again eased his troubled mind. She gave him a smile, and it was then he noticed she was in nothing but a towel draped over her lush frame. A blush was sure to be spreading across his face, so he did his best to keep his eyes on her face and not let them stray further down. Curtly, he finally spoke.

"You didn't look through the peephole to make sure it wasn't somebody else."

He saw her eyes roll and she chuckled.

"Do you ever stop worrying? Besides, I figured you would be coming anyway."

"You did?" He perked up, genuinely surprised.

Lorelei didn't respond as she turned and walked into the room, inviting Daemon inside silently. Sauntering in, Daemon's eyes caught the curve of her breasts in the towel that was barely covering what it needed to.

Dear god...she isn't making this easy...

Before the flush in his cheeks could return, he was grateful to see she was strutting into the bathroom and returned a few minutes later changed into some shorts and a t-shirt. Even wearing that though, with her golden hair still wet falling down her shoulders, she was stunning. Her blue eyes caught his and he was afraid he'd been staring too long. But she smiled at him again and sat down on the bed, waiting for Daemon to join her.

"I assumed you wanted to come check my arm before you went to bed."

"Yes, how is it feeling?"

Lorelei shrugged her shoulders and lifted her arm out for him to inspect. She was doing her best to be strong. If they looked up the definition of strength in the dictionary, Daemon was sure she'd be the picture beside the word.

"It hurts like hell, but I can handle it. I know you're still recovering. I went ahead and ripped up another shirt to use until we can get some proper bandages tomorrow."

Daemon took the pieces of the shirt from her hand gingerly, getting down on his knee in front of her. After looking over the wound while seeing how deep it burned, he gently and silently wrapped her arm back up. He caught the faint sign of Lorelei's breath catching in the back of her throat while his fingers were at work with the wrappings. Making his way up her arm, his fingertips grazing her skin, heat rose into his face and he did his best to control the increasing tumble session his heart was having.

He was kneeling before her, practically between her legs, and the temptation was beginning to make him question if he could resist. The scent of her lotions and perfume pulled him closer, goosebumps forming on her exposed legs where his breath hit them. With his enhanced senses, he could feel the rapidity of her pulse beneath his touch, the way her flowery scent now included another, deeper scent...one that pooled near her core he was so close to. He swore in his mind to keep himself from going there, because he felt a rising *carnal need for her*.

A reaction he wasn't sure was exaggerated in his head or if it was a response he sincerely never felt before with any previous lover. All the carefully curated cool, nonchalant demeanor he'd worked on over the centuries not only for his duties prior, but as the only protection for his most inner parts, couldn't prepare him for the way she made him yearn for her; the desire she aroused to lose himself mind, body and soul; to crave and ***consume*** her entirely.

Composing himself, his mind reeling at what he would love to do to that perfect body of hers, he forced himself to tie off the wrappings and he stood, quite unsure what to do with himself as the distance between them felt like a crater he couldn't quite place. He couldn't bring himself to move further; there was too much unspoken, too much they hadn't had time to discuss. He didn't even know where her head was at, and there was no way he would sully her by ruining what didn't even have time to blossom—*yet*. Running his fingers through his silver hair uncomfortably, he spoke to fill the silence between them.

"I should be alright by tomorrow, I can most likely heal a good portion of it then."

Daemon watched the disappointment cross Lorelei's face; raising an eyebrow at him, a hint of sadness pervaded her words. "Do you think I am going to bite or something? You don't seem to want to get close to me unless you have to."

Daemon shook his head, but noticed he instinctively made his way to the wall across from her already. Stopping himself, he turned slowly to face her.

"No..no..I just...I know we sort of left things unfinished before everything went down and I...I didn't want to.."

Daemon's voice felt small; he was never one to question his actions, or God forbid, get shy around somebody, especially with a woman. In centuries past, he found he was adept in flirtation and seduction, and always had the right thing to say, or the move to make a girl swoon; but Lorelei turned him into a damned pre-pubescent boy, unsure of what to do with his hands. The way she tied a chain around his heart, how his body responded to her without a word spoken, how he fucking stumbled over his thoughts when she was nearby—it was as infuriating as it was enlightening.

Never in his lifetime would he believe he possessed the capabilities to be taken by surprise, particularly emotionally. And yet, here he was. Too afraid to take the next step, getting lost in the eyes of a mortal. Not just for pleasure, but in a way that resonated with his very being. She opened him up in a way he couldn't fully put a finger on to explain how or why. He was stumped by her, and she was totally unaware of the physical effect she instilled in him, fists clenching to keep from grabbing her—holding her and not letting go.

At the same time, they nearly died earlier. On top of a rough moment before where Lorelei called him a dick, the sting of the word still made Daemon's heart sink. It was a dick move to hide that from her, to hide the fact he saved her, that a part of him was eternally connected to her essence. Who was he to keep that from her? She deserved to know. He should've told her from the first moment. He was foolish to doubt her ability to handle such information. There was no way to gauge how she felt with him currently, and he cared for her enough to keep his distance; even if it broke him inside to do so. No lines would be crossed; he would never instigate something he wasn't sure she ever wanted. No. He needed to step back, despite his increasing need to be close to her.

He thought back to the look on Lorelei's face when she realized what he'd been keeping from her. The image of her tears falling still made his chest twinge. Looking down at his feet, he sighed deeply and knew Lorelei was watching him. But before he had time to say more, she was swiftly on her feet and making her way toward him. He barely had time to look up and see that she was meager inches from him. And as he opened his mouth to speak, she placed a soft hand upon his chest and leaned up, placing her lips against his own with a ferocity that startled—and entranced him.

Kissing her sent tingling sensations that filled his entire body. The way their lips moved against each other made it seem like they'd done this a million times before.

In her kiss was the Universe to him. The love he'd never felt until now, the worries of their journey, and the pain of his past melted away; leaving only his purest emotions, his purest instincts, *and the purest passionate love that he was sure there could be no equal to.*

He finally found his own hand on the back of her neck, drawing her closer to his body; he knew that all the feelings he felt for her before now, were true. And he knew she felt the same way. Strengthening the kiss, Lorelei's arms wrapped tightly around his neck, the small of her back curving more to tug him closer. When her tongue swept against his, a growling moan escaped from his throat; his hands gripped her thin t-shirt and found the warmth of her skin beneath it, fingertips digging into her, causing a stirring reaction from Lorelei that reinforced his hunger.

Close wasn't close enough.

His chest pounded, like his heart was doing all it could to leap out and fasten itself to her own. There was never a first kiss before that would measure up to this one. This one surpassed all others, and he knew right then, he'd never get enough of her lips from here on out. There was no more denying it; he was hers. She had him. And he didn't want anything more than to stay hers, this way and every way; for the rest of his existence.

When their lips unlocked, the moment stilled to nothing but breathing and passion, which continued to rage like fire overtaking the field of his centuries long life; putting all else before this to blow away to ash. This kiss, *this moment*, was the light he lost and begged for: the knowing he was where he was meant to be and that all the heartache was worth it. Daemon could see how easily the pain of the years could slip away within that kiss. Lorelei set ablaze to his renewed spirit and hope in a way he feared was lost long ago. He licked his lips, making sure to memorize the taste of her lip gloss; a decadent mixture of raspberry and vanilla he would dream about for the rest of time; imprinted into his psyche like an iron-clad tattoo.

Taking a deep breath, he leaned his forehead against hers, holding her tightly against him. Lorelei nuzzled his nose and he chuckled, finally pulling back enough to see those blue eyes that reflected a beautiful, clear day. When at last she broke the silence, she spoke with a fervent reassurance.

"You have nothing to feel badly about, Daemon. You saved my life and I will always be grateful for that. Because in the end, it brought me to you."

Her words set his heart alight and his mind at ease. She was forgiving him for keeping the secret from her. Daemon cupped Lorelei's face with both hands and spoke tenderly.

"Thank you. You are truly changing me in ways I never thought possible."

Lorelei pulled him down to place another gentle kiss on his lips and grabbed his hand, leading him toward the bed.

"Will you lay with me?"

Daemon nodded, seeing that exhaustion plagued her face, her eyes growing heavier and her body moving rigidly from the ache of the evening's events. He followed her without a word, turning the lamplight off beside the bed and settling beneath the covers with her as she set her head upon his chest. With feeling her heartbeat against his own, feeling the warmth of her soft skin and the steadiness of her breath, he calmed. The mixture of passion and peace he felt with her rivaled nothing else. If he'd never known Heaven before, he'd say now, he found it in Lorelei. He'd never feel the loss of his home realm again. For this girl, this human girl, who has set his soul on fire, would be where he found his strength moving forward. She would be his destiny as he helped achieve hers.

She would not only save humanity, *but save **him** as well.*

CHAPTER 13

LORELEI

LORELEI WOKE THE FOLLOWING morning feeling the best she had in several days. Falling asleep with Daemon and feeling his comforting presence was pure bliss. It gave her the rest she so desperately needed. However, she noticed his presence was gone when she reached her fingers out to find his warm body no longer there. A piece of her felt colder than it had before. After last night, the reminder of his tongue tangling with hers, the feel of his powerful hands moving along her spine, pulling her closer; the memory now laced permanently within her mind. But she couldn't help but wonder if she'd ever get used to the sudden disappearances, the little she actually knew about his life, or the fact he was centuries old while she'd barely begun living. Would she ever amount to knowing all of him? Even the most brutal of details? Although the way her soul sang for him encapsulated every bit of the kind of love or passion she only thought possible in fairytale stories, was that enough? Or would she find herself lost in a flurry of navigating only the bits and pieces she'd find out about him, never fully gauging the sum of who Daemon is or has been throughout his long lifetime.

Not to mention, she would die. And he would live on for centuries more. A sickening feeling erupted in her stomach at the thought; a combination of anxiety and grief, for a life she wasn't sure would be possible with him.

I mean...with the circumstances..is it even possible to have a normal life with Daemon if I won't be around in eternity with him? Will we even make it to "what comes next?"

She knew dwelling on the 'what ifs' was the biggest killer of them all. Her father suffered its wrath, and she has found it to be a relentless companion over the last year since his passing. Her therapist continuously reminded her that to think of a future difficulty, or to reminisce on a past regret, which led to nothing more than the surest way to forever living life as a prisoner to your thoughts. In the situation she was in, there wasn't room to succumb to the unknown, for it was all unknown right now. Lorelei needed to put that away for another day, or she could very well drive away the first true and loving relationship with a man in her life. To worry about the future was a death wish to her wellbeing, and the possibilities of her and Daemon's potential future.

Negativity and self-doubt, be damned. Just enjoy it for the split second, Lorelei. Enjoy the incredibly sexy angel who fucking kisses you like the meaning of life could be sucked off your tongue.

She sat up and stretched, having successfully averted another wave of self-decimating thoughts for now. Although, it felt like it was becoming a little easier to keep those thoughts at bay. Maybe it was Daemon's presence that made her feel stronger, more capable. Less alone.

Lorelei lifted her arm to inspect it, the cloth from another of her ripped up t-shirts was surprisingly unsoaked with blood, but she didn't want to risk taking it off until she had something to replace it.

The early morning light beamed through the sheer curtains on the wall across from her, speckling little shapes across her body as she got out of bed and began to dress. Slipping on a pair of bootcut yoga pants, a long-sleeved red, form-fitting t-shirt and her tennis shoes, she went to the bathroom. Looking in the mirror, she at least thought she looked more alive than yesterday, and decided to leave off the foundation and put on a thin layer of mascara, before brushing her blonde hair that fell into waves down her shoulders, which it always did when she went to sleep with it still wet after a shower.

After brushing her teeth, she heard a knock at the room door. Making her way over, she opened it and immediately smiled, eyeing Daemon over as he strode through the door and began unloading some supplies he had in his arms. Besides his usual stunning emerald eyes that always made Lorelei's heart flutter when she looked into them, and his long silvery locks that whipped around his shoulders, Daemon looked like an entirely different person.

She had only ever seen him in a pair of dark jeans and a basic, grey hoodie. But now, he wore a black leather jacket that fit his form perfectly, a blue t-shirt beneath it, and some black jeans that had a few rips in them. He also donned a new pair of black boots. Lorelei watched as he began unpacking some medical supplies from a bag onto the dresser. He turned to her and with his usual nonchalant manner, addressed her with a broad smile.

"Sleep well, Sunflower?"

Lorelei's mind wandered back to the moments just before she fell away into the soothing depths of sleep. Remembering Daemon's steadied breathing, the warmth of his body against her own, and the gentle stroking of his hand through her hair, she couldn't recall if she ever slept more soundly. Which, considering what they were going through, was a funny thing to happen at all. Lorelei decided it was best to play it cool; give him a taste of his own medicine.

"Oh you know, sleeping next to such a loud snorer will have anybody miserably exhausted when they wake up."

Despite her best effort, she couldn't help but laugh. Daemon pulled her arms to wrap around his torso, and she let him guide her to him, looking up to that perfectly infuriating smirk she adored.

"I'm pretty sure I recall you being the one snoring last night, Madame."

Lorelei smiled in return and nodded.

"You're probably right. It seemed like I slept like the dead!"

Daemon smiled at her, grabbing her chin between his fingers; not roughly, but teasingly, holding her in his grasp until he leaned down and kissed her lips gently. The dichotomy of the firm hold and the gentility he expressed with the kiss sent an array of melting affection that still ignited the match he so easily lit, sending her mind to the image of pushing him to the bed without another thought. *Only this time, she didn't plan on sleeping.* She did however reluctantly silence the temptation for the time being.

"I'm glad to hear that, as I believe you will be needing as much energy as possible today. Let's rewrap your arm, eh?"

Rolling her eyes, his firm grip still on her chin made her toes curl. She wanted nothing more than to fulfill her latest daydream.

"Mm, all work and no play, is it?"

His smile broadened and he looked far too pleased at the effect of his teasing, so much so, he lowered his lips again, but instead of planting a kiss, let his lips trail her chin towards her ear, sending shivers throughout her body. Whispering softly, she gripped his jacket in an attempt to control herself.

"We are on a tight schedule, my lady. I'm afraid *playtime* will have to wait."

Lorelei's heart skittered to unfathomable speeds at being called *his lady*—it was unquestionably the sexiest thing she'd ever heard. To be his was slowly becoming all she desired to be; *and she liked the sound of it on his lips*.

Holding it together felt impossible now, but she knew their time would come and consented begrudgingly. She stole another small kiss, an open act of defiance to the angel's promptness to tending to the schedule of their very desperate salvation, before heading to the edge of the bed. She began unwrapping the makeshift bindings and when her wound was completely exposed, they both made an audible gasp.

The lassoed burn marks that previously ravaged her forearm the night prior were already half-way healed. Although it still sent pangs of pain when he touched it, it was duller than the night before. Lorelei studied her arm a moment when Daemon spoke at last.

"How is this possible? I haven't even been able to use my healing abilities on you yet, and somehow it is almost entirely healed."

Daemon looked like he was in deep thought, doing his best to figure out the puzzle in front of him. When it felt like minutes passed, he spoke again, this time looking directly at Lorelei.

"Lorelei, I want to see something. Do you remember how long it took you to recover after you were hit by the car?"

Lorelei blinked several times and then did her best to remember what happened once she woke up in the hospital all those years ago. The only thing that came to mind was that despite her injuries, the doctors kept saying how shocked they were at how quickly she was healing after something that should've killed her, or at the very least paralyzed her.

"I think I healed pretty fast actually. Why?"

Daemon didn't answer her question but continued to ask his own.

"Do you recall healing quickly with any other injuries you had after that day?"

Lorelei began recalling all the injuries that happened after the crash. There were plenty of injuries playing soccer growing up; cracked ribs, twisted ankle, fractured pinky. As well as the time she hurt her ankle after having a particularly wild night in London on her way back from a pub. She had never noticed before, but she did seem to always heal fast whenever something happened.

"Yes, I do believe I have always healed rapidly...even as a kid, I don't even remember bruises or scrapes lasting very long now that I think about it."

A hint of realization sparked within Daemon's eyes.

"I think when I gave you a piece of my soul that night, its healing power lingered long afterwards, allowing you to heal much faster than normal. Having never heard of any other angel doing this before, I didn't know what the long lasting effects would be. But it seems it has come in handy for you."

Lorelei returned her attention to her arm and it almost seemed like she could feel her body healing itself.

"Well, I suppose I have another reason to thank you for saving my life that night."

She met his eyes and saw guilt hidden behind them still, but she didn't say anything. She only hoped he would see she was no longer upset about the situation soon enough. After Daemon wrapped her arm again, he stood and made his way back toward the door.

"If you're ready, I believe the kid is already downstairs stuffing his face with breakfast at the restaurant in the hotel. We should tuck in and grab a bite before it's all gone. I want to talk over our plans for the day."

There was the slightest notion of disdain when Daemon mentioned Samuel. She didn't blame him; he was skeptical in nature, and to top it off, they were bringing along the son of one of the people most wanting to see their demise. But when Lorelei first looked into Samuel's eyes, she felt something there that didn't make her believe his intentions were false. She really believed he was a kid in a situation and circumstances he never wished to be in. She pitied him, and wanted to help in whatever way she could. Ignoring Daemon's tone, she grabbed her purse and followed him hand in hand, down to breakfast.

CHAPTER 14

SAMUEL

SAMUEL HAD ALREADY SCARFED down half of his breakfast. The food was unlike any he ever had in Hell. Everything on his plate was absolutely delicious and he was finding it hard to pace himself. As he took another large bite of his eggs, he looked around the restaurant. Well, it looked more like what they called a pub up here. It was filled to the brim with deep, rich wood colors and leather seats that were heavily worn down. There was some sort of rifle hung, prominently displayed on a wall, along with various knick-knacks around the place. From what he could tell, the building was old. It had these broad posts that went from floor to ceiling and looked as if they could've been taken off an old pirate ship, at least the pictures of ones he had seen in books. The lighting was so dim that he could hardly believe it was daylight if it weren't for light trying its best to stream through a few windows on the far wall. Despite its eclectic decor, it felt comfortable and homey.

Currently, Samuel's attention was on the tv that was playing some sort of sitcom about an office that sells paper, which he thought odd, but seeing as comedy wasn't much of a genre in Hell, he found it incredibly amusing. Suddenly he heard his name being called from across the restaurant and saw Lorelei's smiling face waving at him, and Daemon's brooding look as he followed behind her. They were holding hands and Daemon looked reluctant to release it as they pulled out the wooden chairs at his table and took a seat. Lorelei sat next to him and Daemon sat opposite from him; most likely to get the best view of him as possible in case he did something fishy. Samuel understood why Daemon was so against him coming along. He just hoped he could prove himself to Daemon in a way that truly showed that he wasn't going to do anything to harm them or ruin their mission. As Samuel was lost in thought, he hadn't noticed Lorelei addressing him, until her and Daemon were both staring at him. He quickly finished his bit of something called "hash" and wiped his mouth before at last responding to her question.

"Huh? Oh yeah, breakfast is pretty good here. And I slept well, thanks for asking."

He watched as Lorelei flagged down a waiter for a menu and began skimming over it. Daemon ordered some eggs and toast with a coffee, while Samuel couldn't hide his surprise at how large a breakfast Lorelei was getting. Daemon must've noticed Samuel's dismay, because he made a point to acknowledge it.

"Yeah, don't let it alarm ya, this one eats perhaps even more than you do."

Samuel got excited at the fact it seemed Daemon might've been being friendly to him, but when he looked up to see Daemon's attention fully on Lorelei, he figured the comment was more directed towards her than him.

"Shut up." Lorelei chuckled into her coffee cup. " You said we had a big day ahead of us. Might as well fill up when I can. Ready to go over the plan with us?"

Samuel's ears perked up, although they had told him what had happened up to this point, he wasn't exactly sure on what they were doing here.

"Alright, well, first things first, I thought we'd go check out Stonehenge after breakfast. I got us tickets for the tour, just to see if anything sparks for you while we're there. I highly doubt it since there will be so many people around. Which is why tonight after everyone has left, we will be returning to allow you to have some alone time. But before we do that, we are going to do some training."

Samuel spoke nervously before Lorelei had a chance to respond.

"T..training?"

Daemon eyed him a moment but kept his attention on Lorelei.

"Yes. Training. It can only be assumed that Hell will send more demons after us once they find out about what happened last night. And Raphael already told me that Heaven was most likely to retaliate as well. There is no denying that if we run into either side, they will be sending highly trained fighters and I know I can't protect you like I previously thought. I plan to train Samuel, assess if you truly lack abilities, and see your fighting skills in action."

Daemon paused, looking Samuel directly in the eye. There was no way Daemon was the type of teacher to go easy on someone; the idea of sparring with him terrified Samuel. Samuel let out a sigh when Daemon's gaze didn't last long, turning his body to look at Lorelei as he spoke.

"And I will be teaching you the basics of the Enochian language. I have thought it over, and seeing as the piece of my soul has helped you thus far by providing you a bit of my healing capabilities, it stands to reason that this part of you might also allow you to use Celestial speech."

"Has a human ever been able to do so before?"

Daemon finished off his cup of coffee before responding.

"No. Not that I know of. But I also had never heard of an angel performing the spell I did to save your life on a human either. So the side effects have been completely unknown until now. If that piece of me is allowing you to use some of my power to heal yourself, it doesn't hurt to try and see if it can be harnessed in other ways, too. This way, if the need arises, you will be able to better fend yourself."

"That makes sense. Do you think we will have time to learn all of this before they send anybody else after us?"

Lorelei was obviously shaken up about the events of the night prior. Her arm was bandaged up, but Samuel knew that the fire lasso used was a brutal weapon that left most maimed for life. From what he was picking up on the conversation, the spell they explained to him that Daemon cast to attach a piece of his soul to hers when she was little, was allowing Lorelei to heal quicker than most humans and could possibly allow her to speak the language of the angels. The only time he himself had ever heard it was when Daemon was using it to help him fight.

When he was hiding and peeking up from behind some tall brush, Samuel swore he could visibly see the magic from the spells hanging in the air around them. It wasn't completely clear, but he could see traces of blue and purples forming spirals and flowy loops in the air like a misty smoke. Yet, it was the final spell Daemon cast that put all the others to shame; the Finishing Spell. Samuel obviously knew about the spell the angels used to kill demons; one of the only ways to do so, but he never could've imagined just how powerful it really was until he saw Daemon perform it with his own eyes. It made the hair on the back of his neck stand straight up and was beautiful and terrifying at the same time. It was something he never imagined witnessing, and definitely something he would never forget.

"Honestly, I think they will take some time to come up with a new plan of attack. I would say until tomorrow at the earliest."

Samuel saw Lorelei's shoulders tense.

"That's not a lot of time." She looked at Daemon with concern flooding her eyes.

"You're right. It's not. I guess that means we're going to be working double time today. And for fuck's sake, let's hope Magnus was right about your intuitive and possibly psychic potential. Time is not our ally."

And with that, their food finally arrived and they ate and chatted about normal things for the remainder of the breakfast. Samuel asked questions about life on the Earth; Daemon cracked jokes at Samuel for not knowing about things; Lorelei scolded Daemon and answered Samuel's questions cheerfully, and so on. This was the first time Samuel ever spent with and around humans. They were not so different from himself or the other demons he grew up with, other than the lack of demon features. And despite himself, a feeling of familiarity rose within him. Even though the situation was far from what most would consider normal. This one breakfast, a time of pleasant conversation, jokes, and good food, made him forget about the hard journey still yet to come. To others looking in and watching the three of them chatting and eating, it would look completely and utterly normal. But to Samuel, it was *extraordinary*, because it was the first time in his life he felt he might actually belong somewhere.

CHAPTER 15

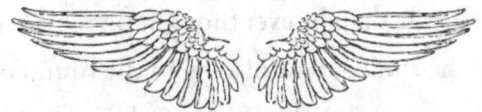

DAEMON

Once they finished their breakfast, Daemon walked them outside to a new car that was in the spot of the nearly-destroyed one from before. He was happy when Lorelei didn't question him about what he did with the old one and how he acquired the new one, because even though he knew she understood he may need to use some unsavory methods to get them through this journey, he didn't want to feel guilty for it right this second. It was only a ten minute drive to Stonehenge and when they arrived, he handed them each the tickets he got and they waited in line to start the tour. As they stood there, he assumed they looked like a family because an old English couple asked him and Lorelei how their kid ended up with such unruly, ginger-red hair.

When Lorelei spit out some lies about how her grandfather had red hair and "how it must've skipped a generation," Daemon found it hard not to blush when they were then asked how long Daemon and her had been married. When Lorelei was responding with some made up number of years, he saw one of the tour guides look their way; obviously intrigued by their conversation, and instantly put a little of his concealment spell around them which aided in concluding the conversation with the elderly couple and in turn, kept the attention of others off of them for the remainder of their wait. Once they were out of everyone's radar, he turned to Lorelei.

"How long have we been married for then, Sunflower?"

He knew sarcasm dripped off every word, but the idea of being married to Lorelei sparked a sense of pure joy inside him. Although their time together had been brief, he knew with his whole heart and soul that he loved her more fiercely than he ever thought possible for himself. When she laughed at him, he smiled, reminiscing in the sound of it.

"I think I said 8 years? But they must've thought we were older than we were because that would've made me be like..." She stopped to count. "14!"

She laughed loudly and the sound of it sent a charge of energy through him. He looked over and saw Samuel was walking through the gift shop aimlessly, obviously giving Daemon as much space as possible. For a moment, Daemon felt badly for how he was treating him. But after reminding himself who Samuel was and more importantly, who his father was; Daemon knew he couldn't let his guard down entirely yet. Shifting his eyes back to Lorelei, she looked stunning. Her eyes were sparkling today even though England had once again gone back to its usual overcast.

Finally, a bit of normalcy. All this sunshine recently has truly made this feel like England flipped on its head entirely. We already have Armageddon to stop—England can't go off the rails, too.

Finally, their tour guide corralled them together and started to explain the history of Stonehenge. As he was talking, Lorelei left to grab Samuel and they all began walking the trail towards the massive stone structure. It was a cold day, and even though Daemon's body ran hotter than humans', he even zipped up his leather jacket and stuck his hands inside its pockets. Samuel walked sheepishly beside Lorelei and was asking her questions.

"The oracle you went to said you might find answers at Stonehenge?"

"Yes, but that's all he said. He didn't say how or what I might discover. Only that I am the only one who can discover whatever it is."

Lorelei did her best to sound confident when responding, but Daemon knew she didn't have a clue what was supposed to happen. Daemon knew that all in all, they had little to no information to go on for what they were meant to accomplish on this journey, which meant they were going to have a harder time figuring it all out with much less time to do so. And although Magnus was an oracle, he was a pretty shit one, so Daemon only hoped he was right about this and Lorelei would be able to "discover" what they needed to. Daemon cut in with an airy tone.

"Well, Stonehenge is one of the places on Earth where the lines between the spiritual realm are far more blurred. According to our history, angel history that is. Stonehenge was originally built to help the ancient peoples of that time craft a space to connect their energies ceremonially to Heaven; a place to receive messages. They are perfectly placed on ley lines, similarly to the Giza pyramids you see in your dream. Angels influenced the humans to build these sites on these ley lines because of the increased energetic power between the realms here, enabling easier influence and more opportunity for ancients to remain connected to the Divine. Or so it's said. In my opinion, they are just a bunch of rocks and stones built in impressive ways; I mean—I was there during the construction of the pyramids; hot as hell, Egypt...Anyways, I watched how meticulously they tried to place the monumental buggers, how much they truly believed the impact of the ley lines would bring them good fortune from their gods. He's never admitted it but I'm pretty sure Raphael played the role of Osiris—that cocky prick. Off point, but still. It was bloody awful in my opinion, the treatment of the slaves who built them; and the Egyptians found out there were no rewards that came after its construction."

Daemon didn't lie, he truly was there when the Giza pyramids were built, or at least right towards the end. It was Raphael and Daemon's meeting point that time, where they would go over their latest missions together.

Daemon finished up a particularly complicated operation in the capital Memphis, Egypt—where the pyramids were being built. He was helping quiet an internal struggle there between the nobles and the poor. The current Pharaoh was losing reign, with the construction of the pyramids, and the fact he couldn't seem to produce an heir, tensions were high in the region, and faith in Pharaoh Pepi II was waning. Daemon was in works to assist the local regime of Memphis to take control from the Pharoah, alleviating stress for the local population and allowing the poor to regain footing with shifting the balance of the workforce to enable the locals more profit.

But when the Nile River suddenly silted up and disappeared altogether, the inability to transport materials and goods deteriorated the entire endeavor. Lack of water meant lack of food supply. Famine was spreading and the main goal turned to helping the locals flee Memphis. Daemon met with Raphael once the last group of humans were well on their way out of the city, and he'd made sure the demons who they found out were responsible for drying up of the Nile, were dealt with properly.

It was a cluster fuck. As was much of this period of time, though.

To Daemon, these "Wonders of the World," often depicted nothing more than some of the worst times in human history. Yes, a feat they were, but in the end, more harm than good came of these strides towards power and prestige that often destroyed the minds of those who initiated the construction. It was hard to think that there was good to these structures when Daemon witnessed first hand the brutality often displayed towards those it least benefited. Usually, Daemon found himself to be proud of the work he did, for he often got to rid the land of these tyrants firsthand, who claimed power over their brethren.

Unfortunately, this was not one of those times.

Many died from the creation of that blasted monument. This was only one of the reasons Lorelei's dream of the pyramids was so perplexing. It was nothing more than a display of grandeur, and some tombs of people who many wished to forget to the winds of history. Daemon included. He still remembered when he did meet up with Raphael as he asked him the point of so much human suffering for a few fortunate. Daemon was met with the dogmatic remark of coldness from his dear friend, whom never deviated from the notion that there must be balance in the world, or else the Good would forever fail.

That was the first time Daemon questioned what he did and the purpose of it all.

Luckily, his thoughts were interrupted by Samuel's subtle voice, the memory evaporating slowly, but evaporating all the same. This entire journey brought up many challenging memories for Daemon, and it wasn't at all pleasant to relive them. He was happy for the reprieve. Whether Lorelei's dream truly pointed them to the pyramids or if they were merely a metaphor for something else—he only hoped he was wrong in their significance, other than being a monument of misery and a damned, bloody pile of stones.

"I've read about those in a book about Earth's geography; I snuck it out of the restricted section at my school's library. Typically, they don't want us getting too familiar with Earth history unless it helps find the weak points in society to better exploit..." Samuel's voice trailed off momentarily, anxiety lacing his words, possibly feeling guilty for the admission, before he continued on. "I also read another book about psychic abilities once and saw something about how some humans have the ability to feel an object's energy, which can sometimes give them the ability to see flashes or visions of that object's history. Clairtangency is what they called it. Have you ever had anything like that happen to you?"

Daemon was quite surprised at Samuel's knowledge. He also figured it would have to be something to that effect. Since the moment he first encountered Lorelei, he sensed she had a highly undeveloped intuitive nature. But he wasn't sure how aware she was of her abilities until they met with Magnus back in London. And with intuitive or psychic powers, the true strength comes with the awareness of the gifts and allowing the information to flow freely through you. So if you're oblivious to it, one would see it as nothing more than mere coincidence or luck. The term "deja vu" has become popular to explain away this very experience.

"I'm not really sure if I've had anything like that happen with objects, but I have always been able to feel when something bad was about to happen. My best friend Xavier back in London who I went to college with, always said it was a spooky skill. I often didn't think much about it. I may not have known what it was until it happened, but I would get these uneasy feelings that would well up inside me just before they would occur. When it started to look like my hunches were right, I couldn't help but believe my feelings were correct. Anytime I told others about it, they told me it was just luck or coincidence."

Daemon nodded, taking in what she was saying before answering.

"All humans actually have access to this ability. It's ingrained within all of you. It's just most people choose to stay ignorant to it or don't believe it is real for one reason or another. Obviously some humans, like oracles or Seers, have more skill than others. But if you are able to recognize it happening, you can work on strengthening that ability like you would any other skill you wished to learn. It's sort of the equivalent of a spiritual muscle. The more you work it out by acknowledging when you feel it, the more it will start to become more of a conscious action rather than a subconscious one."

"Why were humans given this ability?" Samuel's quiet voice hardly broke through the wind that began to pick up.

"Well, it's a little hard to explain but the essence of it all is that each human has a Higher Self; it's the truest form of your soul and is directly

142

connected to the Divine. You know that little voice you often hear? Telling you right from wrong or telling you to feel anxious about a stranger you met on the tube, to find out on the news 3 nights later that stranger robbed a store near you? The very store you were going to and last second decided to go to another? Or how when you're beating yourself up in your head over a mistake, but there's a smaller, quieter voice telling you it will all be okay? That's what it is; in its simplest explanation. Most humans never connect to this Higher Self and therefore don't have access to its knowledge. It's supposed to be the part of you unencumbered by the human ego; the one that isn't tainted by the atrocities of the world or the hardships you face on a daily basis. Are you familiar with the story of ArchAngel Metatron? Magnus mentioned him to us when we saw him, too. Well, he was actually a human on Earth who ascended and was made an angel when he accessed his Higher Self and made a profound connection with God. After that, it became a staple trait that the angels wanted to give humans. A chance at ascension. So, Metatron worked to make it something all humans, if they wished to seek it out, had access to. But like I said, most humans prefer to remain ignorant to it which is why they never try to harness their intuitive powers or remain blind to them all together."

Daemon turned to look at Lorelei. He knew she was worried whether her own intuitive abilities would be enough to access what they needed to learn. Worry was written on her face, so he lifted out a hand from his pocket and silently interlocked his fingers with her own. When she squeezed his hand, his heart gave a lurch. She was so strong in the face of all this uncertainty. He couldn't help but admire her. Then the tour guide's voice rang over the group to announce they were there, the massive structure directly before them. Stonehenge. Daemon knew ahead of time that they roped off a circle around the structure a good distance from it. They hadn't allowed tourists to venture much closer for years now, afraid the stones would get damaged. They began to walk around the perimeter of the rope leisurely, attempting to make some distance between the rest of the large group that were excitedly taking pictures of themselves, trying to get the best angles of the stones behind them. As they walked, Daemon kept the illusion around them.

"Are you sensing anything, Lorelei?" Samuel's voice cut through the silence.

Lorelei stopped several feet behind him and was looking at the stones. Making his way to her side once more, he saw her blue eyes were a pale-ish grey now, almost resembling a stormy sky that hadn't unleashed its deluge yet.

"As a matter of fact, I do feel something. It's like a tugging in my mind but..it's muted. I don't think I'll be able to understand what it is with all these people around. There's too much energy interfering. But, this is definitely where we need to be."

Daemon chuckles, "Well, looks like Magnus came in handy after all."

They continued the tour, believing it would be too suspicious to leave in the middle of it, and chatted about what their next move would be.

"You seriously think you can train me to fend off other demons *and* angels?" Samuel's voice trembled with fear and Daemon smirked.

"Absolutely. I was once the finest trained warrior in Heaven; other than the ArchAngels themselves. Even you and your scrawny self can learn at least some basic defense with me as your teacher. Also, you're a demon. All demons have a singular specialty ability they unlock at some point around your age I believe. These abilities can range from hyper stealth or transfiguration, like shapeshifting. It's about whether or not we can break you down enough to unleash that earlier than wait for it to come out on its own. This will be tough, but not impossible."

Daemon watched as Samuel's expression changed from fear to what appeared to be excitement. Maybe the kid would end up surprising him. Lorelei's voice chimed in.

"Where are we going to train? I mean, with what you're saying, this can definitely not be done near any people."

"I already have that covered. I found a large field, not too far from here, completely empty and far from any peeping eyes. I was already there early this morning putting enchantments up to make sure it stays that way. As well as spells to ensure any damage done to the land will disappear once we leave the area. Like the kid said, we should be safe from Hell's minions until tomorrow. But I'm banking on being long gone from this area before that happens."

Samuel shuffled his feet and grabbed the sleeve of his sweater nervously.

"Is one afternoon really long enough to teach us? What happens if Lorelei can't figure out what is hidden here?"

There it was.

The fear that was settled down deep within each one of them, brought to the surface.

Even Daemon couldn't stop the concerned expression from spreading across his entire face. He let out a deep sigh and went to grab the cigarettes in his jacket pocket, pulled one out and lit it, placing his fingertips precisely lower, so no unwanted attention came their way when his fingertips literally caught fire. More of a reflex than a necessity, a comfort really. Taking a drag, he immediately sees Lorelei's reaction.

She was quiet, but he felt her insides were churning with fear. Fear of whether she was capable enough to do this. Fear of what might be brought to knowledge. Fear of letting down the entire human race. Because that's what they were up against. That was the *true* monument they faced. It was as daunting as it was absurd.

He wanted to comfort her; pull her into his arms and reassure her that everything was going to be okay. But he couldn't. The odds were stacked against them and he didn't know if everything turning out alright would be the case. Lying to her for a moment of comfort seemed worse than saying nothing at all. He only hoped she knew that he wished he had the words to say to make her feel better. Other than her breakdown in the car before the fight, this was the first time he'd seen her faith falter. And it broke him. He decided to finally break the silence that hung dreadfully in the air between them.

"We will deal with it when that comes. But for now, we have to stay focused on what we can do. We can't afford to be weak or let doubt collapse us."

They all nodded, but nothing more was said. It was less a pep talk, and more brunt truth. Doubt their success, and they've already lost. When the tour was finished, they made their way through the crowds, back to the car, and left for the field in which they would begin what may very well be the thing that keeps them alive long enough to reach their journey's end.

If it worked at all.

CHAPTER 16

SAMUEL

HEARING DAEMON SAY HE'D have to learn how to fight, was honestly terrifying to Samuel. He shouldn't be surprised considering they were most definitely going to have a run-in with more demons, if not with any angels as well, which Daemon seemed convinced of. But Samuel had never done well in combat classes back home. He was weak; he'd hardly make a blow, and half the time he was too scared to even try. It was very common for Samuel to be sent to the nurse's office because of a bloodied nose or a mean kick to the cheek. His teachers always saw him as a failure, but would hardly do more than pull him to the side and force him to sit out the activity; no one wanted a meeting with Lucifer to say they failed to teach his only child.

It was hard to think that he was in the presence of one of the most legendary warriors of Heaven. If anybody could teach him how to fight, he hoped it would be Daemon.

While walking around Stonehenge, Samuel couldn't help but become more and more fascinated with what could possibly be there. From what it sounded like, Lorelei definitely had some intuitive abilities, but what if they weren't enough? The "what ifs" of their entire predicament were taking up Samuel's attention when he realized the car pulled off the road and began making its way down a narrow, hand-made path leading to a massive open field. The grass was a dark green color and the few daisies and wildflowers strewn about the area gave an innocence that seemed ironic with what they would be doing here. The swirling dark clouds above them looked like they might soon rain and Samuel wondered how much harder it would be to train if it was pouring.

When they got out of the car, Daemon walked to the trunk and opened it, revealing a basket and a folded blanket. He smiled at them while tilting his head to look over his shoulder.

"I figured we could have a little picnic of sorts before we get the party started. Besides, you're going to need all the energy you can get for training. It's going to take a lot out of both of you."

Daemon eyed them over before grabbing the basket and blanket and walking them out into the middle of the field. Suddenly, a shift in temperature made Samuel look around himself. Daemon noticed.

"That's just the spells I put up to protect this area. Once on the other side of it, no one will be able to hear or see us. Any damage we do to the area will be fixed once we leave here. It also allows only us three to pass through it. In other words, I have made us invisible."

Was Daemon letting down his guard around him? Samuel couldn't be sure yet, but he felt his shoulders relax a little more at the thought and walked alongside the two of them until Daemon picked a spot on the ground and began laying out the blanket and what he packed in the basket. Taking a seat opposite Lorelei, who was sitting beside Daemon, Samuel watched as Daemon pulled out an assortment of goodies: sandwiches, fruit, cheeses, crackers, cookies, and a couple of thermoses, followed by plates, bowls, and utensils. Samuel's tummy growled in reaction, as it was already hours since breakfast. He didn't realize how starving he was until the wafting smell of little finger sandwiches and cake was splayed across the blanket.

"What is in those?" Samuel asked in reference to the thermoses.

"One has a delicious butternut squash soup, and the other is black tea. No picnic is quite right without English tea time. I may be rough around the edges but I'm not savage; missing afternoon tea would be a crime under these circumstances."

Daemon's jovial remark made Samuel laugh; it was nice to see Daemon more relaxed. After everyone grabbed handfuls of food, discussion returned to the kind of training they were going to do. Samuel watched Lorelei add milk and sugar to her black tea; following suit, he took a sip, rejoicing in the delicious combination he'd never had before now. It was delightful. He listened contentedly while Daemon answered his most recent question.

"Well, I know Lorelei has done some defense classes before, so I am not so worried about that. Later I will work with her one-on-one to see if she can speak Enochian in any capacity, but specifically I will be training you. Helping you uncover your abilities, if there are any, and knowing your parentage, I believe there's no shortage of powers lurking beneath the surface."

Samuel blinked in surprise, but nodded casually as he took another bite from a cookie, or biscuit, as Daemon kept referring to them as, He discovered they were lemon flavored, and the combination between that and the warming tea, was a sensation of coziness he relished in. As he shoved the remainder into his mouth, he stood up and wiped the crumbs off his shirt before turning to the two of them. It was so surprising that Daemon's demeanor towards him seemed to be changing. It was less apprehensive and more friendly. Samuel didn't know which was scarier.

"Are we starting training right away? I was sort of interested in examining the flowers in the field, since I haven't been able to see many in person."

Samuel knew his voice was quiet, although he wasn't sure if his uncertainty around Daemon was necessary any longer. Daemon gave him a quirky eyebrow raise before responding.

"No, we will let our food settle a bit. Have at it, mate."

Feeling a sense of relief, Samuel walked away from them, finding a patch of the wild flowers. Kneeling down, he ran a hand along the soft, plush grass beneath him before he pulled a particularly adorable lilac-colored flower out from the ground and sniffed its sweet aroma, smiling contentedly as a light breeze brushed his unruly red locks across his forehead. For the moment, everything was peaceful; a dream came true for him. He had dreamt of the day he could walk here, surrounded by friends, and enjoying the pleasures of human life. He looked out onto the horizon, as the sun did its best to peek behind the clouds above him, and pretended to be a normal human being, enjoying a stroll along the grassy hills of the countryside—if only for this one moment.

CHAPTER 17

LORELEI

LORELEI WATCHED SAMUEL PRACTICALLY skip towards a bed of wild flowers and smiled to herself. It was a moment like this that showed Lorelei how much she took for granted as a human.

Being able to pick and enjoy the sweet aroma of a wildflower, to relish in its beauty and delicacy, was just a simple and easy action for a human. Many wouldn't even think to do it. Forgetting the simple pleasures like picking and smelling a flower was common for humans who don't take a moment to stop in their busy lives. Yet, for Samuel, who has probably hardly seen anything like it in person, it was a pure marvel and wonder to behold. Although seeing the amount of joy spread across his face as he inspected the tiny flower made Lorelei beam to herself, but she couldn't ignore this severe notion of sadness that followed.

Imagine being the son of Lucifer, whose only wish was to see the human world and be among them, when fate dictated you would be part of the side out to torment them. How could such a boy come from such a dismal place? Was it a sign that brought Samuel to them for some reason? What role might he play in all of this? The questions surrounding Samuel and the entire journey thus far were swirling dizzyingly around in her head, and it was beginning to give her a headache, *again*.

Daemon commented more than once about how well she was handling this entire situation, but in all honesty, the anxiety and amount of fear that was welling up higher and higher inside of her, only scared her more. Growing up, she developed a knack for being able to hide her emotions when courage and strength were necessary to get through a situation. But she knew that biting her tongue about her anxieties and fears would only grow to a point where it might result in a breakdown, the emotions becoming too much for her to hold back any longer. Which is exactly what happened 6 months ago.

She'd been out with friends, drinking a little too much, when suddenly she was knee deep in a panic attack about her dad's death; having not really processed it, and found herself shuttled off to the hospital. It was the moment she decided that pushing herself into work to keep herself too busy to think about the sadness of it all, was not the solution. When she was released from the hospital, she called around to therapists all afternoon until she found the first one who could get her in as soon as possible. Suppressing her emotions was the thing they worked on the most in therapy.

She knew this was the pattern that occurred. The same pattern she'd acquired since childhood, when she was old enough to understand why her mother couldn't step up for her, the way every little girl craved. She was 12. This was 3 years before her mother's funeral. She remembered crying for what felt like 2 weeks straight, the emotions totally taking control of her. And although she knew she could probably divulge her feelings to Daemon, for some ridiculous reason, she didn't want him to think she was weak. She wanted to continue to show a brave face because deep down, Lorelei knew the anxieties of the unknown were piled just as high on Daemon's shoulders as they were on her own.

Lorelei sat back and finally took her gaze away from Samuel in the distance, turning to find Daemon watching her. When their eyes met, he smiled brightly at her, making that same immediate effect of feeling as though she was in a free fall, her heart soaring to him with no looking back.

They hadn't been alone together since the night prior, when they fell asleep in each other's embrace. The memory of his strong arms wrapped around her as she rested her head gently on his chest. The slow and steady drumming of his heartbeat that seemed to match perfectly with her own. The soft, hushed breathing while he drifted off to sleep alongside her

Reflecting back on it, it felt more like a dream than reality. A perfect, peaceful dream amongst a cacophony of chaos that enveloped them. Part of her feared it was all just the heat of the moment and they were merely finding comfort in the nearest person.

It surely couldn't be that....right?

Her heart started to flutter at the thought. What she felt for Daemon was unexplainable, but she'd also never felt so sure of her feelings in her life. It was like there was a rope tied around her heart connecting to his. A pull that felt like if broken, she would be untethered from this world altogether.

But what if you only feel this way because you have a piece of his soul?

Now this was the thought that bothered her more than any other. What if it was because of the soul connection? What if it wasn't her own genuine feelings but that of a connection that occurred all those years ago? What if the only reason she felt as strongly as she did for Daemon was because the piece of him that lived within her, only gave her the false notion of knowing him better than she actually did.

No. I can't accept that as the answer.

There had to be more to it. There had to be. Otherwise, her heart might break more than she might be able to handle. Lorelei tried to clear her mind; to think these things at the moment were only hurting her.

Looking into Daemon's striking green eyes, she wanted more than anything to go closer to him; to wrap her arms around his neck and kiss all the uncertainty she was feeling away. To once again melt into his lips and feel the warmth of his body against her own. His silver hair tousled softly down to the tops of his shoulders, glistening slightly as sunshine began to spread across the sky above them. He cocked his head curiously as he continued to meet her gaze.

"You have a lot going on in that pretty head of yours, hm?"

Lorelei felt that familiar hum around her as the energy between them began to undulate and shift. Her emotions were not only written all over her face; they were manifesting again. She wondered how long she had been staring at him, but decided it didn't matter, seeing as he had been watching her as well.

"Yes, I am just trying to gather my thoughts on...everything."

Lorelei hadn't meant to pause before the "everything" bit, and Daemon sat up straighter, scooting himself closer to her, looking around at the energy that moved in the air as he got nearer, obviously feeling it. They faced each other. She watched as he took her hands and held them tenderly in the palms of his own. He continued to stare down at their joined hands, as his left thumb stroked the top of her hand. For a moment, nothing was said between the two of them. Immediately, his nearness calmed her racing thoughts, and the energy between them that started to feel static, quieted. The manifestation of her emotions turned into a physical occurrence that was becoming stronger with each passing day during their travels. Never before did she notice anything similar to this before meeting Daemon. Small recollections of large breakdowns tried to formulate in her mind, one time especially, when she felt like the walls around her in her little bedroom as a child were actually shaking—but these memories were fuzzy. Too hazy to make out or remember for certain. It was draining nonetheless, the more her feelings turned tangible. After the last of the energy trickled down to a dull hum again, she breathed a sigh of relief. Daemon noticed the change in her, and gave a reassuring smile as he spoke.

"Lorelei, I know this is a lot. This entire situation is absolutely mental, and I know that throwing us...on top of all the rest of it must be incredibly difficult for you. And although you haven't said anything, I know you're scared. I know that you're doing your best to hold onto your courage when all the while you are terrified of the outcome. But I wanted to do my best to finally reassure you: *about all of it.*"

She couldn't find the words to respond, and when she continued to blink and stare into his eyes, he nodded; taking that as a yes to continue.

"Lorelei, I know you're scared of being unable to do whatever it is you must do to save humanity. I know that a few days ago you thought you were a normal girl who worked as a writer and lived in London, who would most likely go on to do other normal things in your life. To actually find out that you have a destiny that says you're the only person who can save humanity and you now must run around with a disgraced angel and the son of the Devil to figure out how—is absolutely mad. But, believe me when I tell you that you're one of the strongest human beings I have ever met. You continue to surprise me with your courage and your abilities. And yes, you do have abilities that have nothing to do with the piece of my soul you have; although I am sure it helps in some areas. You are incredibly intuitive; you just haven't had anybody teach you how to harness it. You already have used your intuition throughout your life to guide you where you need to be; which is right here. Despite feeling like you woke up one day and are now an entirely different person, in reality, you are the same person you have always been. Everything that has happened in your life has been leading you to this moment. Something they teach us about how the Universe works, is that nothing is a mistake and everything that happens is the only possible way it could've happened. Which also means there is no mistake you have this destiny. I also believe it means that despite everyone else telling me how saving your life was wrong, I don't think it was a mistake either. Something about you and something about me were interconnected long before I gave a piece of my soul to save you. A force within me completely took over, and I couldn't stop myself from saving you. It sounds weird but I just knew deep in my heart that I *had* to save you. And when I held your little body in my arms, and your beautiful blue eyes stared up at me as the light began to leave them, I saw you in the future. I saw what you were meant to become. I saw the kind of person you would grow to be. It was at that moment that I knew I not only had to give part of myself to save you, but that I wanted to do so more than anything in the entire cosmos. So if there is any doubt in your mind, please believe me when I say it now: my feelings for you are more real than I can express."

Lorelei was speechless. Everything he was saying was as if her own heart was speaking. What she felt was real, and he felt it too; just as strongly. His words about how this was all meant to be; her destiny and them, was exactly what she needed to hear. She took a deep breath and felt her shoulders relax from the tension she hadn't realized she'd been holding there. She finally leaned forward, placing a hand on his chest, and kissed his lips softly. She felt Daemon give his own sigh of relief against her. Daemon's hand moved from her hand to the back of her head. After returning her kiss, he pulled her head down and kissed her forehead. When she finally pulled away, he gave her a hopeful, but tentative look.

"Then, you understand how I feel?"

Lorelei's voice, nearing a whisper, responded confidently.

"Yes, I do."

CHAPTER 18

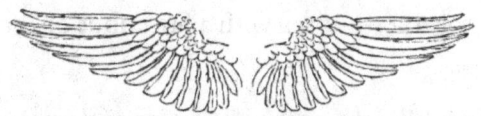

LUCIFER

LOUD, THUMPING MUSIC FILLED the rounded room that was filled to the brim with sofas, floor cushions and poles. In the flashing lights which seemed to coordinate with the beat of the music, one can see many bodies throughout the room. Most were dancing, moving their bodies seductively to the music. Some were huddled around small tables with various instruments and powdered concoctions they were passing around. Some were in the darker corners of the room where the light barely reached them, enough to see bare skin and hear muffled moans. Around several poles were Succubi and Incubi dancing about seated demons who were yelling obscenities or trying to get them to come closer, which many did. Many would look at the scene and sum it up to any normal nightclub. Biggest difference, this was a nightclub in Hell; and Lucifer's personal favorite to frequent.

Lucifer was seated in the back of the club with one Succubus he'd been on and off with for several millina seated on his lap, curling a long dagger-like finger through her purple hair that shimmered when the light caught it. Her name was Catvynia, and she was Lucifer's main lover.

She was a decent companion; she would come to Lucifer any time day or night, even to sit and keep him company as he worked on battle strategies. She had a good sense of humor but knew when to hold her tongue.

Catvynia over the years became one of his greatest confidants, and although he could never say he loved her, he did find her presence pleasant for the most part. But more often than not, a lot of their time was spent doing more...destructive things. Meaning they usually broke several things when they were sleeping together—as sex with a Succubus or Incubus was always a thrilling experience.

Succubi and Incubi's jobs were to lure men and women to Hell's forces through use of their sexual prowess and kinks—mostly while humans were sleeping. The Incubi were the male counterparts to the Succubus. They come to human's in their dreams to seduce them and promise fanciful meetings as well as other lies such as powers, immortality, a place in Lucifer's army by his side, a place as their mates, etc. But they were good fun for demons as well, as they are trained from conception on this particular type of seduction that allows them to take form, shape, or particular fancies and abilities best suited for what lover they are with at a certain time. They can change and adapt to be the perfect partner to who they are seducing enough to even change into the form of the person's most desired traits or looks. Their ability to manipulate is also especially well-trained and mastered in comparison to other demons. Succubi and Incubi spend most of their time convincing humans to not only be their sexual partners, which drains a human's energy, allowing them to be more vulnerable and moldable, to be their puppets of destruction.

Being so irresistible to humans, seeing as they can be whoever the human desires most, they convince the humans easily that what they have is love and therefore, the human is in a sort of trance-like state, willing to do whatever the Succubus asks of them. Theft, manipulation of others, and even murder. These particular demons bring a lot of poor souls over just by merely sitting back and watching them wreak chaos in the name of "love." For Lucifer, they were more used for...distraction.

Distraction from the war. Distraction from the pain. From the *loss.*

Not that Catvynia was his only lover. To his left was his 2nd most frequented visitor, an Incubus named Xinlin, who was different from Catvynia in that he was more quiet, but more ruthless in the bedroom. He didn't speak much with words, but with his eyes he could captivate you with a wink. Beside him were his lovers Syleth and Nyried. Syleth was a Succubus who was the newest in their motley group and the least experienced, which Lucifer enjoyed from time to time. Nyried was one of the oldest Incubi in Hell, but looked to be in his 30s. He was bigger than the others and was the only other dominant lover Lucifer would allow around him other than his good self. Sometimes they would do things all together as a group, but Lucifer got frustrated easily and could usually only tolerate one of them at a time. There was the occasional jealous spat between them, and Lucifer had a different kind of relationship with each of them that he didn't want to intermix much unless he was just in a particular mood for the chaos it ensured. It entertained him, to watch them bicker over him. It typically ended in a rougher fuck for all of them so it was found to be a fun game every now and then.

Xinlin was rubbing the leg of Lucifer that Catvynia wasn't sitting on, while handing a cigarette over to Lucifer who took a long drag of it and blew the smoke out into rings above their heads. Catvynia giggled and tried to suck the smoke into her own mouth unsuccessfully, Lucifer patting her ass with a small smile. The smile was like a cue for Catvynia, and she leaned down and began running lingering kisses down along Lucifer's cheek, chin and chest. With every other kiss, you could hear a purring sound from Catvynia and she proceeded to sink her vampire-like teeth into his throat, which made him let out a low growl. Eyes rolling back into his head, he allowed the pleasure from the pain to run its course through his body. Still allowing Catvynia to leave playful nips, he grabbed Xinlin's hand that rested upon his leg and pulled him in, biting his lower lip and letting the blood that came, drip between their mouths as their tongues intertwined. Blood and saliva tinged with various alcoholic beverages made for an intoxicating mix.

Oh, how Lucifer loved this part. The semi-mind numbing drinks, constant teasing and lingering back and forth, it was one of the only times he felt free from the constant duties. He let his senses run the show, and tonight, he felt it would last longer—*he desperately needed it to.*

Catvynia stood and lifted her hand to the both of them; she was going to take them both someplace more private.

As Lucifer gave a subtle hand squeeze or nod to his other lovers, indicating it would be a night shared by all, a slam of the club door broke the moment and Lucifer sat up abruptly, pushing both Catvynia and Xinlin out of his way as he watched a few of his guards walk briskly over to him.

The first guard who appeared before him was his 2nd in command, Valac. A tall, slender demon with greyish-red skin, yellowy-strained eyes, and curled horns at his temples like that of a ram's. He was the brainier of his command and the one who helped more with strategy than with actual battle. But he was a loyal servant, one that had shown his loyalty several times over the years and one Lucifer trusted. Usually, Valac had a calm demeanor, but now his yellow eyes were full of panic and this immediately sent waves of rage throughout Lucifer's body, tensing his shoulders.

Valac stood and bowed slightly before him and rushed, nearly stumbling over his words.

"My lord, I apologize for disrupting your evening. But I have some news we must discuss about the mission you ordered. May we go elsewhere to speak?"

Lucifer sat up, and Catvynia joined Xinlin on the couch, still sitting next to Lucifer, watching him intently.

Lucifer shook his head.

"If it is so important, speak plainly. We have no time to waste. Tell me now what you must. I have other business to attend to this evening, so please, don't waste my time further than you already have, Valac."

Valac swallowed hard and nodded in return, hesitating and clearly uncomfortable in the club environment. Clearing his throat to strengthen his voice above the blaring music, he finally spoke.

"The mission failed, sire. The angel and the human girl are still on the move and all of our agents were found dead at the scene. We sent a crew out to investigate when the agreed upon communication time was missed. After this discovery, I personally went back to the Oracle Magnus myself, and by our usual torture methods, I was able to inquire the assailants next location. I left him alive, in case we have to use him again. They will arrive at Stonehenge before the morning."

Valac paused, wanting to see Lucifer's reaction, but when his master continued to stare absently ahead of him, he continued.

"Another thing...your son we found, was not one among the dead. A scout was sent to follow the group to Stonehenge, and saw...well..."

Finally, Lucifer laughed loudly.

"So the poor boy was taken prisoner. Wouldn't have pegged Daemon as such a man, but doesn't surprise me in the least. Samuel was always too weak."

Valac coughed awkwardly.

"Actually.....the scout saw Samuel, well...laughing. From what it seems, sir...he has joined their side."

By this point, Catvynia leaned over to Lucifer and stroked his arm.

"I'm sure the scout was mistaken, Valac." She glared at him. "Despite how pathetic Samuel is, he still wouldn't betray his own father–"

Before Catvynia could finish her sentence, Lucifer, without looking, grabbed her throat. She began sputtering on her words, holding her hands over his own, choking violently. But Lucifer made no facial expression, he made no sound or reaction to her feeble attempt to free herself from his grasp. He finally looked up at Catvynia's face, tears rolling down her cheeks. With a graveness, Lucifer finally spoke.

"You underestimate my only child's will to defy me, Catvynia. After all our time spent together, I would've thought you'd know better than to not believe my 2nd in command. The man who saved my own life with his bare hands. The one who has personally seen my failure of an offspring in his classes struggle to grasp the very concept of our war. The boy has always been a nuisance, a disappointment. One I have often loathed over to you during our nightly meetings, Catvynia. Do you pay no attention to your master and lover's plights, that you know so little about me at all?"

Her face was turning purple while she was attempting to gasp out an apology. Lucifer only looked upon her, showing no emotion to his old, longtime lover and confidant as he snapped her neck, and threw her body upon the sofa. Xinlin muffled a yell, holding his hand over his mouth as he looked at the limp body of his longtime friend. He soon gathered himself and walked slowly away from the scene, Nyriad and Syleth close behind him. They said nothing in defense of the Succubus—for the fear they would meet the same fate.

Looking over her body, Lucifer felt nothing. Despite the time they'd spent together, she was only ever a means to an end. She was only ever a pass-time, a way to forget briefly of the true pain and fury that lived at a constant arm's length within him. He turned to Valac, who stood stoically looking down at the floor.

"Gather the rest of the court. I believe it is time to retrieve my good-for-nothing son. I believe his sheer desire to disobey me has pushed my tolerance level to its threshold."

And with that, he walked out of the club. The rest of the demons within it staring as Valac followed timidly. Catvynia's eyes still open from the shock and sudden-ness of her death, stared unblinking after her master.

CHAPTER 19

DAEMON

AFTER MAKING THEIR WAY further out into the field, Daemon watched protectively as Lorelei walked behind them and took out her notebook from that ridiculously old, leather bag. She smiled and waved at him while taking a seat in the grass to watch them. Before starting with Samuel, Daemon wrote down the "Alphabet" as it were, for the Celestial language and some of the more basic spells typically used when first learning. He figured letting her have some time to already look them over and practice saying them, it might spark something inside her. *Anything.*

There was no way to know if what Daemon was attempting to do would work, or if it made any sense at all to try and teach a human how to speak the Holy language of the angels. But Daemon was running out of ideas, and her keen ability to pick things up quickly on top of the fact she did have some of Daemon's essence inside her...it was worth a shot.

Stretching, Daemon lifted his arms over his head, shoulders rolling in circles as he released the tension that had been building up for days. And with his enchantments up to make them and their actions invisible to any prying eyes, Daemon zipped off his leather jacket, the short sleeve blue t-shirt that costed more than what it looked it was worth, stayed behind, and he let his wings unfurl behind him after a painstaking amount of time tucked away.

He turned his focus on the lanky, red-headed teenager across from him, who looked absolutely terrified. Daemon's angel perceptiveness thought he could see the boy's knees shaking. How this kid could be the Prince of Darkness, son of Lucifer, the most powerful once-angel, and now ruler of Hell—it seemed like a cruel prank. Samuel was so unlike his father that it was a wonder he'd survived this long.

But, Lucifer wasn't always so bad...maybe Samuel embodies what Lucifer was supposed to be like: innocent, kind to all, curious, but not defiant or in need of power.

Daemon cocked his head and as he felt the tension recede in his body, he smiled broadly. This was his element. This was where he belonged: on a battlefield, using his powers and strength in fighting. Here was the arena he hadn't had in so long to use these skills he spent his existence curating, nurturing, and implementing.

Until your services were no longer needed...

He chided himself in his mind; there was too much at stake to let another of his debilitating emotional potholes steer him anywhere but straight. It was time to focus. That pain and self-loathing would always be there for him later.

Turning his attention back to the shaking boy, Daemon cleared his throat and stood in a battle-ready stance.

"Alright, mate. Let's do this. Now, I know you said before you have no abilities, but no child of Lucifer would be so unlucky to receive none of his accosted skills. Have you ever been able to dream-walk? That has always been a particular favorite of your father's. Or perhaps shadow magic? No? Okay, how about emotional manipulation, sword work? Your father was pretty wicked with a blade if I recall. No?"

Samuel shook from head to toe, shame washed over his features as with every question Daemon posed, he reluctantly shook his head "no" and stared at his feet. Poor kid. To have such a powerful, renowned, and substantial father and to come out with nothing.

No. There can't be nothing. There just has to be something in there...some spark....

Opening his eyes wider, Daemon snapped his hand. He remembered one skill Lucifer used a lot back at the beginning when humanity had barely gotten its feet off the ground.

Elemental magic. Weather manipulation. It is never written about in texts, but Daemon saw Lucifer do it once. That flood was a right, nasty piece of work.

"Have you ever noticed the weather changes with your emotions?"

Samuel's head peaked up and with a look of confusion that turned into what looked like a lightbulb going off in his head, he nodded vigorously.

"Actually, if I think hard about it...it could be stupid, but once I was getting beat up by some of the kids at school.."

Daemon's heart clenched at the confession. This kid was pulling on his heart-strings, and Daemon had even started to grow fond of him. He was sad to realize what a lonely and difficult life Samuel has known. Daemon crossed his arms, listening to Samuel as he began walking closer while he finished.

"And I remember feeling so alone, and so angry at the world. But just as I was about to get hit by the final blow from the biggest guy, a giant storm began and they all ran for cover. I guess they figured I was already down in the dirt, it didn't matter if I drowned, too."

Samuel sighed and pulled on the sleeves of his green and brown striped sweater that Daemon grabbed for him when he got his own clothes; something told Daemon green was Samuel's color.

Before Daemon could respond to Samuel's remark, Lorelei spoke up.

"There are storms in Hell?"

Daemon turned back to her and held back a smile. That curiosity never seemed to leave Lorelei's eyes. Her blonde hair fell in waves over her shoulders, although a little frizzed out from the humidity in the air, she was so beautiful. Her mind never stopped, and he thought it was adorable she could fully focus on the alphabet Daemon gave her and was still somehow able to keep up with their conversation as well. He wished he could go to her, lift her up, and kiss her again. Breathe in her scent again and be there with her as she studied; but that would have to be later.

Samuel answered Lorelei eagerly. He always seemed to perk up when she was talking with him.

"Yes! Well...no? My dad said there didn't used to be. It started only..I don't know...a decade ago or more? I'm not really sure. But there used to be no storms, and one day there was. The demons were shocked when they started. Hell isn't all what the books say it is. It is actually sort of like an oasis. Yes there are cities sort of like your New York, but it's also filled to the brim with wildlife and flowers. They are not like Earth's though, because they glow and apparently are not real or living—but the growth has never needed rain. They grow all year and never need to be taken care of. It's rather fascinating and no matter how many times I have bugged the librarian at my school, there isn't a lot of information on these plants. My dad does have some environmental control and told me it was his gift to us who followed him to never need to live in a place that wasn't beautiful. He believed we deserved that. He's very loyal to his people if nothing else. Anyways, yeah, the storms started not long ago but no one can figure out why. Not even my dad. It's been a source of constant frustration for him."

Daemon spun on his heels and looked at Samuel.

"Did this start before or after you were born?"

Samuel paused to think, "I guess it was after. Why?"

Daemon's brain clicked and he knew what he needed to do. He winked at Lorelei, and she blushed.

If only I could make her blush for other reasons...

Soon, Daemon thought. And he took that as motivation as he paced around Samuel in circles.

He didn't speak, didn't say a word to the kid; he just kept pacing. Soon, Samuel's reaction became more and more nervous. He began shifting on his feet, playing with the sleeves of his sweater so much he could've put a hole in them from the constant tugging. All the while, Daemon could feel the fizzling of his emotions begin to boil inside him. Angels could perceive emotions, and although most demons were excellent at concealing them, Samuel put up no shields to cover it: and honestly, it was written all over his face. When Daemon thought he might have to come up with something else, the *drip, drip, drip* of a soft rain began; and he knew he figured it out. Daemon needed to push him harder. He just hoped Lorelei would forgive him for what he was about to do.

"You know, I knew your dad...in the old days. He was admired by many and he was powerful. Nearly untouchable in strength and ability..."

Daemon drawled on as he kept circling Samuel like a vulture about to pick up its prey. Out of the corner of his eye, he tried to give Lorelei a look to let her in on his plan, hoping she would understand, but she was now too fully engrossed in her studies to look up.

Please...let this work....and for fuck's sake, don't let Lorelei hate me afterwards..

Fear was obviously the catalyst to pulling out Samuel's abilities, but anger, that's where one's true self could be revealed. All was told in the heat of anger. That's where Daemon needed to push Samuel. He needed to be angry; that's how his powers would be forced out.

Daemon continued on.

"Yeah....your dad was one of a kind...it's too bad, really." Daemon paused before his first strike, "Considering you're nothing like him."

Daemon paused again, waiting for that first cut to meet its mark. Samuel's eyes shot open in shock and Daemon was sure Lorelei gasped behind him, but there was no way he could look her way after what he would need to do. When Samuel didn't say anything, he kept going—driving the knife of shame deeper, for he knew it all too well.

"Pity for ol' Luci. Having a son like you as the ruler of all Hell; it's got to be such a blow. I mean, look at you, you're pathetic. Weak. You got nothing to show for all your dad's efforts."

"What the hell are you doing, Daemon?!"

Lorelei's voice rang out, anger laced with utter disbelief etched in her usually sultry tone, and instantly Daemon regretted this tactic—but they were running out of time, and he needed to get Samuel to find the power he had. But, he could use this to his advantage...

Are you ready for her to truly hate you? Because this one is going to hurt.

Daemon turned his attention to Lorelei and tried to let his eyes show differently from what his mouth was about to say; screaming an apology in his emerald irises in hopes she would understand this wasn't real.

"Oh Lorelei, so naive! Look at him! You really think this scrawny thing could ever amount to anything other than an absolute nuisance to everyone he comes in contact with?"

Lorelei's eyebrows furrowed, and he thought tears might come. But she kept her mouth shut.

She'd gotten his message he'd been trying to plead with his eyes—she understood what he was trying to do. She didn't like it, but she went silent and nodded slightly.

"SHUT UP! I'm not nothing!"

Daemon turned on his heels to face the now half-sobbing, half-raging young demon behind him. Samuel's hands that were before gripping for dear life on his sweater sleeves for comfort, were now balled into fists. Breathing heavily like he couldn't get enough air, his body was visibly shaking from anger; Daemon nearly expected for him to combust entirely. Just when Daemon was thinking all he would have to do is hurl one more remark to finish this, there was no need.

Above Samuel, the small drizzling rain clouds had begun spinning into thick, black and grey monstrosities; it looked to be the start of a tornado. But just as Daemon readied his wings incase of needing to take off and get Lorelei to cover, instead of gusting winds and torrential rain, lightning is what came from the sky, cracking the air around them so loudly, even Daemon had to cover his ears.

Surrounding Samuel in a semi-circle of lightning bolts, they snapped and crackled like a barrier of electric warriors standing guard over their master. Daemon smiled knowingly and nodded at the boy, hoping he now understood why Daemon attempted to rile him up. Samuel did not return the smile.

Instead, his face was plastered in a warped, twisted snarl that Daemon didn't think resembled Samuel at all. It did however look familiar to someone Daemon had seen this way before: Lucifer. For the first time since meeting, Samuel finally looked like his father. Each lightning bolt struck the ground and made miniature craters in the earth beneath his feet. The light barely illuminated his face as he finally spoke, not a yell this time, but a steady, seething tone of voice that sounded like it was coming from elsewhere. His eyes now pure, black pits.

"Try smiling at this, *Daemon*."

Samuel lifted a hand and caught one of the lightning bolts coming down beside him in his hand, and like a nuclear explosion in his palm, he held the crackling light a moment, eyeing it fondly. Then when Daemon thought he might change his mind, Samuel stared at him directly and tossed his hand outward, sending the bolt directly at him.

"Shit. I think I pushed him too much."

Daemon barely had time to spread his wings and push off from the ground, narrowly evading the lightning bolt; but he forgot who was behind him.

He heard her scream and Daemon tried as hard as he could to get his feet under him fast enough to turn back to block the bolt. Even if it meant taking the full force of the strike himself, he couldn't let Lorelei be electrocuted!

Another scream came, but it was Samuel's.

"Nooooooooo!!" Daemon sprung forward, twisting in a flip through the air like a torpedo, his wings encapsulating him in a cocoon with enough room to block Lorelei. He felt the heat of the light closing the distance behind him and the zapping sting of its force. Closing his eyes, he braced for the impact: suddenly there was silence. All he felt was a huffing small frame buried against his chest, hands gripping his shirt tight. Daemon sighed in relief, cupping the back of Lorelei's head, his fingers locking in her hair, close to desperate as he stepped back to inspect her and make sure she was all in one piece. Steadying her as she gave him a weak smile of reassurance that she was alright, Daemon turned to see what happened. The ground near their feet was singed entirely; Samuel averted the bolt at the last moment.

Samuel was running towards them, *the usual Samuel*. His eyes were back to their normal red color, and as he reached them out of breath, wanting to go to Lorelei to hug her, he paused and stopped himself short in front of Daemon—waiting.

"Lorelei...Daemon. I am so sorry. I didn't know I could do that, and it wasn't until after I sent the lightning at Daemon that I realized what he was doing. That it was all just to get me to find the power....but once I got so angry, I couldn't stop myself! It's like I was clouded by this darkness, and what Daemon was saying brought up all the hurt and shame I have been made to feel my entire life...I didn't mean it." Samuel paused and looked directly at Lorelei.

"I understand if you never forgive me."

Daemon hadn't realized he was keeping a protective arm shielding Lorelei across her chest until she patted his arm to move, walking over to Samuel and bringing him in for a hug.

"You don't need to apologize. Controlling negative emotions is hard. And you have endured a lot of heartbreak and neglect. I will always forgive you, Sam. It's okay."

Samuel hugged her back and his shoulders released their tension. As they stepped away from each other, they both looked at Daemon. Running his hand through his hair, he chuckled and smiled at them both.

"Well then, let's keep going, shall we?"

PART 2

CHAPTER 20

LORELEI

LORELEI'S NERVES SETTLED, AND she continued to watch Daemon teach Samuel tips to better control his power and how to recall it without having to resort to anger, while another hour passed as she studied and they trained. Samuel was able to call forth two more lightning strikes with enough focus and sent them flying in different directions with success, none of which was towards either of them, thankfully.

Lorelei set the notebook down of the ancient, otherworldly language she had been studying and rubbed her forehead. The same notebook that once held her mutterings and research for myths, was now filled with an ancient language she never knew existed; she was a part of what felt like a myth all her own and was curious how so much had already changed. Staring harder at the letters on the page, she felt like her brain was going to explode. The Celestial language, otherwise known as Enochian, was intricate. Consisting of 48 "letters" compared to the English 26. They paralleled symbols rather than what she was used to as a common letter, resembling a combination of Egyptian hieroglyphics and ancient Greek.

I bet Dad would've loved every second of this.

If her dad were still here, he'd be in his own version of Heaven just reviewing the ancient letters, more than likely able to decipher them better than Lorelei can right now. Because in the end, although Daemon wrote pronunciations of the symbols, Lorelei had been muttering to herself relentlessly trying to form the syllables; it felt foreign and wrong. She tried and couldn't get her mind to wrap around the strange language. She felt something inside her call out to them though, like a knowing of something she couldn't remember, but it was just out of reach. Every time she said a word, nothing happened. She looked around to see if she made anything appear, made a small spell like the one Daemon used that brought forth a barrier shield-but nothing.

At this point, the symbols were blurring into each other and she didn't think this idea was going to pan out. Daemon was sweet in believing in these abilities he thought she might have, but at some point, maybe they were all kidding themselves. Feeling a bit defeated, she didn't realize that Daemon was standing in front of her. He smiled and sat down beside her, grabbing her hand, giving it a squeeze before he reached into the basket he'd brought for a bottle of water and wiped sweat from his brow.

"The kid's getting it. Pretty impressive actually. I think we should explore what other types of weather manipulation he could do. But right now, I believe this is as good as it's going to get considering the limited daylight we have."

Neither of them had discussed the disturbing accident earlier where Samuel nearly electrocuted Lorelei, and honestly, she hugged him and told him it was fine; but at the same time, it was so odd to see the usual shy, cheery teenager morph into a dark, almost scary fragment of the Samuel she had come to know. Seeing as Daemon wasn't mentioning it either, maybe it was a conversation for another day.

Daemon stretched, his wings laying out on the ground behind him, his wings glistened in the pools of light that peeked from behind the clouds that Samuel brought forth. Every time she saw him like this, she couldn't help but stare. It made her wonder what it'd be like to attempt to draw him. But there would be no way to capture the power that dripped off him like honey. The muscles in his arms shifted, covered with a sheen of sweat, making him even more beautiful to behold. Her hands itched to reach out and run her fingertips along it.

She only came out of her daydream when she heard Daemon speak something she couldn't understand in a deliciously, seductive tone, causing her heart to race even without knowing the words; he must've been speaking Enochian.

"What was that?" She asked, wondering how long she'd been admiring him.

Daemon flaunted a rare smile that illuminated his entire face, his silver bangs sweeping playfully over one eye before he pushed it behind his ear, his teeth nipping at his bottom lip, making her ache in a lower place..

"It means, if you keep looking at me like that, Sunflower, I think we may be having a different lesson altogether this afternoon than the one we are supposed to."

His voice trailed off, eager and hungry-sounding as she saw him look her up and down.

God, he is going to bring me to my knees.

Suggestion oozed from him and she felt her legs closing tighter together, unable to take her eyes away from his mouth. She remembered the feel of his hands on her the night before, the intensity of this pulling sensation she experienced ever since she ran into him at the pub back in Inverness. Daemon ignited something inside her and eased her worries at the same time. How that was possible she didn't know, but right now it was less calm and more releasing molten lava in her veins if she didn't have him this instant.

Daemon raised his eyebrow at her, having read her mind. His emerald eyes burned with the same intensity she was feeling. He scooted closer to her, looking to see Samuel had taken a break and was now lying on the grass watching the clouds above him, resting. Daemon moved close enough to brush his lips against hers, teasingly. His tongue shot out to lick her bottom lip, and she sucked in air, her body now trembling with the need for him. There couldn't be a second longer. She needed to close the gap. But as she tried to, Daemon smiled cruelly and spoke again in Enochian.

She could still feel his breath against her skin, his mouth now trailing down her chin, his hand having found its rightful place on the back of her neck. Lorelei arched slightly to give him more access, her fingers gliding up his pant leg.

"Please...don't stop."

Daemon clicked his tongue and a laugh rumbled against the base of her neck sending goosebumps all down her body. Just when she thought he was going to kiss her again at her collarbone, instead, he gave a small bite that made her yelp slightly, and it fueled the raging fire even further. He pulled himself up and kissed her lips softly again before sitting back.

Lorelei's chest heaved from the adrenaline rush, and while her heart thudded violently, she attempted to regain a semblance of self control; there was a teenage boy not far off out here for Pete's sake. She looked into Daemon's eyes and playfully smacked his arm as he spoke again in Enochian and then in English.

"Okay, so what did I say now?"

Trying her best to ignore the intoxicating British accent that swept her into a near-frenzy moments earlier, she shook her head and recalled the sounds of the words he was saying.

"Err...I know the second word was "a" and....the last word you said sounded like "repeat?"

Daemon laughed, causing those little eye crinkles from happiness that appeared only briefly with him; she wasn't sure he was used to laughing. Or if he was, it had been so long since he did. And that made her leap with joy to know she could make him laugh; it was a beauty to her ears.

"Sort of. I asked if you needed a *release* or if you were fine with me tormenting you a little longer." His tone changed again to playful seduction and that same tingling feeling low in her belly made her squirm under his gaze.

"Are you always this much of a tease?"

Daemon raised an eyebrow at her, that suggestive smirk reappearing. *"Who said I was teasing?"*

Her heart quickened but she ignored him and studied over the notepad again when Daemon followed up and told her to repeat a specific spell when he knew she wouldn't give into his game so easily. It was the same damned spell she'd been trying to do for the last hour; the Barrier Spell. Looking up from her page, she mustered her strength and tempered her embarrassment at the sure butchering of the words, and repeated the spell aloud.

This time, it was different. A feeling of pressure came from her chest and grew to encase her entire body. Looking like a blob of translucent jelly, it edged further away from her. The concentration on the effect made her eyes strain. It felt like a piece of herself was no longer attached to her body—and it fluctuated in and out, until with surprise, she willed it to hold in place, forming a perfect bubble around her. Her jaw dropped at the sensation of feeling like the world around her was now muted, and she poked the formation; it rippled in response but did not break.

She'd done it. She was able to speak Enochian and successfully do a spell!

Daemon smiled at her from ear to ear and clapped proudly. But the moment she met his eyes and literally jumped for joy, her concentration ebbed, and the bubble popped. Lorelei groaned in frustration.

"Ugh! Just when I had it.."

"Hey! You bloody did it though! I couldn't be happier. For your first attempt, you held it well."

Lorelei smiled; it wasn't perfect, but she now had the capability to speak Enochian, and with more practice, possibly use more of the spells Daemon did for protection or to help him in a situation. She would never be fluent, but she could put up a barrier if need be for now. That was a success.

She felt a sigh escape her, her hope at their prospects renewing. She picked up her notebook again and raised an eyebrow at Daemon over it, deciding to see if she could practice her fluency further by giving Daemon a taste of her own teasing. She skimmed the words a moment and lifted her eyes to match him again. The words felt stronger this time, and they flowed easier than before.

"A crip mir da trian noan i ds capimao ol zir c top c g."

Lorelei stumbled through the words and the sounds that felt like snakes slithering on her tongue. In comparison to Daemon when he spoke, it sounded like classical music. She only hoped any of what she said was right, and by the look on Daemon's face, **it was**. Daemon didn't respond in words, but when he bit his lip in frustration, she knew she'd relayed what she'd wanted to.

She told him in Enochian that he could *release* her anytime, anywhere; as long as he dragged the release out for ***maximum pleasure.***

She brushed her shoulders in smug retaliation, wondering what fun response he'd have or how impressed he would be with her efforts. But she gasped when he moved so fast, pushing Lorelei down to the ground, one hand finding its way up her side until he wrapped his fingers firmly around both of her wrists. Hunger emanated from him, every inch of him throbbing with desire for her; she could feel it pulsing against her skin as her own famished eagerness matched his, creating a delicate dance of pushing each other to the absolute edge.

It felt carnal, raw. It felt like if they went any further, she might become undone from this world. She wished to bond herself in every physical way possible to him. She wanted to explore it *all* with him. Every sensation, every way they could fulfill each other's desires, every way she could make that perfect man moan in response to each touch she aspired to perform.

Lorelei had obviously been with other men, but she had never encountered this enticing combination of pure, unfiltered, lustful desire; at the same time, she felt her own soul begged to intertwine in such a spiritual, emotional capacity. Her body heat rose sharply and she knew her face must be flushing red as her eyes lingered first on his demanding eyes, then his lips that pleaded for her own.

She didn't want to fight him—*he could pin her and take her as much as he wanted.*

Daemon's voice was haggard, rushed, his heart beating as fast as hers. "Passion...like anger, is often a catalyst for powers to emerge...looks like we got you there."

Of course. Daemon always had a tactic. He knew that his teasing kisses before she did the spell would help her produce it. But she also knew it wasn't just a tactic. It was indulgence for them both, as he too, could hardly restrain himself around her.

Two birds with one hot angel, right?

When Lorelei thought he'd finally release her from the torture building up, a barely audible coughing sound came from behind them. Samuel stood a few feet away, doing his best to not look directly at them as he spoke.

"Uhh...I think I'm done with the drills you needed me to do."

Daemon ignored the uncomfortable teenager and leaned down, kissing Lorelei softly; the humming of the energy between them felt like a shock the moment they disconnected for only the briefest of moments as he quickly hopped off her and pulled her up as well. Lorelei at last looked at the boy who'd seen their near indecent act and covered her face in embarrassment.

Who is the adult here, huh?

She continued to scold herself but Daemon shrugged it off as no big deal; although, Lorelei could still see him shifting uncomfortably, also trying to calm himself from the moment earlier. But he winked at Lorelei behind Samuel's back before responding. Her heart fluttered and she stifled a laugh herself.

"No worries, we've finished our lesson, too."

CHAPTER 21

LORELEI

AFTER RETURNING TO THE hotel bruised and tired, the three of them ate dinner at the restaurant again. Gathered around the little booth where they sat earlier, they chatted over their progress during their training and surprisingly, Daemon couldn't stop complimenting Samuel on how well he did.

"You were far better than I expected. You really impressed me, mate."

Lorelei watched as Samuel turned a bright red that matched perfectly with his flaming hair. Samuel smiled proudly, and Lorelei wondered if that was the first ever compliment he's received for anything he's done in his life. The sad thought told her it was likely, and she hoped he was soaking in the true success of this day as much as possible.

Today had also been a major success for her as well. Daemon's hunch of her being able to tap into that connection between them, to speak Enochian and perform spells, had been true. Although it was too fresh, and her ability to do larger spells was nowhere in sight currently, it was a start. And it was the first time she didn't feel totally helpless in this entire endeavor. She felt true strength in the moment she conjured the barrier around her, and it gave her hope. She couldn't believe what was happening still, but as long as she kept hope, as long as they all did, they could do this.

She'd looked over the notebook of symbols the majority of the dinner while Daemon and Samuel grumbled about sparring and angel abilities versus demon ones. It was cute to see them getting along. That too, gave her immense amounts of rejuvenated hope.

When Daemon asked Lorelei to attempt to produce the Barrier Spell there at the dinner table, she hesitated, but she spoke the words softly and lo and behold, a barrier formed around herself again. Daemon coached her to think of the bubble expanding, and with a bit of effort, she was able to push the bubble to encompass them all—if only for a moment. Samuel and Daemon congratulated her on the result, and she couldn't help but feel such a sense of power and relief; perhaps, she could do this after all.

She swore to herself silently that she'd practice the words and spells every chance she had until she could do more than just produce a barrier to avert eyes and dull ears. Maybe one day, she could even perform something as strong as the Finishing Spell Daemon used to eradicate demons.

The thought of killing another person—or demon—or whatever, made her stomach instantly upset. That was the situation they were in though, the possibility of needing to defend herself to the point of taking another life. Lorelei's hope wavered; there was no guarantee she'd ever be able to find the strength or willpower enough to do it. But, if she didn't, the world ends. It was all overwhelming.

Welp, there's that headache again.

Pushing the recent walk down misery lane away in her mind for the time being, Lorelei looked to see Daemon smiling at Samuel. She honestly never thought Daemon would come around to trusting and liking Samuel, but then again, Daemon seemed to be shifting before her eyes in his own way. The hard, untrusting, always joking demeanor was washing away slowly. He was opening up more, trusting the both of them, and starting to believe that despite his past, he too deserved happiness in this world. Her heart felt so full while sitting there laughing and chatting with the two of them that for a little while, she found herself forgetting the treacherous situation they were in altogether.

After having stuffed his face more than they had even seen him do prior, which was saying a lot, Samuel left them to go take a nap before they were to head back out to Stonehenge late that night. When Lorelei finished her cup of tea, her and Daemon walked back up the stairs to Lorelei's room.

Walking in, the light she left on in the bathroom was casting odd shadows around her room. Her suitcase was nearly spilling out on the floor opposite the bed. Daemon walked back over to where he set the supplies to wrap her arm up and started to pull out another piece of gauze and some wrapping. Lorelei sat at the edge of the bed and watched him meticulously cut the right length and then turn to her arm already, outstretched for him. As he unwrapped her arm, he raised an eyebrow and chuckled to himself.

Lorelei looked down to see what amused him.

Her arm was completely healed. There was nothing left now but some circling white marks left from the lasso that was sure to stay with her the remainder of her life. Daemon's hand found its way to the mark, and gently ran his fingertips along the raised skin. She immediately felt a pulse from his touch radiate up her arm into her entire body, as if she were buzzing. A breath caught in the back of her throat as she spoke.

"I guess I will have this as a reminder of what we have gone through during this, huh?"

Daemon's eyes lingered on her arm a moment longer before he finally drew his hand away and nodded.

"Yes, I am just sorry that this had to happen to you to begin with. If I had been more careful, or even been better prepared, I might've been able to..."

Lorelei instinctively reached out for his hand and interlocked their fingers.

"You need to stop beating yourself up about that. You did protect me; you already did everything you could've."

When he only sighed and said nothing in return, she figured changing the topic might be better than trying to convince him further.

"So, do you have any idea how I healed so quickly? I mean, I recall healing fairly fast before, but never this fast."

Daemon blinked and nodded, continuing to keep his hand locked with hers.

"Yes, I have a theory. I already told you that I believe the piece of my soul I gave you has been helping you heal before. But now, I think because we are...together. Near each other, working together; I think the link between us is stronger than when we were apart before. It would make sense to think that piece of myself within you sort of reunites with my half, and so being together actually reinforces the power it gives to the both of us. I am not sure I explained how I killed off those last couple of demons when you passed out that night; but I performed a Finishing Spell. One strong enough to kill them both off at the same time before ever having to weaken them. I honestly figured it would kill me, and although I was weakened by it, it was not to the extent it should've been. Since it didn't kill me, I should've at least been taken out of commission for several days, perhaps longer. But I healed much quicker—all things considered. I was also thinking that could be the reason why you're able to speak the Celestial language despite being human. I have to wonder if there are other possibilities of this reunification that we might find out about, too."

Lorelei listened intently; it did make sense that being with each other, the pieces they shared were working together and making them both stronger in some way. Lost in thought, she hadn't noticed Daemon's hand releasing hers, and looked up at him.

"We should probably both get some rest before we leave later. I'm sure you're exhausted. I'll come by your room when it's time to go."

Leaning down, he placed a kiss upon her forehead and was already walking back toward the door to leave. The fire between them from the field earlier was gone and replaced once again by doubt and guilt; she could see it riddled his face, and her heart sank to the floor. A feeling of loss overwhelmed her. After falling asleep in each other's arms last night, the thought of being without him now was suffocating. Before she knew what she was doing, she was sprinting across the room after him.

"Wait, Daemon!"

Daemon's arresting emerald eyes met hers as he stood with one hand on the handle of the opened door. They stood in front of each other, neither saying a word. Feeling almost embarrassed now for not wanting to be away from him, she tried to come up with an excuse for why she called out to him—but before she could, the hand not holding the door open pulled her by the arm and let her body collide into his own, kissing her fiercely.

Lorelei weakened at the knees slightly before meeting his intensity with her own. Her arms found themselves wrapped around his neck, trying to make it so there was no space between them any longer. Everything in her screamed to have his body against her, to feel the warmth of it; the muscles beneath his clothes moved beneath her fingertips. The eruption of desire from the teasing earlier in the field was now unraveling tenfold within her.

It was like a storm of passion opened from the sky and consumed them both, enveloping them in the tornado of all their feelings for each other they hadn't yet been able to express.

Lorelei's mouth was greedy as her tongue met his in a flurry, and it wasn't until she heard a low growl escape Daemon's throat from her biting his bottom lip that he finally slammed the door he had been holding shut, without even having to stop kissing her to do so. His hands caught at the small of her back and he hoisted her up. Lorelei wrapped her legs tightly around his torso as Daemon walked her hastily over to the bed, gently laying her down and climbing on top of her.

Their legs intertwined, and Daemon's lips moved their way down her chin, placing small kisses and bites along her throat. Lorelei's body was burning up, and sensations from his lips on her neck sent tingles throughout her. Her hands were balling up the fabric of his shirt on his back, and when he bit around her collarbone playfully. She let out a soft moan, which seemed to only intensify Daemon's own efforts. His hand trailed up her thigh and gripped it hard. Unable to take anymore of it, Lorelei brought his head back up to meet hers. Both of them were breathing like there was not enough air left in the world. He smiled at her when she took the handfuls of his shirt and lifted it over his head.

The moment his shirt was off, his wings unfolded themselves from his back; although not fully extended, they were so large in comparison to his body. They lay strongly behind him, cascading off the bed. Lorelei's eyes were immediately drawn to them, recalling the first night she'd seen them. Without realizing, her hand reached out to the one on her right, and her fingers ran over the feathers delicately. They were soft, and responded to her touch as if they were an entity all their own. Seeing him this way—he was absolutely striking. He definitely looked like any angel she could've conjured in her head, but even more spectacular than that. Many might think him a bit scary looking—what with these massive black wings and those alarming green eyes, but to her, he couldn't be more perfect.

Sitting up, the moonlight was shining from the window, illuminating Daemon's perfect form. The ripples in his shoulders and chest, his defined abs—she let her hand move from his wing and work its way down his body. Daemon bit his lip as her fingers skimmed the top of his jeans.

Suddenly, the energy changed and Daemon was tenderly bringing her up to meet him. He went quiet and was merely letting his eyes wander over her face, like he was doing his best to memorize what she looked like in this moment. He let his hands cup her cheeks, bringing their foreheads to rest against each other. She could tell he was still catching his breath. Lorelei tried to look at him to see if something was wrong, until he broke the silence at last.

"Lorelei, I love you. I love you with all that I am and more. I love you so much that it almost hurts...My heart aches for you in ways I didn't think existed."

Lorelei didn't say anything, but she knew what he was describing. This constant burning feeling in her chest that was getting hotter and brighter with each moment together, as if it might ignite and burn wildly out of control. The need to be with him was overwhelming, and the feeling of emptiness when he was away was almost too much to bear. Daemon continued, his voice softening.

"I can't imagine not being with you. The pull to you that I feel is as if I was always meant to be with you. I didn't stop...yanno...what we were doing because I didn't want to keep going. In fact, it feels like I might explode from wanting to be with you that way. But a part of me feels like we should wait until this whole mess is over with. The connection with you is beyond me. You are far too precious to me to rush this. I want to be yours. Bare my soul to you. Open up and reveal the shattered pieces I thought deserved to remain hidden forever. I want nothing to tug any part of our minds away from the moment, where there is complete confidence that we are safe and can be in each other's embrace until eternity takes us."

Daemon leaned back and brushed a hand through her hair, gazing into her eyes.

"I can't rush making love to you, Lorelei. It wouldn't feel right. I want to savor every single milli-second of it. I want to take my time, taking you fully as *mine*. But I can't right now—not this way."

Lorelei's heart felt like melted butter. He was absolutely right, even if her body ached to be with him, with her heart still pounding beneath her chest and the pulse like electricity from his touch lingering, she placed her hand over his and smiled.

"I love you too, Daemon. And you're right—we should wait."

A wave of relief washed over Daemon's face when she returned the words she knew he longed to hear back. Finally having expressed their love for each other, there was nothing more to hold back. Nothing separated one from the other. While the world remained wild beyond them, here, in this time, they were together—in mind and passion. Daemon brushed her hair from her face behind her shoulders, and the touch on the nape of her neck making her shiver, as did the confession they both gave. Love was conquering here, in the middle of the end of the world, and it was stronger than what she'd felt before. Daemon kissed her, the fury of passion still dictating the movement of his lips on hers. She fell away in his kiss, letting her shoulders drop, breathing him in. Only him.

When he pulled back, he kissed the tip of her nose and settled on the bed, pulling her to fall on top of his chest, his eyes filling with pride and affection. He said nothing aloud—feeling all they would ever need to say silently. Daemon let his hand run through her hair, and she just laid there looking up at him, saving his features into her memory. The way his silver hair glowed in the moonlight. The way his eyes flickered slightly as they moved to scan over her face. How his mouth curled at the edges, the shape of his lips plumper when he was still. The way his cheekbones looked even more defined by the pale halo of light around the outline of his body coming from the window. His wings were wrapped around them like a blanket. They were warm and comforting, and although trying her best to stay awake, she could feel her eyes getting heavy. Daemon chuckled under his breath, whispering sweetly.

"Sleep, Sunflower."

And with the sound of his voice and the light peck she felt upon her forehead, she drifted off to sleep.

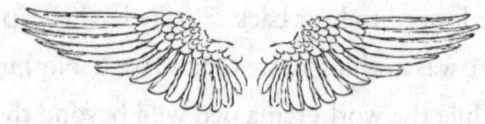

I was looking to the right, where Daemon's hand was in mine. He gave me a comforting smile, but I felt it deep in my bones that everything was about to explode around us. A crack of white and red lightning flared across the sky above us. Daemon took in a breath, squeezed my hand, and let his enormous black wings unfurl from his bare back; soared into the sky, leaving me worriedly staring after him trying to make out his figure amongst the thousands of others.

*Suddenly, I'm flung into a different place, one of bright, golden light —and yet, the feeling from the place is ancient and **dark**. Blinking my eyes several times, I make out Daemon kneeling on the ground a few feet from me. I smiled and ran to his side, stopping abruptly.*

Circling his arms, legs, and throat, were heavy duty chains that linked to large beams on either side of him. Other shadows now emerge from behind him; I can make out two angels and two demons. It was confusing seeing them together without chaos ensuing. One of the angels muttered something too soft for me to hear to one of the demons, who gave a peculiar smile in return. They gathered on either side of him, lifting his wings out, which were white now, and with two of them on each side, began ripping them from his body.

The agonizing screams ushering from Daemon made me wrench in horror and disgust. Blood spurt all around him until finally, Daemon lay slumped in a pool of his own blood; his wings tossed aside as if they were nothing more than a piece of a broken toy, no longer useful. Bile filled my mouth as I tried to keep from vomiting. At last, Daemon raised his head to look up at me, and the sound that came forth was one of pure defeat and hatred.

For me.

*"You....you did this to me. YOU **DAMNED** ME!"*

"Daemon, no! I never meant for this to happen! I'm so sorry!"

I was on my knees, arms wrapped around myself and weeping. Weeping because I knew he was right. I let this happen to him. If I had only given myself over—let them kill me—and let the war happen, this would've never happened to him.

Daemon's usual beautiful emerald eyes now burned a fiery red. He was laughing hysterically and only shook his head.

"Apologies are worthless now. I am nothing because of you. Nothing."

And as he uttered these last words, he vanished into a smokey abyss, leaving me on the floor, crying so hard that the tears began to sting my face.

When I opened my eyes again, I found that I'd been transported to another place again. This time, it was central London, but it was on fire. People ran screaming through the streets; bodies lay dead all around me. Panic was starting to take over. I felt a small tug on my pant leg and looked down in horror to see a small body, still alive but unlike anything I'd ever seen before. It looked like the body of a child, but its eyes were gouged out, a black sludge streaming from them, and its body was horribly disfigured. Although it looked like it should be dead, it was tugging fiercely to get my attention. But when I asked what I could do to help him, he merely screamed,

*"You were **SUPPOSED** to help me, already. **YOU** were supposed to save us from our destruction. But look at me; look at the result of **your failure**."*

Looking up from the boy to the rest of my surroundings once again, in an instant—nothing at all remained. All that was before me was a desolate, decaying world. And I am the cause of it all.

I fell to my knees and screamed.

CHAPTER 22

RAPHAEL

RAPHAEL WANDERED CASUALLY THROUGH the southernmost gardens; the one that Ariel spent the majority of her time in. The luminescent glow of the plants surrounding the pathway brightened as he passed them. All gardens in Heaven glowed, as did most anything else here. This garden was named "The Garden of the Virtues," for it was created by the Virtues themselves to tend to and spend time when they were not on Earth.

The Virtues were the angels who preceded over the elements of the Universe, making sure everything in the cosmos remained intact. They were also in charge of keeping nature on Earth in balance. Ariel was the ArchAngel in charge of the Virtues, for she was the overseer of all plant and animal life on Earth. This garden was her sanctuary in Heaven, and one she went to whenever something was troubling her mind. Raphael found his way to a small pond near a gazebo and saw Ariel holding a petal of a blue flower that glowed brightly at her touch.

Ariel was petite; some would say she resembled a fairy. She had fair, ivory skin with deep golden hair that fell in waves around her and down the length of her back. Today she was wearing a warm pink dress that clung to her small frame, long, draping sleeves that fell from her arms, and her head was adorned with a matching crown made of blushing roses. The one thing she never wore was shoes; she said she preferred to be barefoot to connect to the energy within the ground. Her cheeks were always warm with a flush pink hue that matched the mixture of pink and green aura that engulfed her body. Everyone in Heaven exuded a colored aura, and the color depended on their rank or duties; for instance Raphael's aura was yellow, for he was the analytical one, the one tasked with overseeing projects, dictating orders, and keeping other lower-leveled angels in line. Ariel's showed she was a mixture, because her duties were plentiful; the green was for her connection to nature and overseeing the Virtues, and pink was because of her compassion. She was often brought in to help the new angels or angels struggling emotionally, acting sort of like a human therapist.

She was highly empathic, and was able to discern emotions of those nearby her, as well as soothe others easily and with an air of maturity that Raphael felt surpassed many, even other ArchAngels. ArchAngels were powerful, but this did not mean they were the most caring of beings. Often, ArchAngels ruled with a cold indifference, a harsh hand of justice—not one of emotion.

As Raphael approached Ariel, she lifted her head and met his eyes with a smile. Returning one, he stood by her side and watched as she delicately released the flower she was holding and let the now free hand loop into his own as she leaned on her tiptoes to kiss his cheek. Raphael ran a hand through her curly golden locks and cupped her face gently.

"You ran off so fast after the last meeting—I was worried about you."

Ariel sighed and nuzzled her face into his hand.

"I'm fine, Raphie. I'm just a little overwhelmed by these delegations. I'm not sure why, but this instance of attack seems profoundly wrong to me. I know we have never been ones to shy away from doing what must be done for the good of all the Universe, but this girl, Lorelei...she doesn't deserve this fate."

Raphael did his best to not wince at the pet name Ariel used for him, because although she'd used it from the start of their relationship a thousand years ago, it still wasn't preferred. He nodded and let his hand find hers again, leading her to the bench under the gazebo that overlooked the glass-like pond.

Although she often had the personality of innocence and sweetness, her dress spoke nothing of this; she was sultry and elegance at its finest. The pink dress clung perfectly at her small curves, hugging every inch of her body, its fabric made of divine silk, making Raphael's hands roam on her waist; imagining how easily he could tear it, and bring her close. It'd been awhile since they were intimate, and she was gorgeous beyond reproach; they made a miraculous pair together. But he steadied his thoughts, for this was all a delicate and difficult situation, and Ariel's mind was saddened by the processions. He cared for her deeply. She was the first being Raphael actually fell in love with, and she was precious to him beyond all others.

Personality-wise, they were vastly opposite. Raphael was calm and calculated, run by logic and confidence. Ariel was all passion and emotions, run by the need to express herself. She always acted more with her feelings than her head, but that's also what made her so different from the others; she was kind, to the point he would do everything in this Universe to protect her, hold her close, and hope that her kindness would never be sullied by another being ever. And that ability to express herself helped him do the same, little by little over the centuries—but only when they were totally alone, making love, sipping wine and duties were momentarily put aside. Otherwise, he remained composed: the perfect angel to enforce duties.

Sitting beside her, he adjusted his white linen suit, picking lint off his shoulders before pulling her closer to him. She let herself fall into the crack of his arms, and he hugged her. He didn't often show such physical affection publicly, but he too, felt his heart needed reassurance. It was taking a long time for the ArchAngels to deliberate on what to do about the situation pertaining to Lorelei and Daemon. Time for angels ran differently seeing as they can operate on multiple planes at the same time. This is why three weeks had already passed in Heaven's time since Raphael gave the warning to Daemon, when for them it had still only been a few days. Half of the council, including the head, Michael, were in vote to attack them and take them out by whatever means necessary. The other half, including Ariel and himself, were on the fence about that tactic. The deliberations were starting to get tense for everyone, and so a recess was set to allow time to think on what had been argued thus far.

"You're not the only one thinking that way. Although it's not the majority's opinion, a few of the others have started questioning the point of the war. But I don't think anyone will speak up about that on account of what happened to..."

Raphael's mind went directly to Daemon, remembering the day he had condemned Daemon for the very thing the others were now rethinking, and turned his wings black—marking him as one of the Fallen for all eternity.

It was one of the most difficult days of Raph's existence.

Daemon was his closest friend and therefore, Michael decided that the person to carry out the ruling against Daemon would be him. To become a disgraced angel, there is a hearing in front of all angels—but there was hardly ever a verdict of not guilty once a hearing was called.

The accused angel would sit in the middle of a glass courtroom, where the walls and floors shimmered in the light and reflected strange, distorted faces on the walls from those around you. Michael was the judge and final decision in the matter, but the ArchAngels would proceed to vote on the punishment. The only ArchAngels who didn't vote guilty were Raphael and Ariel. Michael saw this as being sympathetic to his friend and thus forced

Raphael to carry out the next phase: blackening his wings and condemning him to a life on Earth.

Blackening an angel's wings is a very grueling and painful process. It requires the accused to be chained to large pillars to keep from escaping as they are "stained." Staining was a marking of not only the outer appearance of the angel's wings, but would leave an inner mark or wound of sorts within the angel as well. This inner mark was said to be damaging to an angel's very essence. The screams still haunted Raphael to this day. **Daemon was the first ever angel to survive the ceremony**. Nobody could say for certain they knew what the long-term effects were. They casted him out, and he has been living on Earth ever since; unable to return home.

Most angels never questioned their orders; they trusted what they were tasked to do, whether good or wrong in their eyes, believing the higher-ups knew what should be done for the good of all. They were doing the Divine's will; how could it be wrong?

But Daemon had always been different. He asked more questions about his missions rather than the others who would take their assignments and go. He would always eventually shrug his shoulders and take the task, but it wasn't until he was assigned to make sure Lorelei did indeed die from being hit by that car that he instead, saved her. He didn't just question it, he didn't follow it at all—which to the ArchAngels, was instant mutiny. There hadn't been such a blatant disregard for orders since Lucifer.

Over the millennia, there were occasionally other angels who questioned an order, but never to this magnitude. Not to the point of allowing the prophesied girl, the only one who could stop the Great War altogether; continue on. *That was out of the question.*

It honestly broke Raph's heart to have to do it, and although Daemon believes that not a single person was on his side, he would scoff to find out that about half the council was on the fence about a very similar predicament.

He'd probably say something snarky and ironic about it. Even Raph couldn't help but think similarly about whether or not they should send an attack on Lorelei and Daemon, or let what unfolds come to be.

Raph hadn't noticed that Ariel was saying his name. Her soft, gentle voice could sometimes make it difficult to hear her when he was deep in thought. Blinking a few times, he turned to her and gave a faint smile.

"Apologies, my darling. I was only thinking.."

She went to take his hand and place it on her lap.

"I know, I know you were thinking about Daemon. I am sure all this happening is stirring up feelings from the past around you two's relationship and what happened. Daemon is your best friend, more like your brother, and you have to know he doesn't actually hate you for what you had to do."

Raphael thought back on the look Daemon gave him when they met outside that restaurant in Inverness. Daemon's usual bright, green eyes narrowed over Raph and he could see the momentary joy at seeing his old friend pass through his eyes, and then fade swiftly to betrayal and pain. Seeing his friend look at him as though he were the scum of all creation was harder for Raph to handle than he thought. He figured Daemon would still be angry with him, but he hoped after all the time that passed, perhaps he wouldn't feel as much animosity towards him. When Raphael returned to Heaven, he sat quietly in his chambers for several hours. It was only when Ariel came knocking on his door, he realized how long he had been in there mulling over the interaction. Ariel was the only one to know that Raphael defied the no-contact order to warn Daemon of what was to come. If any other ArchAngel found out what he did, he'd meet a similar fate to Daemon. It was the first time Raphael disobeyed an order; it weighed heavy on him. She was the only one he could trust, and the only one who knew how much it scarred Raphael to lose his friend forever.

"You didn't see the way he looked at me, Ariel. I think if you had, you might not be saying that."

Ariel squeezed his hand and looked like she might say more, but her gaze moved from Raph to the figure over his shoulder. When he turned, their fellow ArchAngel, Gabriel, was standing there. Gabriel was beautiful for a man. He had a sleek, angular face that always seemed stern to Raph. His long, straight white hair went below his shoulders, and he was wearing a fine white suit with gold trimmings. The pants were hemmed above the ankles and were fitted to his thin, but fit form. His white aura surrounding him made him even brighter against the white suit and hair. As he approached, he eyed them both without emotion, and spoke.

"We are being called to come back."

Pausing, he measured his words before he continued.

"And it doesn't look good for Daemon and the human girl."

CHAPTER 23

DAEMON

DAEMON CONTINUED TO RUN his hand through Lorelei's hair as she fell asleep beside him. He couldn't help but smile to himself, the blonde strands of her hair silky to the touch as they fell between his fingers. *She loved him back.*

Something he never thought he could have this deep of a connection with somebody—was right there before him. He'd been with other women before, but the feelings never lasted. He didn't ever aim to fall in love, not with anybody. But with Lorelei, it was a totally different world. The way she made him feel, he could do no wrong in her eyes; even if he did fuck up, she would always love him. When she looked at him with eyes like a clear ocean when the water was still and breathless, he saw the infinite possibilities with her. The joy, the laughter, the love. It was all there in those eyes. For so long, he was convinced he was meant to be unlovable, meant to live with the guilt of his past and merely exist. But now he knew that to exist wasn't enough; he wanted to *live*. Live a life with the person he most cherished, because now she was showing him that he deserved to.

To her, he was worthy. And to him, she was worth more than anything else in the world.

Was he always meant to fall the way he did so that he could be here now to help her? Only those much higher than himself would ever know the Divine purpose of others, even the purposes of certain angels. Daemon always thought that his purpose ended when he was cast from Heaven, but what if that wasn't actually the case? Could there possibly be a destiny for him with Lorelei beyond all the turmoil? And was he actually strong enough to protect her as she protected the world? Despite the odds stacked against them, he wanted with all his heart to believe they would achieve their goal. To even think about the alternative was too terrifying to dwell on. But luck would have to be on their side, and that very well may not be how the cards are drawn.

Plus, time was waning quickly. The demons will have regrouped soon, and that means the angels may be finalizing their plans as well. Raphael had said the hierarchy of angels were to meet to decide what they were to do in regards to Lorelei and Daemon. That was 3 days ago now, and time moved faster in Heaven. They were bound to make their decision by now. So why weren't they attacking? What was keeping their hands steady? Surely they knew about the first demon attack which would only push them to act sooner rather than later. But perhaps, like Samuel today, they'd be surprisingly better than he thought. He only hoped it was enough, because if it wasn't—if there were more coming at them than the four demons before, from either side, they probably won't stand a chance.

Getting back to Stonehenge as soon as possible was their next goal, but they were having to go in the dead of night to make absolutely sure no humans would be lurking about. He'd fortified the field earlier with wards and protections, but it severely drained his magical energy; he wouldn't be able to do the same tonight.

He thought perhaps he might need to sleep, but he was so wired from what happened earlier with Lorelei, he was content to just lay beside her. She was always beautiful; he thought he hadn't ever seen anything so lovely before. Of course angels were lovely, but they were also terrifying in their own right. Vampires were usually pretty, but had a sinister side that always showed itself eventually, and other human women just never seemed worth the time.

But Lorelei was more beautiful than ever expected. Never before had Daemon become so completely attached to a human. And now it felt as though if he ever parted, the loss would never make him feel whole again. Because for the first time in centuries, he *did* feel whole.

Even many of the angels spoke of true love as an almost folly pursuit, one that would only end in heartache and suffering; but perhaps that was more because for an angel, the heartache felt from a breakup or are loss of love would be felt indefinitely, seeing as angels live on while their loves are lost to time.

Daemon always believed that's why angels usually had short, playful relationships rather than long-term. With humans, love could always be fleeting, and yet their first instinct is to jump head-first and love as deeply and truly as possible—despite the fact that it might not last. It was a trait Daemon always admired in humans, and now he understood just how much you want to give of yourself when you finally find the one you feel you've been waiting for. For so long, he never thought he deserved to be loved by anybody for the shame of his past seemed to spill over in all aspects of his life following the incident.

Suddenly, a shifting from Lorelei brought Daemon out of his thoughts. Lovingly turning to look at her face, he immediately drew in breath as she began to toss and turn. He tried to sit up slightly, but was taken aback when Lorelei screamed aloud and began to cry, whimpering into his arm.

"No please! I never meant to hurt anyone! Please....please! I'm begging you! I'm so sorry, Daemon! I am so sorry..."

Tears ran down her face, and Daemon gently tried to wake her.

"Lorelei...Lorelei...Please wake up."

Lorelei's eyes remained shut, the curtains on the wall behind them starting to move, slowly at first, but the longer Lorelei screamed out, the more intensely they moved, flipping about wildly, nearly seeming to pull themselves off the curtain rod.

Her emotions were producing energy that was making the entire room shake.

The desk opposite the bed rattled on its legs, causing scratching sounds and thumping as it hit the wall. The bedside lamp flickered on and off, making it resemble a scene in a ghost horror film.

At last, Lorelei's eyes shot open fast, but when she blinked several times as if she didn't remember where she was, Daemon placed both hands softly on her arms and attempted to get her attention on him. He needed to calm her before the room was destroyed.

"Hey there, hey. It's alright. It was just a nightmare. You're okay, I'm here with you."

When Lorelei finally looked at him with recognition, he breathed a sigh of relief and gave her a small smile. She was breathing heavily, like she finished running a marathon, a look of horror upon her face that made Daemon's stomach wrench.

What did she just see?

After several more breaths, Lorelei reached for Daemon and hugged him tighter than she ever had before. Wrapping his arms just as tightly around her, stroking her hair soothingly, he wanted her to feel safe again. Between gasping breaths and tears, Lorelei buried her face into his chest and sobbed. The energy shift ebbed the longer he held her the more she calmed, the effects of her emotions causing a rippling in the energetic field in the room, stopped. All was quiet. Lorelei was becoming stronger, her intuitive and empathic abilities growing more powerful.

"Daemon...I saw....I don't even know what I saw. But I know I saw you. You were hurt because of me. Because of who I am, and the danger you're in from helping me. I saw the fate of the world if I failed. I saw the horror of it all before me and I could do nothing to stop it! It was all my fault and all I could do was watch! It was the most terrible thing I have ever seen and...and it was....all my fault..."

Her sobbing worsened as she tried to utter the last few words. Instinctively, Daemon pulled her to him as he sat up against the backboard of the bed. She curled her legs around his waist and sat in his lap. Making a soft shushing noise without thinking, he continued to hold the back of her head tenderly and whispered.

"Lorelei, it was only a dream. None of that stuff you saw was real. You haven't hurt me; and I genuinely don't believe you ever could. I know...I know that this is more on your shoulders than anyone should ever have to bear. But you of all people **can** bear it. You are so strong and so capable, and I know you can do this. It's going to be alright. I'm with you, and we can get through all this together. I'll never leave you to face this, or anything else alone—ever. You're my light, and there is no longer a future I can see and want that doesn't have you in it."

He heard an indiscernible mutter against his chest between another wracking sob, and although he couldn't quite hear her, he knew what she said.

"Because I believe in you. I believe in this cause we are fighting for. I believe that it can be done and that you can save *everyone* with your light, not just me."

He waited another minute before saying more, continuing to hold her tight against him. It killed him to see how much pain Lorelei was in—to witness her self-doubt and fear of the possibility of failure render her like this. All he wanted was for this mess to be over and to love her and give her the life she deserves—to protect her. But how could he protect her when the very thing they were trying to do, might not work out? How can he reassure her that it will all be okay, when there is a chance it won't be? He was racking his brain for the right thing to say when her sobs lessened, and she was breathing more steadily.

"Lorelei..."

She finally looked up at him with a tear-stained face. Her eyes grey like a storm, he put a finger under her chin.

"I believe in you."

She merely stared into his eyes.

"But...what if you get hurt—because of me? I couldn't forgive myself if that happened."

Moving his hand to cup her face, he spoke softly.

"I would die for you, Lorelei. You are my path now. I willingly follow you anywhere, even if that means I lose my life. Because for me....life without you in it wouldn't be worth living. I chose this course. I choose you and everything that comes with being with you. I will continue to choose you until my last breath. And if I can keep choosing you beyond death, I will do that too. "

Her tears finally ceased, and she leaned her forehead to rest against his. He breathed in her sweet scent, now mixed with the saltiness of her tears, and closed his eyes as she spoke in a hushed tone.

"I love you, Daemon. I love you so much...I never thought I would find somebody like you. Someone who believed so whole-heartedly in me. Someone who saw my potential more than I saw it myself. I am thankful I do have you. I choose you, too."

She kissed him fiercely. The lingering taste of salt from her tears upon her lips didn't bother him. He returned the kiss just as passionately. After a moment, he drew back, but the feel of her lips could still be felt on his own.

Hesitating before asking, "Do you want to talk about what you saw in your dream?"

She shook her head "no" and Daemon nodded. He was curious to know what particularly about him freaked her out so much, but respected her desire to not discuss it. Leaning over to look at his phone, he slowly turned to face her once more.

"It's time to get going. I'll go wake up the kid."

Placing a kiss on her forehead as she got off of him, he walked out the door of the hotel room to get Samuel. And although he hadn't experienced it nor knew what the dream was about, a part of him feared Lorelei's intuitive abilities were now allowing her to see what could come to pass, and he didn't know if it was better that way.

CHAPTER 24

LORELEI

LORELEI SAT IN THE car patiently waiting for Daemon to come back to let them know the coast was clear, so they could make their way back to Stonehenge. Samuel yawned in the backseat, still waking up from their nap in between dinner and their return here.

The dream she had earlier was spiraling over and over in her mind, the grotesquely disfigured child, Daemon's screams as his wings were ripped away like paper. London, *her home*—on fire. Daemon comforted her when she woke screaming and sweating in his arms. She had nearly knocked him off the bed with how frantically she'd awoken. The panic must have alarmed him because Daemon's eyes quickly went a dark green color and the protectiveness in his voice, although reassuring, still wasn't enough to calm her for several minutes as she wailed and whimpered about the possibility of hurting him and failing to save everyone.

He reassured her that she could never hurt him, and although she nodded silently, she wasn't so sure that was true. His very being near her meant he was a traitor, a betrayal to his kind, a rogue on the wrong side. The sheer truth of what they were trying to accomplish meant he was always in danger. Daemon tried to get her to tell him what she saw in her dream, but to speak it made her feel like it would come to life, and she couldn't bring herself to discuss it. With their connection, she knew it hurt him that she was shutting him out. Keeping it from him seemed wrong. But she was too afraid of the consequences that may come if she told him.

That wasn't the only thing on her mind. Lorelei was mulling over exactly what they were doing here. When they were at Stonehenge earlier that morning, they were seeing if something would happen to her while there, something that might give her a clue as to what the next step in their mission was. And to her shock and dismay, something *did* happen. It felt like a whisper; it was quiet—subtle at first, and it sounded like a buzzing bee was in her mind. Slowly, as she breathed and focused on it, an almost ethereal melody arose. It was beautiful and eerie at the same time. It was calling to her, inviting her in to see more. A flash of bright blue came across her eyes, although they were closed, and the melody intensified. But soon, it faded and was no more. The buzzing ceased. The moment passed. When they were walking back to the car afterwards, she was unable to hide her frustration.

"It was your first time trying to connect to it. Don't beat yourself." Daemon said, hopeful at her attempt and that it meant that they were indeed at the right place.

Looking out the window, she saw a shadowy figure approaching and when Daemon's face finally came into view, he opened the car door for her.

"No one is around. I put up a couple of protective spells to enhance our chances of going undetected, but they're not a guarantee; they won't be as strong as the ones earlier today. It's best we all stay on guard while we're here."

Daemon reached a hand out to Lorelei as she stepped out of the car. Taking it, she gave a soft smile and he squeezed her hand gently. Samuel scuttled out of the backseat and stretched before walking alongside them. When they arrived back at the stones, they hopped over the roping that originally kept them several hundred metres before, and as they walked nearer, Lorelei felt the hair on the back of her neck stand up. A vibration or sort of static feeling enveloped her body, and it was as if the air around the colossal structure sensed her presence. Daemon finally let go of her hand once they reached the center of the stones, and unzipped his backpack to pull out several various sized candles. He started laying the candles around in a circle, matching the placement of the stones, and lit them one by one with the flick of his fingers, stepping back once finished, looking at the both of them.

"The candles help with clearing the energy left before. A sort of cleansing to help set the tone for you, that way, you don't get lost in there."

Samuel spoke up before Lorelei.

"Lost? Lost where?"

"Exactly my question. What are you talking about Daemon?" Lorelei looked at him, his face lit by the surrounding candles, but shadows danced and moved across his striking features as he turned to face her. His silvery hair caught the light just enough to look like the tips of it were on fire. His glowing green eyes shone brightly, almost glowing in the dark. He beckoned with his hand for her to sit down on the ground with him within the circle of candles. Sitting quietly, afraid to disturb the peace of the moment in fear that something dastardly could pop out from behind one of the large stones, Lorelei faced Daemon and Samuel in the circle.

Daemon looked around them, purveying the area again before speaking.

"I know that you feel a connection here, I feel one too. But it's faint, almost illegible and far off. I had a thought earlier to try something that could possibly help us connect with the force here better, quicker. I could train you to meditate and allow yourself to come to this connection on your own, but we just don't have that kind of time. So I have another plan...one that is possibly a long shot and one I have never achieved on my own."

Daemon's voice went quiet, ashamed that he was admitting that his plan may not work at all, although it seemed to be the only plan he had.

Lorelei steadied her breathing and nodded.

"A plan is better than nothing, even if it's a long shot."

Daemon turned to Samuel.

"Unfortunately, with you being a demon, you will be unable to join us. Therefore, your job is to keep a lookout and protect us while we go in. We are both going to be in a trance, unable to hear much or feel grounded to where we are. That's one reason the candles are here, but we also need your help if we get too deep, or if something happens while we are gone; you will have to pull us back out. You will be the bridge back to this plane so we may return. That means you have to do everything in your power to "wake" us in a sense, so we don't get stuck. It's imperative you do so, or else we may never be back in this dimension again. We are also counting on you to defend our bodies if anybody should show up to attack."

His voice was grave, and it sent shivers throughout Lorelei. Samuel was equally panicked.

"What are you talking about?? I know I did alright at training today but that doesn't mean I could fight and protect you all by myself! And what do you mean you won't come back? Where are you going?"

Daemon hesitated before answering, "We are traveling to the Akasha, to attempt to access the Akashic Records."

Lorelei stared at him dumbstruck; this was not a term she'd run across in all her studies. Daemon noticed and continued quickly.

"The Akasha is a higher dimension than the one we are on now. It's a place that exists on a different plane from our own, but allows you to move through time. Every thought, action, and idea from the past, present, and future are stored there. In essence, it is sort of library of what *will* happen, what *is* happening, and what *has* happened in all of the Universe, for all time. Similarly to Heaven, time can move all at once or not at all. The rules of time don't apply to you there like they do here. You can be in the present time but see clearly what came to be in a moment a thousand years before, and you can be there like it was happening right now. Each person or soul has their own individual record they are able to access here. It can tell a person exactly what the trajectory of their life could be—if they stay on that particular course 10 years from now. It can also show you potential outcomes of scenarios or reveal not only your history, but of those most closely connected with your own journey. Pretty much, it's the biggest book keeper of all time. I figured we had no other leads, no clue as to what to do next, and perhaps the best bet would be to access your Akashic records and see if we can learn anything from there."

Samuel looked between them and hugged his arms across his chest.

"But what does that have to do with you not coming back? Daemon, I can't fight off demons or angels if they come and you're not here!"

Daemon was concerned and Lorelei could tell the thought of Samuel's chances of fending off whatever possible assault that comes, may have run across his mind as well. But surprisingly, Daemon smiled brightly at Samuel and patted his shoulder.

"You got it, mate! The way you moved today on the field, no matter what, you have speed on them for one. And two, your ability to manipulate the elements will be your biggest strength. Just slow down and don't think too hard, alright?"

For the first time, Lorelei could see a companionship between Daemon and Samuel. Daemon was showing a protectiveness of Samuel she hadn't seen before, and it made her heart feel warm witnessing it.

Finally Lorelei found the courage to accept it; she didn't have a clue where she was going, and it didn't sound real; but she had to believe Daemon knew what he was doing, and she believed him completely.

"Okay. Let's do it then."

Daemon winked at her and turned his attention to Samuel.

"Samuel, I need you to stand outside of the circle's perimeter. Do not, I repeat, **do not** let any person or thing enter it until we are out of the Akasha. You got that? Once we are there, there will be no way for us to return to our bodies quickly. Until I finish the meditation ritual, our souls will be trapped there. It isn't an evil place, but it is tricky. It's not like we can just waltz in and get what we need; we will have to earn it, and that takes time. So give us all the time you can."

With that, Samuel began walking out of the circle, his hands balled into fists by his sides, shivering from fright. But he took a position beyond the circle of candles and stood, steadfast and strong. Lorelei's heart went out to him; he was being so brave. Glancing up, she turned to look at the stones towering above them. She remembered visiting them when she first moved to London for school several years ago, and the effect was still the same—pure awe. Stonehenge, along with structures like the pyramids, were some of the most theorized structures in the world. Nobody knew exactly how they were constructed, or what their true purpose was. It was said the stones themselves are a type of rock that were brought from over 15 miles away from the site; and during 2500 BC, that is a feat of ingenuity experts still couldn't figure out how it was accomplished. It fascinated her to no end. Her little history buff heart did a flip in excitement.

They are like the silent guardians of this place...but what exactly are they guarding?

Lorelei was surprised by the thought, not believing she ever considered that question before. She looked into Daemon's eyes; he was seated a couple inches in front of her, and they faced each other, continuing to hold each other's hands. This comforted her greatly, making the tension in her shoulders release a bit.

Daemon cleared his voice, which was barely audible over the wind that had started to pick up. The firelight from the candles flickered wildly, casting strange shadows over the stones surrounding them. Lorelei wondered if she could see figures dancing in those shadows, swaying and moving to music she couldn't hear.

"Close your eyes, relax your body. I need you to try and clear your mind; focus only on my voice. You won't understand the words, as it will be in Celestial speak, but I need you to let whatever feelings and emotions, that rise up inside of you upon hearing them come forward, I need you to feel them completely. Let them overtake your body. Likewise, any images you see—let them come. You may not understand them but that isn't what matters. It only matters that you don't force them away or overthink on them too much, okay? That is how we get to the Akasha; we ride the waves of your thoughts and emotions there. Because I am sort of the conduit for the ceremony, I will be able to travel with you as long as we touch. It may seem....scary, at first. But don't be frightened. When you feel scared, just tune back into my voice, the feel of my hand holding yours. The fear will pass quickly and it will be over. Do you understand?"

She could feel that fear creeping up inside of her, but she pushed it down and squeezed his hands, "Yes." With her acknowledgement, Daemon closed his eyes, and began to speak.

His words felt like a warm hug, surrounding them in their embrace. As the words flowed from him, a prickling sensation rushed through Lorelei's body, similar to the masking effect Daemon had when he was putting a sort of film surrounding them from others. But this was stronger. The air around them hummed along with the melody of his voice, the words almost echoing around in her head. They were striking, demanding, yet beautiful. Suddenly, she became overwhelmed with a feeling of elation. She could feel herself smiling, an instant rush of happiness filling her up from within. But a moment later, anxiety rose to meet it—anxiety that made it feel as though her heart might burst out of her chest. Sweat was starting to pour down her forehead, pooling at her temples. Lorelei knew she was tightening her grip on Daemon's hands, the urge to run all-too-consuming. She tried to remember his advice: to ride the feelings but not take too much stock in them. This was easier said than done.

As Daemon's voice grew, so did the visions.

Dark figures lulling out of a long slumber, coming out from the shadows in the corners of her mind. Hulking, lurking things making noises Lorelei thought she would not soon forget. But as soon as they arrived, they vanished. And suddenly, she saw the face of her mother, staring down at a sleeping baby. Singing and rocking the baby to sleep in her arms, she was smiling, joy radiating from her face as she looked upon the child.

That same joy transmitted to Lorelei. She could feel it working its way from her toes to the top of her head. This feeling of lightness, of sunshine.

She had to assume the child was her, but she never even imagined seeing her mother this way. Seeing her—*happy*.

Lorelei wasn't sure from what direction she was looking in at the scene happening before her. Was she all around? Was she seeing her mother's face from the child's perspective? Was she above it all? She wondered if this is what people described as having an outer body experience. She was all of it. In every instance she could recount, she was seeing the scene from every angle, reliving it as a pure moment of time like it was yesterday, and seeing it happen from all around. But the mood shifted all too suddenly.

Lorelei's mother abruptly stopped singing, and looked directly at Lorelei herself, not the baby. But the smile that a moment ago illuminated her face was gone. Lorelei's heartbeat felt like it was sputtering out of control as her mother spoke, her voice haunting.

"It's time."

Lorelei shook her head.

"Time? Time for what?"

214

Her mother gravely responded.

"The truth."

Before Lorelei could ask for further explanation, Lorelei's voice was drowned out by screams, her mother vanishing into smoke in front of her eyes. At last, Lorelei heard Daemon's voice above the screams she hadn't realized were her own.

"Lorelei! It's okay! Don't let the images scare you! I am still here! Lorelei? *Lorelei!*"

But it didn't feel like Daemon was there at all. Lorelei felt lost in her mind. More visions kept coming, seeming endless as a black sea. Some good. Some grotesque. Angels falling. Demons with ghastly features. Her father's face the last time she saw him, sipping a cup of coffee contentedly as his glasses fell to the brim of his nose. Her friends from college, who clinked their glasses together, having a drink to celebrate at the pub. Her childhood dog, Buddy, ran happily in the backyard behind her home. Daemon standing with a bloodied sword at his side, looking at her menacingly. A throng of people scurrying in a bustling city; but the people looked off. Distorted. Like the ones she saw in her dream.

It was beginning to make her feel sick, like she might be physically affected by the torment of images. She could hear Daemon still calling for her, and she realized she was in a long, dark hallway. Dozens of doors lined either wall, and all the voices from the images she was hearing were coming from behind them, banging on the doors to be let out, but they were muffled now. She was safe. From the first time since the meditation started, Lorelei felt like she could breathe.

The hallway was fairly bare; everything was vintage and there was a tinge of dust upon the paintings on the walls. The paintings looked like depictions of moments throughout history. As she walked along the corridor, she saw cavemen off on a hunt, Native tribes in ceremonial garb, the Battle of the

Bulge, the first plane flight, the building of many worldly monuments, various treaties signed, the beginnings of religions, wars, and many things she couldn't even recognize.

She arrived tentatively at the final door at the very end of the hallway. There was a white glow escaping the edges of the doorway. Slowly making her way up to it, she could tell the door was incredibly old. There were strange markings carved into the wood that Lorelei couldn't make out. They didn't seem like any signs that she had seen before, and the same glow that framed the door also lit up these markings. The doorknob had a large, golden knocker, with the face of a lion. Its mouth open wide, teeth bared, and its eyes glowed with a sense of knowing, like they were looking into Lorelei and could see everything about her that she couldn't even see herself. At last she pushed open the door, and walked into a bright, white open space. Blinking several times at the intensity of light, once her eyes adjusted she looked around. The area was vast, and felt endless. It wasn't a room, but just continuous white space that had no beginning and no end.

There didn't seem to be a floor she could visibly see, but she was able to walk easily forward. After a moment she was afraid she wasn't in the right place as there didn't seem to be anything here at all, but then she saw it; a massive white structure like those of ancient Greece or Rome. It was made of what looked like marble, with large columns that rose from floor to ceiling. Lorelei thought it looked like many of the Roman pantheons she saw in history books and historical etchings in her father's work at the museum. She stood at the bottom of the stairs that led upwards to the entrance of the structure. On either side stood a statue, the base similar to those of the pillars supporting the structure up, but it was topped with this strange geometric symbol. At its core were six circles, one in the center and six others surrounding it like flower petals. Connecting the 5 circles was a near star shape. This pattern repeated again, a larger surrounding the original. It spun and rotated, making it mesmerizing to watch.

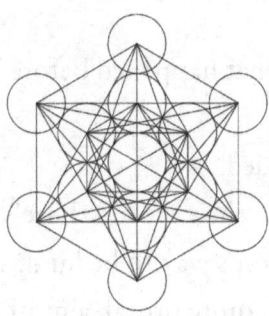

She hadn't realized the dark, silent figure that stood behind her. Lorelei turned to finally see Daemon, his bright green eyes standing out spectacularly in this place full of white. He raised an eyebrow at her and tilted his head toward the spinning shape.

"That's the symbol for Metatron's cube. Because of his ability to access his intuition, he is the keeper of the Akashic records. He monitors all things here, and protects the information. This cube is like a protection as well as the representation of all things. It is the representation of the knowledge and unity of the Universe itself."

Lorelei looked once again at the symbol, and then turned to look around, wondering if Metatron was there watching them right now. Daemon walked forward and kissed Lorelei's forehead softly, looking down to meet her eyes.

"I'm sorry the journey was so difficult for you. I could feel your fear and anxiety, but each person has to make it past their own mind and challenges; they can't be assisted once they have asked for access into the records. Every person's entry is different from another's, as it is concocted out of each individual's thoughts, their past experiences, biggest fears, dreams, nightmares, and current reality."

Lorelei tried to think back to what she even experienced but it felt like static in her mind.

"I don't remember what happened before I got to the hallway to be honest."

Daemon merely nodded.

"Yes, once you enter the records there's a form of amnesia you experience. It was Metatron's way to be kind; some peoples struggles to get into the records can be quite brutal, almost traumatic and terrifying. He wanted everybody who could brave their minds enough to make it here, to be able to be free of what they experienced on their journey. He figured they could fully receive the information they were so desperate to seek without those negative emotions from their arrival here to block their minds as they move forward inside the records."

Lorelei looked into Daemon's eyes again, searching for a sign as to what his experience getting here was like. Was his journey more terrifying and brutal? She only knew tidbits of what he'd told her of his past, but nothing in detail. She could only imagine what he saw as he made his way here. She was also curious if the amnesia only affected humans, or if he got it as well. Instead of asking, she turned to look up the stairway to the entrance of the building.

"I'm assuming what we need is in there?"

Daemon nodded, grabbing her hand, as they both started towards the steps, when a figure dressed all in white armor, fell in front of them, blocking their way. Daemon pulled Lorelei back, away from the figure standing before them. When Daemon acknowledged the figure, his voice was filled with a mixture of admiration, and fear.

"Good evening, Metatron. We have come for information."

Metatron loomed above them, having the higher ground on the steps. He was twice as tall as Daemon, with a floor length gown trimmed in gold, a golden plate of armor on his chest that attached to large shoulder protection Lorelei recognized as a pauldron, a type of armor that covers the shoulders and most of the back and chest. Pauldrons were popular in the 14th and 15th centuries, one of the many articles of history her father inspected and studied during his 20 years at the museum. The ones Metatron donned were far superior to any she'd seen when her father worked. They were made of pure gold, cascading down his shoulders in a way that resembled the shell of an armadillo. It was both striking, and menacing to behold. Metatron eyed them both, turning directly to Lorelei.

"Hello, Child of the Prophecy. You've made it to the Akashic Records."

Chapter 25

Lorelei

Lorelei hesitated. Hearing the title "Child of the Prophecy" felt more disconcerting even though she knew it was technically true. The words spoken aloud felt foreboding, and far too great a title than she deserved. She was the one destined to either stop or start Armageddon; but that didn't mean she could. She thought she might get sick right there on those beautiful marble steps at the feet of an ArchAngel.

"Headline, read all about it: Chosen One pukes all over mighty being's shoes!"

She didn't feel like she could respond; what do you even say to a Celestial being? Although she'd met Raphael, nothing compared to Metatron. He was powerful and cunning, at its highest level. His power seeped from him, making the energy in Lorelei zing in response; it was *strong*. Whoever this was, mortal turned angel, was different from what it felt like to be in Daemon or Raphael's presence. Lorelei was frozen in place, but a comforting squeeze of her hand brought her back. Daemon stood beside her boldly, and he too, looked immensely powerful in this place. When she thought the silence between them all might go on forever, Metatron spoke again.

"I know why you have come, but I am not sure you will find what you seek. You should know, the Council of ArchAngels has made a ruling against your cause. There will be no protection for you from their wrath."

Daemon stepped closer to Metatron, his voice lowering to match the tone of authority of the formidable ArchAngel.

"If you'd allow us, we'd like to discover that for ourselves. You know what we face, Metatron. You know this is our best and only option to find answers. Would you not allow us to enter to do so?"

Lorelei's heart jumped when Metatron's piercing gaze made her uneasy as he pondered Daemon's words.

"What say you, child? Do you wish to find the answers to who you truly are? Do you believe yourself capable enough to handle the answers that come?"

She hadn't thought how what they came looking for would be so defying in the basic knowledge of who she was as a person, but perhaps, she was naive to believe this. She was the girl who was proclaimed to be the only solution to ending the Great War. Lorelei was way farther out on a cosmic limb here to truly believe what she would be facing wouldn't be redefining. They were here to find out how to stop the war, or at the very least, where to go next. What more would she find out?

A trickling fear began to encase her heart: the fear of what she couldn't face, the fear of what was to come when she stepped through the giant marble archway at the top of the stairs. The archway resembled the buildings and columns often found in Greece and Rome, and although they brought a sense of security, having often studied the structures with her father as a child, and having visited similar in her adult years; she feared to step beneath it. For a moment, the longer she stared at the entryway, the more she felt her eyes were tricking her. Cracks began forming along the beams, and could even hear the sound of fracturing stone. As the cracks descended, bluish light peeked out from within at the top, but lower down the columns, dark red light fought for a way out. The sounds intensified, forcing Lorelei to close her eyes in pain. All at once, the sound stopped. When she opened her eyes, there was nothing more than pure, polished marble columns. No cracks. No light.

Was that a sign of what I am to find out once I enter?

Lorelei mustered up what strength she had left, finally looking to Metatron. Willing herself to temporarily put aside the image she just saw—seeing as no one else reacted to it—she knew only her eyes experienced the phenomenon. Looking to Daemon, his green eyes eased her and she blew out a calming breath, facing Metatron like a warrior ready for battle.

"I'm ready. Humanity needs somebody who will face their fears, even when it becomes hard; someone who can see the light through the darkness in the face of the end of it all. I don't know if I will ever be the hero people need; but I know that there's not a chance in this world that I would ever give up on them. Humanity deserves to live on. We are gravely flawed, but we are also resilient. We can find beauty in the depths of despair, and shake hands with it if need be. I watched my father do it, and even strangers have had the power to keep me from falling into a darker place with nothing more than a heartfelt smile. We may have the capacity for great evil, but equally, we have such a capacity for love and understanding. We could be better, yes. But we have much to offer still. Not all humans are so bad that they deserve nothing but death. I believe no matter what, I'd rather know the truth, to be able to give this my everything, give us a chance to continue to try, than to sit by and watch people I care for suffer for a war that isn't even theirs."

Metatron crossed his arms, looking at Lorelei severely, until he sighed.

"Those, my dear, are the words of a savior. You face death, and you face the discoveries lying behind that archway that will make you question the fabric of who you are as a person. You face scrutiny and the fact you won't know until the very end, if things will work out. That is what a Chosen One does. They try. Until there is no other alternative."

Lorelei turned to Daemon smiling, and he nodded reassuringly.

"See, Sunflower? I couldn't have said it better myself."

Lorelei returned her attention to Metatron, and a sense of renewed hope flourished in her chest.

"Are you with us? Do you believe what we are trying to do is worth it?"

Metatron smiled, and Lorelei couldn't help but find it comforting; like the way her father's smile relayed a message that she was where she was meant to be.

"My dear, I was once human. I see no purpose in their destruction, which is what I told the Council earlier. There is a movement, hidden and silent within our ranks, who are against what is deemed to happen. Once we find a proper footing to assist, we will. You are not alone. Your path is a righteous one. But be wary, you may find yourself lost once you enter the Records. You, of all people, have a past riddled with conflict before your very conception. Take heed, but remember who *you* are. You know who and what you are better than anyone could ever write about."

Daemon bowed to Metatron, Lorelei following suit. Metatron extended glorious, white, glistening wings, and flew upwards into the vast white of the Records, looking to become one with light itself.

Lorelei let out a sigh of relief; although Metatron was on their side, it felt odd and unreal to be in the presence of such a renowned, and powerful being. He was the first human to ascend to the status of an ArchAngel; he followed his intuition to one of the grandest positions in the Universe; *and he believed in her.*

We're not alone after all. We have a following. We have others who see that humans should live on. We have hope—hope in me! Perhaps...I could do this.

Daemon held her hand as they began making their way up the grand stairs. When they were about to pass through the arch, Lorelei's heartbeat thudded louder in her ears. She touched the marble column to her left, felt a thrumming of energy zap her fingertips. But there were no cracks.

Stepping inside, everything remained white, but overhead the ceiling was glass, resembling the roof of a greenhouse, and although there didn't seem to be a sun, rays of brighter light shone upon different areas around them like sun peeking through windows in playful arrangements. Lorelei saw that the area was incredibly large, and resembled an old-fashioned library. Rows and rows of bookshelves aligned either side of the room, while a large study-like area sat in the middle. Long tables lined with chairs filled the space. Large pedestals with books on display sat in various positions around the room. It sort of reminded her of the library she had at university. The Akashic Records were just a giant library of knowledge—but this was definitely not what she expected. She asked Daemon if this was always how it looked.

"No, the Records look different to most people. In essence, it's similar to how it is now, but it caters to each person who enters. Whatever would make them most comfortable, represented in a way more familiar to the traveler. Since this is your passageway, and I was the conduit, it looks like what feels more familiar to you. Which seems to be a University library, perhaps like the one you had in school?"

Nodding, Lorelei looked around, totally captivated by the place. It really did look similar to the library at journalism school. She found herself relaxing the longer they stood there.

But what truly caught her attention were small specks of light in ball shapes that bobbed and weaved around the room. Although they were without hands, some could be seen pulling books off shelves and flying them back to a seat at a table. Others were gathered around a large book at one of the pedestals, and Lorelei could hear a humming sound, like whispers, coming from them.

"What are those?" Lorelei asked as Daemon continued to hold her hand. It was comforting, and it eased her racing thoughts and confusion of what was to come.

"They are souls. When people come into the Akasha, they shed their human forms and return to their essence essentially. We look the same to them. Little balls of light."

Lorelei looked at him confused.

"But I still see you as I always do. How does that work?"

"When souls know each other in life and are here together, they see each other as they have known them on Earth. Like those groups of souls over there."

Daemon pointed to the group of three glowing souls surrounding the one book on the pedestal.

"That is a group of souls who probably know each other on Earth as well and are here to find answers to a question that concerns them all. Sometimes people can do that if they are highly in tune with their intuition. Some people can travel here together and find information that better helps them in life: couples or soulmates, families, best friends. Most people are not able to do this, but a select few can. In fact, not many people on Earth are even aware the Akashic Records exist, and therefore it isn't common practice for many to come visit here at all. Most people discover it by chance during meditation, or some are spiritual teachers who train for this. Others are just higher-level souls who are more in touch with their true Soul Self while on Earth and therefore have an easier time remembering this place, and are more capable of crossing through this plane."

Lorelei looked up at him, still incredibly confused. "What do you mean higher level souls?"

Daemon sighed and rubbed his hand on the back of his neck like he usually does when an answer is hard to explain.

"It's a bit complicated but the easiest way is that each person, or soul, is at a different level of existence. The more lives you live, the more experience you gain as a soul. With each life you choose, you choose it to try and learn a particular lesson to better enhance yourself- just like how on Earth people will go to therapy to work on their past trauma or start working out to feel healthier in their body. How can you do things to grow as a person? Well souls do that too, but over lifetimes. And the obstacles and challenges each soul faces are totally based on each individual. So if a soul has a tendency to pick lives with negative, self-destructive habits like alcoholism or drug abuse. They will continue to have similar lives until they figure out the root reason why they keep facing this problem; it could be something like not having enough self-worth or discipline to resist temptation. Anyways, the more challenges you overcome in life to better yourself as a soul being, you move up levels. And don't think it's like one level is better than another. It just means that that soul is closer to reunification with God....or some call it Source. Bottom line is it's the place of all creation, the very beginning and end of existence. It's where we all come from and where we all go when our time as souls has ended. And when that time comes is totally different for every soul. It's a hard thing to explain because it's the basic concept I know of. I was never a high enough angel to know the complete inner workings of Universe things like this; I only know a baseline of what happens. But in the end, it's said nobody truly knows what happens or how it works other than God themself. And there is an extreme hierarchical line to him; I have never met an angel high enough to have a personal connection with him other than ArchAngel Michael—and even his, I have heard, is limited."

Lorelei took a final glance at the bundle of souls gathered there and tried to take in the new information Daemon was revealing. It made sense. To Lorelei, religion was a complicated subject growing up because to her, at the core, she always believed there must be truth; even a small amount to every religion and belief system. The idea that a soul could possibly live multiple lives, was incredibly compelling to her. It was hard not to wonder if she had lived any previous life before, or if the same concept worked with angels or demons. Adding that to the prospect that even in life, souls want to grow and learn to become the best version of themselves, made the afterlife and purpose of life in general, seem less scary and finite. There were chances to continue learning, continue helping others, and to Lorelei—that was a beautiful thought. It raised so many more questions but she knew they neither had the time nor was Daemon perhaps privy to that information anyway.

Daemon guided her through the throngs of bookshelves, seeming to go on for ages. When they finally turned to one, he began scanning over the books until he pulled one out and handed it to her. The book was light as air; it almost felt nonexistent. But it was warm to the touch; it felt familiar. The cover of the book at first looked to be white and transparent in nature, the edges and lining glowing similarly to that from behind the door when she entered the hallway to get here. She traced her fingers around these beautifully intricate letters that went across the cover, the same as those on the doorway here. Daemon came closer and pointed to the letters.

"Recognize any of these symbols? Eh, perhaps not many since we didn't have much time to study. This is your name in Enochian. This book is all about you: your lives before, your future. Just focus for a moment on the words and you will then be able to read it."

Daemon's voice trailed off which suddenly made Lorelei realize that her heart was racing a mile a minute inside of her chest. After a few more seconds of observing the words, they slowly changed to English, and she read her name: *Lorelei Alexander*. She had a sudden sensation also bubbling up within her; rising higher and higher; but she couldn't pinpoint the feeling. The fact that she was holding in her hands the very thing that would tell her who she really was, what she was meant to do, and why this destiny had been chosen for her long ago—was almost more anticipation and anxiety than she could handle. Her hands began to shake, causing the book to nearly fall from her hands. Daemon softly placed his hands beneath hers to help support the book. His thumb rubbed gingerly along the back of her hand as he steadied his voice.

"Lorelei, it's okay. This is what we came here for, remember? No matter what that book says, you will at least have some answers. Good or bad..."

Daemon cleared his throat, seeming to regret his phrasing choice.

"What I mean to say is that no matter the outcome of this, I will be right by your side. I will protect you and love you. *Endlessly.* You are not alone in this."

Taking a deep breath and attempting to steady herself, she opened the book fast, like ripping a band-aid off to get it over with sooner.

Once looking upon the contents of the book, she furrowed her eyebrows in confusion. She was expecting pages and pages; chapters of her soul's journey, lifetimes to assess like so many other souls. But instead, what she found was one single chapter; and it was marked as the date of her birthday. December 31st. She flipped quickly through the pages, her eyes scanning the text wildly as, just like the cover, the text changed from Celestial speak to English. But the chapter was no more than 100 pages long...not long at all if you were to have lived as many lives as it seems most souls do.

Because, the conclusion was clear; she was living her first life **right now.** She never reincarnated before. She had no prior lives as a soul. This was her only life to have reference from.

There would be no help from past experiences.

Lorelei's breathing intensified again. Moving back to the first page, it resembled a biography page or "stats" page: physical features, birthday, where she was born, and more. But it was the "Parents" section that made her heart stop.

It was divided into two sections. The first was her parent's names: William Alexander, her dad. And Amelia Alexander, her mom. But beside each name in parenthesis was "Earth."

Earth? What does that mean?

Lorelei finally looked below it, seeing that it was the general information she already knew about her parents: their background, careers, and even the dates and causes of death. Finally looking to the second section, her breath caught in the back of her throat making her feel like she would choke. She dropped the book entirely and fell to her knees. Daemon rushed to her and grabbed her shoulders, trying to get her to look at him. But she was in shock. And the information from the second column was repeating over and over inside her head, she could hardly hear Daemon saying her name.

Daemon reached down to look at the book, and he too, couldn't believe his eyes.

Reading opposite the information of her parents, the ones who she *knew* as her parents, was this:

Celestial Parents:

ArchAngel Ariel, Mother

Lucifer, Father

Lucifer, father. Lucifer, father. Lucifer, father...

Over and over the words rang in her mind like the tolling of a bell. None of it made any sense to her. None of it could possibly be true. But yet, here they were, in the records of everything ever known.

And now, *she knew*.

She couldn't bring herself to keep looking at the book. She only had strength enough to softly ask Daemon to read it for her, and relay back the information he found. He didn't respond other than a nod. His eyes were swirling with equal confusion as she watched him read the contents. Holding her knees against her, she waited. What only took Daemon a few minutes to read the books in its entirety—felt like a century of time had passed to Lorelei. But at last Daemon closed the book, placed it back on the shelf, and stood silently for a moment before speaking.

"You are the true daughter of the ArchAngel Ariel and Lucifer. A long time ago, when humanity was first created, Ariel and Lucifer fell in love. You know the story of how Lucifer didn't always used to be bad, right? Well, he was God's top angel at the beginning of it all. He was practically God's right hand man. And in the early days, before more angels were created, mostly there were just the ArchAngels, and a few others. Ariel and Lucifer were together for centuries before God decided to create humanity. At first, he was loyal, compassionate, and trusted by all. This is what Ariel fell in love with. But over time, his vanity and pride slowly began to skew his judgment. When God declared to the angels he would create humans, and that angels would serve and protect humanity, Lucifer disagreed. To him, a superior being serving a "lesser" race was not what he had in mind for his eternity. This of course is where we know he tried to take over and was cast out of Heaven. But, when he was banished to Hell, he didn't know that Ariel had fallen pregnant; and she never revealed this information to him, or anyone else for that matter. Ariel is the first angel to ever become pregnant, as it was always assumed, we couldn't. Instead of giving birth to you as an angel...or as a demon; seeing as there was a chance you could be either, she preserved your soul energy and kept it in the spirit realm. She taught you things of life, of the Universe. You studied with her when she would come to visit you, all the while keeping you a secret from everyone by refusing to let you incarnate into either angel, demon, or human life. She believed she was protecting you from the other angels and Lucifer as well, as she knows the angels would never be able to trust your existence, and Lucifer might have tried to take you for himself..."

Lorelei couldn't speak when Daemon paused. He looked at her with worry in his eyes, but continued on.

"Remember how I told you there has always seemed to be sympathizers amongst the angels for humanity to live on? Well, Ariel is one of a small, secretive group of those angels. She believed that humanity should never have to be sacrificed for the sake of Heaven and Hell's war. Like Metatron said. She also had grown fond of humans, believing them to be good and full of bright and beautiful ideas. When recent talks of Armageddon coming sooner than expected arose, she in secret, transferred your soul; which had been living life for countless centuries since almost the beginning of creation, and finally allowed you to materialize in a life. *A human life.* And that is why you only have a single life to recount and access. When the prophecy was foretold right before your birth, none of the ArchAngels took it seriously. There was no possibility for an angel to produce a child."

Lorelei swallowed, but it became a thick lump in her throat as she spoke.

"What did the prophecy say?"

Daemon rubbed hand on the back of his neck, sighing, and repeated the words Lorelei dreaded to hear.

"For all the world, the Other must burn
Innocence beyond compare, no lifetimes earned.
A child becoming of Angel-born
Ever-changing future sworn.
The child shall seeketh the truth unknown
A weighted burden in Kingdom Come.
Realms at war in bloodshed and strife
This child destined Reclaimer or Undoer of all Life.
The Human Element, the Universe proclaims

A beacon of hope if the world remains."

What does it mean, the Human Element?

Lorelei's brain was scrambled. This was the prophecy thrusted upon her; one she never wanted or believed to be possible. She couldn't pinpoint one thought from another. But she managed to ask the one question she needed to know: why she was chosen to save humanity.

"Who spoke the prophecy?? Why me? If I have no past experience, if I was merely a soul for forever and never lived before, how could I possibly be the person to save humanity from the end of it all? Do you understand at all what it means, "The Human Element?""

Daemon's eyes dropped and he shook his head.

"I don't know either of those answers. It doesn't note who spoke the prophecy and there wasn't any information on why you were chosen nor how to stop Armaggeddon. And no...I can only guess it's just stating you're human born to angels. Other than that, no..it doesn't make much sense."

So, there it was. They still had no answers on what to do next. They still had no idea how to stop the war or save humanity. They were still in the same situation, *with no way out.*

And now, everything she ever thought about herself, broke in an instant. Everything she thought of her parents, her life, her upbringing, felt like one of those movies where the character starts confusing reality from fiction.

Which was the fiction and which was the reality?

Not to mention, not only was her true mother an angel, her father was the bearer of all evil in this world. He was the ultimate sinner, the ruler of the damned.

Lorelei tasted something bitter and putrid in her mouth at the thought. Of all things they came here to find out, none of this was at all what she anticipated. And she felt empty inside; like she no longer knew who she truly was. But all at once, she experienced this sense of knowing in a way that made her feel a weight off her shoulders, as if she found the missing puzzle piece of the story of her life, the piece that she felt was always missing or unexplainable before, now was back in place.

But knowledge is a burden. Once you know something, you can never *unknow* it.

CHAPTER 26

SAMUEL

SAMUEL STOOD IMPATIENTLY NEAR the outer edge of the circle of candles. Inside the circle sat Daemon and Lorelei, both of their eyes closed, like they were sleeping. When they were beginning the mediation, Samuel thought his heart was going to stop the moment he heard Lorelei screaming out. Quickly Daemon responded, trying to soothe her, but Samuel couldn't make out much of what was being said. The wind started to pick up and the candles flickered wildly, close to going out. He carefully tip-toed around them, without touching, and kept checking to make sure if he needed to quickly relight one. It had already been an hour since they started the meditation; and Samuel was getting anxious. He knew that his father would be sending out another search team once they discovered the bodies of the demons from his group when they were originally following Lorelei and Daemon. It was only a matter of time until they were found again. His father wouldn't let an assault that led to several of his finest warriors' deaths go unaccounted for. Samuel knew this incident would only enrage his father.

There would be no one safe from his wrath. Not even him.

Samuel would now not only be known as the disappointment of a son, but as a betrayer and sympathizer with the enemy.

The enemy...

The thought forced Samuel to look at Lorelei.

Although Samuel had only ever seen humans from the books in Hell; which didn't usually depict them in what he believed to be accurate light; having come across many now in places since his time here, he knew Lorelei was a lovely one. Her face was a soft pale, with a hint of honey color mixed in, which gave her a look like she'd been out in the sun recently. Her blonde hair was pulled up in a ponytail, and if it weren't for her eyebrows seeming strained; like she was struggling with a headache, she would otherwise look quite peaceful right now.

How could she be the enemy?

Lorelei was the first human he ever came in contact with, and he wasn't sure he would ever forget it. Despite having been a part of the onslaught of demons against them, the first time Lorelei made eye contact with him in the field when the fight was finished, Samuel felt less afraid. She looked at him with such sincerity, such compassion. She didn't fear him at all. And without knowing him, she offered him sanctuary in the motley crew and he hadn't felt safer, or more alive in his entire life. A familiarity grew around her, like she was some old friend or sibling he never had, but always dreamt of.

Samuel often wondered why his father never had any other children, considering he was definitely not the son Lucifer wished for. But, like almost all conversation topics, this was one his father simply waved off as nothing of consequence and responded with some variation of "Well, if I am stuck with you, best be sure you make it worth it for me."

Getting to know Lorelei made Samuel start to imagine what having a loving, older sister might look like. He couldn't imagine anyone kinder and more warmhearted than her. All of this business of what they were trying to accomplish, was something he never dared think would be a possibility; let alone him being a part of it. Yet Lorelei made him feel like he understood humanity and what makes humans so wonderful. Although, Daemon tended to remind him there were lots of horrible humans and that the good ones were harder to come by these days. Samuel wasn't sure if their end goal was even possible; most likely it would end in all their deaths. But he would follow Lorelei and her kindness anywhere. If to live a brief life meant he got to meet people like her, and experience the things on Earth he has already; prove to his father that not all humanity was worth damnation; it would be sacrifice enough.

Suddenly Samuel got a strange feeling. Just like angels could smell demons, angels themselves also had a very particular smell. There wasn't anything Samuel could say smelled similarly, but if he could describe it, the best thing would be if Light had a smell—or maybe pine? Even though he'd never been face to face with one before now, the instinct of detecting the smell of an angel was engraved deep into his DNA; he was born and bred to recognize it, even without confronting one before.

He knew the smell wasn't coming from Daemon; although an angel; since his falling, he no longer had the same smell. Samuel's stomach turned inside-out and he swallowed hard, putting on a strong face as he turned slowly to see an angel in an all white suit, standing a few steps away. The suit gleamed against the clouded darkness that surrounded them. Behind the angel, the looming stones of Stonehenge seemed to cast menacing shadows against the moonlight; only making the angel look larger than he appeared.

He looked like a model who walked straight off a high-end fashion show. But unlike Daemon who usually kept his wings hidden, this angel stood boldly with them displayed, the wing tips draping softly to the ground. The angel's face was defined and angular, with swooping ash blonde hair that formed waves upon his forehead, whipping around as the wind blew threw it. The man stood with one arm across his chest, propping the other up, making Samuel feel as though he'd kept him waiting far too long. His facial expression wasn't harsh, but it was deliberately stern, although there was no wrinkle that marked his face. Samuel began to shake, not from the cold, but from the intimidating angel he faced. Samuel waited anxiously, he was definitely not going to be the one to speak first. As the angel eyed Samuel up and down, the angel gave a pleasant, but intimidating smile.

This was a game of cat and mouse.

"Interesting...a demon, hm? This surely adds intrigue to this developing situation, now doesn't it?"

Samuel dared not speak. And although all he wanted to do was run and wake Lorelei and Daemon, there was no evidence of threat yet, and he didn't want to ruin their chances of obtaining all the information they could. That meant he would have to stall somehow. The angel continued, never expecting a response from Samuel anyways.

"You're a young thing though. Curious how you would join this duo on such a perilous journey. Do you not wish for a long life, my friend? As I assure you, you will not find one if you remain with your companions."

The angel's voice shifted, not quite a threat, but the undertone of the words indicated the friendly nature would soon pass.

"I see that you are no ordinary demon though...red hair, freckles, severely fearful gaze...you wouldn't happen to be Lucifer's boy, would you? You smell exactly like him."

Samuel shifted uncomfortably in his spot before clearing his throat.

"I am. And who are you?"

The angel nodded, the confirmation of his identity not seeming to change anything for him.

"You can call me, Raph. I'm an old friend of Daemon's. I recently came to him and Lorelei to give a gentle warning about the state of the "mission" they endeavored to pursue. I see now that there was no swaying their minds as to reconsider. My fellow ArchAngels will be highly disappointed to hear that."

ArchAngel Raphael. Oh we are in far deeper trouble than I thought...

Samuel thought his knees would buckle from the weight of the information before him. Daemon and Lorelei both told him that Raphael came a few days ago, but to face the being, was something Samuel didn't expect so soon.

"If you're a..a friend, does that mean you're here to help?" He stuttered, unsure if he would be able to get the words out at all.

The angel smirked and raised his eyebrow.

"In a way. I have a proposal. And I think, considering your desperate situation, he will find it a suitable one."

Samuel attempted to think of a response but before he could, he watched Raph step to the side and reveal something Samuel had not noticed before. About 50 metres behind Raph, stood a large group of angels. Their eyes pierced through the fog that began to form around them. Samuel couldn't help but hold his breath, the sight catching him completely off guard. He felt stupid that he hadn't checked to see if there were more of them around.

So much for being a lookout..

Returning his attention to Raph, who had taken notice of Lorelei and Daemon sitting within the circle of candles, Samuel began to speak when a loud wailing sound ruptured the night sky. Raph looked up to see where the sound was coming from but a crash into the stone behind him knocked Samuel to the ground hard, skidding across the grass and throwing him far. Looking up to see where Raph was, Samuel saw him narrowly avoid the collision by swooping quickly into the air, his wings flapping hard, spinning to look around him. His group of angels in the distance were all on guard, some in the air trying to get a better view as well. The stone that was hit was now in a million pieces.

A monument that prevailed through so much of Earth's history, was now partially destroyed in a fraction of a second.

When dust finally began to clear, Samuel saw what hit the stone. Within the wreckage of stones and debris stood a menacingly large demon whom Samuel instantly recognized: Volgoth, *the Slayer*. Although not high ranking within his father's army's higher council, he grew to be an essential asset when pure, brute strength was needed. Although typically Samuel's father preferred smaller, stealthier, more quietly lethal tools in his armada; occasionally he needed ones with more bulk, to more quickly wreak havoc and devastation without worrying about losing his strongest minds in the process. Volgoth was the size of a SUV, bulbous in weight, but within that fat, were muscles that were bigger than Samuel's entire body.

Unlike most demons whose "demon" features didn't amount to more than a fang here, wings, varying skin colors, and maybe some small texture difference, which generally didn't come off as ferocious or scary, allowing more likelihood to be concealed or pass as an average human—Volgoth was one of the demons where there was no hiding what he truly was; a monster.

His skin sagged under the sheer weight of him, dripping off him like candle wax melts. A purplish-grey color, his skin was rough as dragon scales that rippled down his arms, legs and back like a suit of armor, but far thicker. Scars were running all across his body showing the amount he'd faced and conquered in battles. His face is a gelatinous thing with a chin that drooped, his eyes small and pure black, a smile full of jagged, razored teeth inside a mouth that seemed to have been slit further than your typical smile, taking up more space than it should've. Finishing the terrifying look, two bat-winged horns protruded from the sides of his head.

Volgoth was made to send the masses screaming. He was made to beat down everything in his path; and who so happened to be in his path now? Samuel quickly realized how close to Volgoth he was and began to panic. Volgoth was launched like a cannonball into the stones and didn't seem to have a scratch on him, the armor-like skin having done its job. Quickly,

Samuel turned to his right to see where Volgoth came from, and his heart dropped.

At the edge of the field where they entered, stood a large section of demons that had also gone unnoticed—or did they just arrive? In any case, Samuel, Lorelei, and Daemon were now fully surrounded by angels and demons, all there looking for them.

When Samuel was looking back at Raphael, trying to gauge where his mind might be; Volgoth roared a deep, guttural noise that shook the air around him and charged directly for Lorelei and Daemon. His massive feet left imprints with each lumbering lunge forward, and it wouldn't be long until he was barreling his tank of a body into them. Samuel's breathing stopped as he began to attempt to match Volgoth's pace and meet him head on.

His mind raced uncontrollably, screaming at him to run in the opposite direction, the direction *not* towards sure death. But his body moved on, determined to save his friends. As he ran, he shouted Daemon's name in hopes to stir him out of his trance. In hopes his eyes would spring open and he'd rush head first to the colossal demon and take him out in seconds. Daemon's eyes did not open, he did not spring forward to rescue them all. He sat motionless and unhearing to Samuel's shouts. Samuel was on his own.

Taking a final glance at Lorelei's face, Samuel tried to quickly etch her features into his memory, hoping to remember until his final moments the kind, sweet girl who made him believe everything he always hoped for in humanity, in Earth, in being surrounded by people who actually cared for him. She was the reason he found his strength, found his courage and confidence in himself—to see he was more than just the Devil's son.

Seeing Lorelei's face rejuvenated him more. The thought of her death being the end of all humanity as they know it, and the end of his first true friend; was not something he would let go without a fight. Because this time, he would fight. Fight with all he had left within him, even if it meant his own demise in the end.

Samuel threw his hands out, panting as he ran towards Volgoth. That same tingling sensation he felt before when training with Daemon surged in his body, and pressure built at his fingertips. Afraid it didn't have time to build the force up enough, he grunted and felt a more shocking sensation spread and warm his body. It couldn't be enough to do much damage, but maybe enough to keep Volgoth's attention on him until he figured out how to get his friends awake. Without second-guessing, Samuel breathed deeply and focused his mind on the palm of his hand; heat rose in his fingertips, and as before at the field earlier, swirling clouds darkened the sky further, and a lightning bolt surged down for a brief moment; he looked up to see the bolt zooming towards him, and holding his out out, he caught it.

Grunting as he held it, the feeling was a combination of pin-pricking his skin and blazing heat; although at first the feeling was alarming, he was now beginning to tolerate it more. Samuel frantically searched for Volgoth, and throwing his hand outward, propelled the bolt in his direction. The lightning missed, searing the grass instead, cracking the ground under his feet and Volgoth's until the very ground was singed and burning. Volgoth covered his face and came to a sliding halt as flames started to overtake the field.

Uh oh. Not exactly my intention there.

Samuel surveyed that Volgoth would have to try to find another, less direct route to his friends, so he possibly had a moment to make another go at waking them before Volgoth; although large in size, he was not large in brain, and Samuel should have an upper hand on him for the time being. With his fingers feeling burned from the electric charge; he was proud and terrified of what he'd done. He had a very special power, as Daemon told him before, but it was nowhere near under his control yet. Thus, the fire and lack of aim—definitely not part of the plan. But it did the job for now, and all he could do was focus on how to get them to wake up; because he didn't think he would be able to keep any others away much longer.

Although, he hoped he was able to wipe Raphael's smirk off his face a bit and show that he too, could be intimidating.

Samuel reached the edge of the circle when he began to scream as loud as he could, hardly able to draw breath. He didn't know what else to do. Looking behind him, scanning the area for more threats, he could see that the groups of angels and demons were now fighting each other. Taloned demons of various sizes lashed like animals at the elegant, deadly angels who moved like dancers rather than warriors. But even with all the angel's fighting beauty, this fight was nothing beautiful to witness; gnashing teeth, blood splattered across the ground, necks twisted and wings laying limp in piles taller than himself.

Samuel shuddered, holding back vomit, watching as one angel tore the head off of a demon, its greenish-black blood leaking wildly as its head, mouth agape and eyes with a look of horror, rolled along the dirt and landed to stare in Samuel's direction. Like a deadly warning saying, ***"You're next."***

*That could be **me.***

For the first time since he joined Lorelei and Daemon, he felt the intense realization that he was the enemy to more than one lethal and powerful group. He was attached to a cause that although he believed in, the end for him was in all likelihood just that—***the end.***

Daemon has his weaknesses and couldn't protect both Lorelei and Samuel from every threat. And the sad truth was that Daemon would always choose Lorelei over saving Samuel if the choice had to be made. Samuel squeezed his eyes shut and took another breath in an attempt to calm himself. These kinds of thoughts were no friends to him right now. His friends; and himself; were in serious trouble. He had to wake them. And quick.

Samuel took one final glance at where he left the behemoth Volgoth, and saw he had made his way through the flames and wasn't far behind.

Frantic, he kept screaming Lorelei's name. To his relief, her eyes shot open and the candlelight flickered wildly in the wind. She looked around, and as Daemon also came back to consciousness, they both leaped up, panting. Lorelei caught Samuel's eyes and he thought she might collapse right there. Her eyes looked hollow and she seemed to have aged somehow, like she lived through something that took her youth away. And the way she looked into his eyes, she looked like she had a million things to say. He wondered if she'd call out to him, but all their attention was taken to the chaos ensuing behind them.

The fight between the demons and angels was turning uglier by the minute. Piles of bodies lay upon the ground as a torrential rain swept across the field so suddenly that they were all fully drenched in seconds.

Great! I caused a freak storm!

While Samuel's focus was on the downpouring rain clouds he tried to will to relinquish, Volgoth grabbed him from behind and hoisted him into the air. How Samuel hadn't noticed, was just another indication that he wasn't his Father's son who could detect a presence from miles away. He didn't have skill enough, or strength enough to hone the skills he *did* have, to stand a chance in a war like this.

Because that's what this is. A war. One he was starting to think they wouldn't win.

Volgoth's hand wrapped tightly around his torso and squeezed him until it felt like his lungs might incinerate him from the inside out, as he feebly attempted to suck in enough air to alleviate the burn. It felt like a million suns exploding in his chest—but he couldn't get the saving breath he needed.

Tears rolled down his cheeks, trying with the little strength he had to push against the beast's fingers, but to no avail. Spots danced around his eyes, and the last thing he saw before a choke barely escaped his throat, reaching an arm out towards Lorelei, was the horror on her face. She screamed so loudly he thought it rang and reverberated in the the air.

It looked like she had so much to say; her eyes held it all and he'd never know what she knew. He'd never be able to thank her for her kindness. The kindness she showed him proved to him that humans were nothing like his father drummed into him and the rest of the demons. He was wrong. Humans were strong, compassionate, and sacrificed everything for the ones they loved. Samuel wanted to be like them. *Like Lorelei.* If this was the end, the sacrifice would be worth it. Because for the first time in his existence, he experienced love. Love for Lorelei and for all humans who didn't deserve this fate that awaited them.

These were his final thoughts before his body went limp and the darkness descended over him, claiming him like a cocky friend who always got what it wanted.

CHAPTER 27

LORELEI

LORELEI'S SCREAMING CONTINUED, AND she turned to Daemon, who was already flying into action. He flew towards the biggest demon Lorelei had ever seen, and with all his strength, catapulted himself, kicking the creature in the face. It let out a deafening roar, stumbling backwards and falling to the ground. Lorelei watched as the beast's hands dropped Samuel's unconscious body. Daemon left the demon riling on the ground, howling and holding his face at the tremendous damage Daemon inflicted on his cheek. Daemon dropped down and caught Samuel inches before he hit the ground, and flew back towards Lorelei with him in his arms. The tremendous creature got to its feet and gave one last menacing look before heading in the opposite direction, like he'd been called away.

She watched as he held Samuel so closely, so gently. She hadn't expected that he would come to care so much for him. *For her **brother**.*

How had fate brought them together in this way and then viciously rip it out from her grasp so quickly? Before she even had time to enjoy it—before she had more time with him, to actually be his sister. Tears welled in her eyes and she couldn't believe what all had happened.

Daemon laid Samuel at her feet and she crouched down, lifted his head, and wrapped her arms tightly around him, sobbing.

"Please, Samuel, please wake up!"

Lorelei's heart was breaking; it hadn't felt this much loss since the death of her beloved father. She already felt alone before, and now without even the kindness of time to allow her to heal before losing another she loved dearly, she was utterly alone again.

She looked pleadingly at Daemon.

"Please, do something."

Daemon shook his head, kneeling down to Samuel and inspecting him all over.

"I can't. His wounds are too great; demon anatomy is different, and they don't respond to our magic the same way humans do. It wouldn't be so simple."

Daemon's eyes wanted to tell her he was sorry—that he knew how much it would hurt her if she lost Samuel, too. But before he could speak again, he looked around the chaos of entangled limbs, wings, and snarling teeth towards the far end of the field where what looked like a lighthouse was standing—blissfully untouched—a beacon of white salvation.

Raphael.

Just as she had seen him back in Inverness, Raphael appeared to act as though he was seemingly unaware of the madness going on around him. Completely out of place in the bloody, mud-flying mess of the fight between the angels and demons. Just when Lorelei thought that he was possibly standing in his own dimension where he couldn't be touched, a rapidly approaching demon with several sets of eyes, that of a spider's, came barreling towards him at a speed Lorelei was sure couldn't be possible if she had not seen Daemon do something similar on more than one occasion.

When Lorelei felt she needed to scream to warn Raphael, with a single hand outstretched from him, he caught the demon's face, its bone-thin arms with razor hooks for fingers slashing at him with a need that was only fueled by the smile Raphael gave him, as he was able to keep the creature from landing a single blow of his unruly talons. With a single squeeze, the demon's head turned to jelly and dripped between his fingers; the rest of its body dropped to the ground in one quick smack.

Looking more annoyed by the dreadful mess of his hands than anything else, he waved the blood and brain-matter-covered hand and in a flash it was clean, as if the terror Lorelei just witnessed hadn't happened at all. Within moments, Raphael shot for the sky and landed nearby. A foot tapping at the ground impatiently.

Finally looking away to Daemon, who had stood without her noticing, she continued clutching Samuel's limp body closer to her. An aching in her chest was starting to take over, and she watched Daemon continue to look at Raphael.

Please, please don't.

She wondered if she was in such a state of exhaustion and despair that she had actually spoken the words out loud. But when Daemon didn't look her way, she realized that her heart must have known what he was about to say next.

"Lorelei, I need to speak with Raphael."

"But why? Look at us! We need to get out of here, Daemon!"

Kneeling down once again, he came closer to her and held her hand, rubbing the back of it with his thumb like he typically did when he knew she was in distress. It sent that familiar tingle through her veins that did, in fact, make her shoulders ease. He kissed her forehead and she sighed in relief. It seemed crazy and absolutely maddening that in the midst of this literal throat-ripping battle, she could still be made feel so safe by him. But Lorelei would always trust him. Always.

"I promise, I won't be long."

Nodding, she relished the feeling of her hand in his until the connection was broken and she was left with an empty feeling she couldn't quite place.

This didn't feel right. Something was even worse than the fact they were surrounded by such a horrible sight. The feeling was deeper, in the pit of her stomach. She thought she might be sick. It festered inside her and if it wasn't for the tangible feel of Samuel tucked in her arms, she wasn't sure she'd be able to hold back a panic attack. The feelings that rose as she watched Daemon walk away, like she'd never see him again, or he'd lose his way back to her; was all her mind could imagine.

Thinking she could easily be sick, she took a deep breath and cuddled Samuel closer to her body. Watching each painstakingly lonely step Daemon took further away from her, the more she yearned to run and pull him back to her. She knew she had no further strength to even stand, and decided to table a conversation with him later about leaving her in the midst of a god-forsaken battle.

The sun was already beginning to rise again, the air getting cooler, the storm clouds were dissipating. She held Samuel and looked down at his face, bruised and cut up. She had no idea what he endured while they were in the Records, but it looked like far more than he should've had to. She cuddled him tighter, and spoke barely above a whisper.

"Don't worry, Sam. It's going to be okay. You'll be okay, we all will be...okay.."

She hesitated, unsure she believed her own words. She stared longingly at the unimaginably real pair of angels standing in the distance and shivered.

But she knew it wasn't from the cold.

CHAPTER 28

DAEMON

DAEMON KNEW IF HE looked back at Lorelei, he might lose his nerve to do what he was about to do.

It's the only way I can save her.

How could he be so stupid? There was no way in Heaven or Hell that Raphael would consider his request. But with each passing day, Daemon was becoming more and more unsure they would be successful. And after what they learned in the Akashic Records, there were things going on under the premise of this war that were far deeper and far more complicated than he could have ever imagined.

There was no way he would be able to save humanity. This was, as he was beginning to see, inevitable.

Although it always has been, huh?

He shook his head as he thought to himself: what he did all those years ago—he did out of this enormous instinct. This need to save a girl because he couldn't possibly believe one little girl could really be what stood between the Great War. And yet, now knowing who she really was—she was human, yes, but she also wasn't. She was so much more.

She was a combination of humanity that was pure, innocent, new. One that hadn't yet been so tainted by hardship over many lives. To top it off, she had the psychic abilities that allowed her to perceive things, whether she understood them or not, before it happened, and was able to speak the language of the angels, which no human was said to have been able to do before. And then, she was apparently the true firstborn of evil incarnate.

Lorelei? Evil?

There's no way. She was so caring, Daemon was sure there couldn't be a mean bone in her body.

Daemon knew that DNA traits from such a strong and formidable person like Lucifer were very unlikely *not* to manifest in some capacity.

No. That won't be the case for Lorelei. Look at Samuel. He has always been against his father, and Lorelei can be too. She won't change now.

Daemon would protect her, save her from having to do anything that might change her to become colder. He must. She was too precious. He knew he'd risk it all to save her from this unwinnable war.

For he knew now—this was unwinnable.

He wasn't strong enough to help Lorelei with her task. It was bigger than anything he anticipated and he'd already failed her once when she was harmed the first time the demons ambushed them on the way to Stonehenge. Never before did he question his abilities to fight. But after what happened, after the information they discovered, this was beyond him.

The gut wrenching shame and guilt threatened to overwhelm him as he approached Raphael; shrieks and clashing of claws against swords, screams of pain and sudden lapses of silence echoed around them as they stood before each other. This reminded him all too much of the many times in the past they had been somewhere similar, experiencing what they were now, total bloodshed, and brothers in arms putting up the good fight.

Because that's what they always were: brothers. Raphael, although far outranking him, never made him feel lesser. They became close friends in the early days, not long after Earth's creation. He remembered exploring the cities and monuments the humans created—many with some of their help. Wandering about the newly constructed markets filled with color and delicious foods of all assortments that made your mouth water. Exploring the cathedrals where humans tried so desperately to grasp the concept of the Divine. He remembered they would sit and criticize the stained glass artwork within them, joking that if angels looked like that then they would never be able to get girls—and always wondered why they made Lucifer look so damn attractive in his caricatures if they wished for nobody to follow him. Memories of laying underneath the moonlight and stars together as they recounted their recent missions near and far, attempting to help gauge civilization and steer the unholier side clear; their jobs being what made the most sense to them; at least back then.

Raphael suggested one night they make a pact—swearing to always come if the other should need help. And after each mission, they would meet up and vent about the crisis they averted or enjoy a new human treat that'd been invented.

They would take care of the other, for some of the things they were tasked to do, were not so easy on the mind. You needed a friend, so that the darkest parts you played a role in, wouldn't fully devour you.

For as long as Daemon could remember, it had been that way; until the night Daemon made the choice to save Lorelei's life, and Raphael seemed to change. He recalled it'd been several missions since Daemon and him got together. Daemon would meet at their designated spot and wait, but for three occasions in a row, Raphael never showed.

Until the night he went against orders. Raphael appeared before him in the street, just after he saved Lorelei and the ambulance drove away to take her to the hospital. Daemon was flooded with relief at seeing his friend. Having started to worry about him after the last few no-shows, he hugged him tightly, a sob escaping his lips. Daemon knew that he had gone against an order for the first time in his existence. He was scared. But Raphael would understand—he would know what to do.

No comfort came from his friend though. And before Daemon could figure out what was happening, he was transported by his friend in an instant, a trick most upper angels could do, and brought to where he would be unforgiven. Made a Fallen.

By Raphael himself.

Something changed his friend that he was unaware of in those absences before that. Daemon knew he could never fully hate him, but it was hard to be in his presence now. Especially when he was going to ask a favor from the one who hurt him the most. Raphael crossed his arms in the usual way that suggested he was irritated. He was never the most patient of angels.

"Dae, I thought you were smarter than this. You can't believe that after the last time you decided to change things, this outcome would turn out any differently; did you?"

"I don't have time for your cocky fucking opinion today, Raph."

Raph held his hands up in defense.

"Fine, yes I suppose you're right. Seeing as things are escalating around here. What is it you summoned me here for?"

Days earlier, Daemon sent a message to Raphael after Lorelei fell asleep in his arms. It's less a message and more a mental ping that was created after their pact: a special kind of magic that allowed them to notify the other in case of emergency. After Daemon was exiled on Earth, he thought the bond was broken. But seeing as he may need a backup plan—he tried, and to his surprise, was able to still use it to get a message to Raph: to meet him there at Stonehenge when they finished the ritual.

Daemon knew if Lorelei found out, she'd be pissed as all get out, but, there was no way around it. Holding Lorelei in his arms, her nightmare waking her, shaking violently against him—he couldn't keep doing this to her. He decided then, he would do anything, *anything* to protect her, even if that meant betraying her trust.

But nothing had gone as planned. They were in the Records longer than he anticipated, and from the look on Raph's face, the demons showing up at the same moment was a happenstance he too didn't see coming. Daemon wanted to make a snarky remark about the amount of angel power Raph decided to tag along with him, mentioning he must've been asking for trouble like this, but in all retrospect, it was more likely for protection. The demons weren't really after the angels; they were after Lorelei.

"I reached out because you're right. We won't win this."

The admission felt like a punch to the gut, harder than he thought it would be, but there was no denying it. He needed to save Lorelei, and he wasn't capable of doing so on their current course. Daemon expected Raph would laugh or make another snide comment, instead, sadness filled his eyes and a sense of wanting to comfort Daemon came instead.

"Dae..my friend, thank you for coming to this realization on your own. I know what happened before, you do not trust me much. But I care about you. I always have. And to lose your friendship was the hardest experience of my existence, but to lose you entirely in the Universe—to know you were gone because you couldn't win this fight and lost your life—that would be worse."

Daemon's heart clenched at the softness from his long-lost friend. He wanted to embrace him, forget the past and allow movement to a better relationship. But it wasn't one of those simple moments; there was still work to be done. Work to ensure Lorelei's safety. That's what mattered now.

"You need to protect Lorelei, Raph. She didn't choose this destiny. She didn't choose to be the "chosen one." If we get out of the way, and let the war happen as planned; there's no need to kill her. You know that. Just take her somewhere safe, and I promise, we won't try to stop it anymore."

Raphael let out an exasperated laugh.

"And how would I go about doing that? It's not like I can take her to Heaven and just keep her there. And what—I'm expecting you want me to protect you *and* our archenemy's child there as well? Like a little resort? Ha! Okay you have always been the funnier one, Dae, but this takes the cake. They are not angels. They can't be in Heaven without turning into a puddle."

Daemon shook his head.

"They can, I think...Lorelei isn't what you think. She has abilities that are not fully formed but I promise you, she can be in Heaven safely. And the boy, he can too. We already know there isn't damage done to demons in Heaven unless they have ill intent, which I promise you, he doesn't. It's sort of complicated to explain it all in this same second Raph, but she can speak our language. She should be fine there."

Raphael's mouth opened slightly and he blinked at Daemon several times.

"What did you say?"

"It's true, Raph. She can speak in the Celestial tongue. I taught her. I swear on my life. If she can do this, that means that she also has the capability to withstand the dimension change and effects in Heaven."

Daemon waited for Raphael to say something else, but he didn't. He just stared at his old friend, and Daemon's heart beat faster in the waiting, so much so, he could feel the hastened thumping loudly in his ears. When Raphael finally spoke, Daemon was certain he had been holding his breath.

"Okay. I will take them somewhere safe when this settles down. As it happens, you're in luck. Michael wants to see you. And when I received your message to meet, I figured it was the perfect timing to let you know."

Daemon took a deep breath, but it wasn't one of relief. ArchAngel Michael was the ruthless leader of the ArchAngels and ruled with an iron-like fist. He wasn't cruel, but Daemon always felt he was often harsh in his rulings and plans. Michael had also been the one to make the order of his fall-which Daemon found out afterwards.

"What the fuck does *he* want?"

"Michael wants to give you an offer. He didn't tell me specifics, but from what I gather, you two are on the same page. I believe he's offering you a deal for no further interference in exchange for asylum for the three of you."

Daemon's heart lifted and he finally breathed a sigh of relief. If Michael was offering asylum, then their chances of deflecting Armageddon were none. Because Michael had never offered asylum to a Fallen, a human or a demon—***ever***. This was their chance to survive. And stay together.

Raphael scoffed, "What of the rest of humanity? Haven't you become their sort of puppy dog? Always at their rescue?"

Guilt continued to try and sway over his mind about the little piece of this puzzle he kept ignoring—which was the rest of humanity's destruction—but he couldn't think so much about that if the one human who meant more to him than life was also gone forever.

No, they would regroup. Maybe he could speak to Michael about the possibility of no war, or at least, sparing humanity. Whatever happened, he would keep Lorelei safe. And keep her with him. Was it selfish? Of course it was. But he would move Heaven and Earth for her. Even when it might break her heart.

"I can't let you kill Lorelei. Humanity may burn, as they always have. But she—***must*** live."

He wouldn't lose her. Not now, not ever. He could pay for his sins later.

Daemon looked back to meet Raphael's gaze, knowing he'd said exactly what he wanted to hear: Daemon's defeat. "Alright, let's finish up this lot of demons and we can figure out our plan to meet him."

Raph shook his head and smiled. "Foolish, twat. You always think everybody waits on you. Michael doesn't wait for anyone. We leave now."

Dameon rolled his eyes, "Fine, I'll get Lorelei and the kid, who's hurt by the way, so I'll need to get some of the healers to see what they can do."

Raph surprised him when Daemon turned around, finding Raphael standing before him again in an instant, hand upon his shoulder. He used his Transport Spell, one only ArchAngels could use, teleporting in thin air and reappearing again anywhere.

"This initial meeting was said to only be for you. We will come back for them. There's no time to waste."

"You're fucking mad if you think I'm going to leave her here in the middle of a goddamned onslaught!"

Daemon was about to push Raphael out of his way and tell him off, that he wouldn't go anywhere without Lorelei with him; when the sadness returned to Raph's eyes; and as Daemon blinked—the field around them, the last glimpse of the blue crystals of Lorelei's eyes shining brightly in the middle of darkness, the sun leaving its duties for the day, met his before she, and the very world around him, vanished.

CHAPTER 29

LORELEI

LORELEI SAT STUNNED. ONE second Daemon was standing beside Raphael, the next she could tell they were arguing—not that the two angels ever seemed to *not* be having an argument—and then Daemon poofed. Literally. He was there, and in the same half of a blink, he was gone. Her heartbeat hastened as she swiveled her head in circles to see if by any chance he had just gone to another part of the field. But the longer she looked, the more her heart throbbed against her ribcage, rattling her already icy-cold body that now felt like it would never be warm again.

"He left me."

Lorelei knew she was talking to herself; Samuel was still passed out in her lap. She thought if she weren't holding his limp body, she would collapse altogether, the fabric of her being wrenched apart by the abrupt absence of Daemon which threatened to seep into her heart and wrench it clean from her chest.

She couldn't stop herself as the tears streamed down her cheeks, her eyes stung as the wind whipped her hair about her face, the tears feeling more like acid on her skin than saltwater, sliding in cascading zigzags downwards towards her cracking lips. The burn of the tears hurt as they dropped to her mouth, making her snap out of her momentary lapse of reality.

No matter how hard she tried to fight the blasted emotions, she was done for. The Daemon she knew; *thought she knew;* would never abandon her like this. He would never leave her alone, stranded in the middle of nowhere, in the midst of a fight between beings she still barely wrapped her mind around. He wouldn't leave her to figure out how to heal Samuel alone. He wouldn't leave her inches from Death's fingertips freezing to the point she didn't know where the teeth chattering ended and the racking body aches from exhaustion began.

Just shut up and think. What can you do, Lorelei? What the fuck can you do? Nothing. Absolutely nothing. I am a human sitting in the middle of a blood bath clutching the near-lifeless body of a helpless teenage demon. I have no idea how to help him and Daemon...Daemon is..

Lorelei choked. Even the sound of his name in her mind made it feel like she was about to hyperventilate. Panic was setting deep into her bones and she shook fiercely, because Daemon was gone. And she had no idea why he left or if he would come back. Her heart ached at the thought of having possibly been deceived by him. Had she been so lonely and lost since the passing of her father, that she fell into the traps of a man who didn't actually care for her? Could everything between them be a lie?

"No. You can't think that. We need to get a grip. He will be back...he will.."

Lorelei took several deep breaths. But she knew she wasn't convincing anyone. Her mind could be playing tricks on her right now. She was in a horrid state: bruised, battered up, and tired to the point that if she closed her eyes long enough, she would most likely pass out. Lorelei knew it would be a death wish in this situation, as the very real reminder of snarling and slashing of flesh not far off, made her take another deep breath and steady herself. Laying Samuel's head on the ground, she tentatively stood to see if there was somewhere she could drag him further away from the fight until she figured out a plan. If Daemon was here right now though, she knew he would say she needed to find a safer spot, and quick. She couldn't lose faith in him now. She had to keep fighting. For Samuel's sake.

Or until Daemon comes back...

Then Lorelei had an even better idea. *An angel*. If she could just get the attention of one of them out here fighting, she could have a chance of getting out of here. Turning to look for the glowing white wings that would be her redemption, her mouth dropped as she surveyed the field.

Nothing.

No white.

No wings.

No angels anywhere.

They were all *gone*.

She was alone, facing a group of demons, the last ones left of the fight. Particularly, one rather nasty one resembling a dog-if a dog were more dripping skin and bones than anything else. And teeth. Lots of teeth.

The dog demon growled, licking its non-existent lips as its glowing yellow eyes that looked like bottomless pits, locked onto Lorelei. Breath caught in her throat and she nearly yelled for help when she recalled—there wasn't any. The realization that no one, not even Daemon was there to save her, made her think she might puke. In all the craziness of the last week, at least Daemon had been there. To hold her, protect her, be that guiding support, and a reminder that she wasn't alone in the madness. Now it was only her, and this rabid, terrifying creature, and a swarm of dozens of others, and no one to come swoop in at the last second to save her.

At that last thought, the dog demon came clawing its way across the field towards her and leapt at her before she even had a chance to react. Barking, growling, and chomping jaws snapped at her head while she skidded across the ground, tumbling several times as the beast had dug its unruly claws deep into both her arms. Screaming, Lorelei struggled to see what was truly happening in the dust flying, pain-searing chaos until she was pinned underneath, with no way to move.

Lorelei tried to twist and turn beneath the creature to get lose, but with every movement, its nails dug deeper into her flesh; she glanced down to see her jacket was in total ruin, and she saw her own skin flayed open and shredded along her biceps, but she tried to not focus on that and instead looked up at the beast, its mouth dripping with greenish-yellow saliva. A long tendril of it dripped onto her collarbone and she yelled out in pain—*acid*. She could feel her skin bubbling in response to the saliva that caused her to scream out in agony.

She waited for the creature to finish it: tear her head off, play with it like a puppy with a tennis ball, pull out her stuffing and watch as she goes limp like a ragdoll along the field. But it didn't move. It just held her there in place like this was what it was ordered to do, not to kill her, but capture her.

A loud whistle rang in her ears, but she couldn't move her head to see what it was. The dog demon immediately let her go and the snarling face that once hung over hers, was replaced by refined, human-like features. Swooping black, slicked-back hair, beard cleanly shaven and defined, and menacing red eyes now stood over her in an all black suit tailored perfectly. The hair on the back of her neck stood up in recognition, not from having actually met this man before, but a deeper recognition. Unexplainable but all too real. Lucifer stood above her. And although black spots threatened to overtake her vision, she knew it without a glimmer of doubt.

She watched, saying nothing, daring not to move as he made a clicking noise and looked at the state of her—which she was sure was nothing pretty to see. But it wasn't embarrassment that took over her, but a disgust as his eyes lingered too long in certain areas. Although, he made no indication it was lustful—purely observant, like studying a specimen in a lab, which somehow made her feel even more vulnerable. Without any emotion whatsoever; those red eyes revealing nothing, he finally spoke.

"Hello, daughter. It's time we talked."

CHAPTER 30

DAEMON

"ARE YOU OUT OF YOU FUCKING MIND, RAPH?!"

Daemon huffed in frustration, his hands curled into tight fists; the whites of his knuckles stood out prominently. He was pacing in circles around Raphael who stood impatiently, seeming unaware of the ridiculousness of forcing Daemon to leave in the middle of a bloody fight. Lorelei was there completely alone, and no matter how much Daemon berated Raph for his stupidity, Raphael merely responded with his usual superior complex and bullshit.

"It was strictly Michael's orders, Daemon. I'm sorry. I am sure they will be fine for a few minutes."

A few minutes? A few minutes could mean life or death in the middle of a pack of blood-thirsty fucking demons, arsehole.

But Daemon didn't say this, there was no point. He had no idea how to get back to Stonehenge with Raph's power blocking his own. "Procedure" is what he claimed it to be. If Daemon wanted any chance to get back to Lorelei quickly, he needed to calm down and play his cards right. Besides, no matter how obnoxious Raph could be, in all honesty he was only the messenger.

It was Michael who would get the brunt of his words, or his fist, without a doubt.

Even with anger growing, there was anxiety as well. The last time Daemon saw Michael, was the day he was condemned as a Fallen—by his own best friend nonetheless. He was following orders, just as Daemon used to. No matter the consequences, that was an angel's duty. And Michael, being the leader of the ArchAngels, was apparently closest in lineage to God themself. So it was said. It had always been this way, with Michael in charge and dictating orders from Up High. Daemon was always Michael's least favorite angel to deal with, at least that's how it seemed. Michael was always chiding him for asking too many questions, which Daemon would rebuttal with more. Like, "Why do we never see God?" or "Are you sure there isn't anybody else higher up in the chain of command than you?" or "Why are you such a wanker, Michael? Don't you ever relax?"

All of which were met with a heavy-handed, mostly indecipherable riddle of responses that typically made Daemon up and leave before Michael even finished his convoluted retort. It was a contentious relationship, but it wasn't until Daemon defied a direct order from Michael to eliminate young Lorelei all those years ago, when Daemon really saw how the ArchAngel could be.

Daemon was not looking forward to coming face to face with him again. Raphael assured him it was protocol and formality that forced Daemon away at such an untimely moment. Daemon mumbled under his breath as if it was really decorum Michael was so concerned about or if it was having another upper hand. Michael always had to have the upper hand. This is why Daemon never trusted him. Still, Daemon could never decipher if it was distrust of Michael or the anger and shame over what occurred all those years ago. To distract himself from the worry of whether Lorelei would be okay, he figured he'd talk to his long-lost 'bestie' in the meantime. Gauge what he knew about the upcoming war. Whether it was happening soon, if there was a date, what he knew. Any information might help.

Help what? You're the reason you're here with this fucker instead of protecting Lorelei, remember? You didn't have faith you could come out of this alive. You wanted a bargaining chip—now you got one.

Daemon's guilt tugged at his mind violently, but he endeavored to wrestle it back for the time being. He desperately needed to keep his wits about him here.

"How are things, Raph? Any news about your 'precious' war?" He hoped his mocking tone hit its mark.

Raphael was examining his perfectly manicured nails, picking out dirt from beneath them—or perhaps it was blood—and shrugged his shoulders absent-mindedly.

"Soon. Word is there will be confirmation of the exact date in the coming days. That's all the information you are allowed to know anyways. But why do you care? You are here to get an out for you and your little world-saving posse. Isn't that right?"

Daemon wanted to go over there, take that absurdly clean hand and crush it with his own. Change that look on his face from carelessness to excruciating pain, but decided it wouldn't be in his best interest at the moment; even if it might be satisfying.

"Hmm...so you don't know. That's just a long-winded "I have no fucking clue but I am going to pretend like I am above you" response. Typical of you Raph. Typical of all of you."

Raphael at last turned to Daemon who stomped around the arena he had been brought to, it was the same blasted arena he lost his status: the colosseum in Rome.

Figures.

Angels always liked to put on a show or meet in places of significance; it seemed Michael was driving the dagger in his wound deeper than even Daemon thought he was capable.

Never thought Michael to be one to make a joke.

If this was Michael's way to get to Daemon or have a show of power: it was unfortunately working. Daemon hadn't felt this small or uncomfortable in a long time; but immediately the memories of that dreaded day came in like a firebomb—blowing his once neatly placed wall to keep those bad memories at bay, wide open. Before the day he was brought before the Council of ArchAngels for his Fallen ceremony, the colosseum was filled with a lot of happy memories. Although often times absolutely barbaric of the humans to partake in some of the events put on there; especially the hunting of the animals or public executions. A lot were exciting to watch and at times; for shits and giggles; be a part of.

There was one particular time Daemon and Raphael competed in one of the gladiator competitions and Raph swears he "let" Daemon beat him; but Daemon was always a better fighter than Raph. They laughed about it for weeks afterwards. A stinging sensation now replaced the guilt. The memories of this place were overwhelming, good and bad.

Nice play, Michael...

"You can be angry all you want from the past, Dae. But at the end of the day, you made your choice. Now you have to face the punishment. Your snide comments do nothing for you."

Chuckling, Daemon finally leaned against one of the many pillars and kicked one foot over the other, arms crossed.

"Ah, like I haven't already endured enough punishment all these years? Right'o, mate. Excuse my remark. I am sure you are a well-valued member of this cog in the grand scheme of the Universe after all these years. Has Michael given you so many duties now you have forgotten how it is on Earth or how good humans can be? He's kept you in Heaven like a fucking prisoner after what you did to me, Raph. Don't deny it. You haven't stepped back on Earth until the day you showed up in Inverness. At least back when we toured

Earth together, you knew how to live a little. And you knew when something was wrong, even if it meant defying orders to protect someone who meant anything to you."

Daemon paused after this last remark, and seeing by the concerned look on Raphael's face at the suggestion of him being the one to have broken rules, Daemon knew he got under his skin. ArchAngels were not supposed to be together intimately after what happened with Lucifer before. Lucifer fell in love with somebody, and when he became all too obsessive, was the first sign of when he began to defy his orders.

But Raphael broke the rules once getting together with ArchAngel Ariel. Granted, the two were perfect for each other, and Raphael was always way better at shimmying his way with words to get on Michael's good side to make an exception, claiming the bond between ArchAngels was "too sacred" to deny them—it worked out in his favor. Daemon wasn't sure Michael ever truly forgave Raph for upstaging him in front of the other angels though. Yet, nothing bad came from the incident. Either way, Daemon wanted to make sure Raphael remembered: he wasn't the perfect angel he thought he was.

Now, after what happened in the Akasha, Daemon knew it was Ariel who was the mystery angel with Lucifer before his fall. Raphael may not be the most emotional of angels, but he loved Ariel deeply, and to know she kept such a secret would kill him. Not to mention to know who in fact she had Lorelei with. The situation was becoming messier by the minute, and Raphael would be hurt.

I wonder if I should tell him what we saw?

Daemon felt uneasy not letting Raphael know, but with everything going on, Raphael wasn't much of a friend currently. And perhaps it could be a card played later when Daemon needed it more. For now, it was the only card he held; even if it meant keeping this secret about what Ariel did and who Lorelei truly is. Daemon was pissed and there would be no way he'd be the first to tell him—not when Daemon had too much pent up anger towards Raphael—not when the sting of his actions left scars he never apologized for. With clenched fists, Daemon brought an arm down, slamming it against the pillar he leaned on. His words were barreling out before he could calm himself.

"And if I remember correctly, you used to talk to me all the time about how you didn't see the purpose of this war. Now he's got you chained here like a goddamned dog. *His* dog, Raph. That's all you are now. I may have changed, and even with all my years of relentless shame, I am beginning to think I am starting to change for the better. What about you? You've only changed for the worse. A dainty, pompous, head-in-the-clouds, arsehole."

Raphael's face turned into a scowl, and as he was about to return an insult, a hush fell over the air around them. Michael arrived.

Walking slowly across the arena floor, Daemon could barely make him out as it was shadowed heavily along that end of the space across from him. Raphael composed himself and stood in attention, continuing a conversation they were definitely **not** having.

"Like I said, Daemon. Michael has come with a proposal for you, the human girl, and if you so insist, Lucifer's boy. He will explain it all himself, but the deal would be an asylum for you all as long as Fate and the Great War are no longer interrupted by your plotting. Is that understood?"

Daemon hardly heard what bullshit Raph was spitting out to save face. The only thing in his view was Michael, his long, cascading bronze-toned hair in curls that lay neatly upon his shoulders. He wore battle attire that consisted of a mixture of a gold and silver-breasted metallic suit of armor, similar to how they saw Metatron. Michael's never-ending stern facial expressions sat prominently as always, and Daemon wondered if there was a place to avoid his gaze as it pierced through him directly. But it wasn't the ostentatiousness of Michael's entrance that had Daemon's mouth agape: **it was the group of demons trailing behind him.**

They walked in silently, standing on either side of Michael, who had yet to speak. Daemon immediately recognized one of them: Zanul. The demon who pursued him before and who Daemon thought had successfully performed a Finishing Spell on. No demon survived the Finishing Spell once in place—how he was possibly alive when the last Daemon saw was a pile of ashes, was nothing short of a miracle.

Miracle. Of course...Michael performed a miracle to bring Zanul back. But why? Fuck, this is bad.

Zanul smiled a jagged-toothed grin at Daemon and waved. The rest of the assortment of demons stood patiently behind the two. It was Raphael who, surprisingly, spoke first.

"Sir...What is going on here? You specifically told me to bring Daemon alone. Who are these demons and why are they here?"

Raphael's voice cracked as he spoke.

"Indeed, Brother Raphael, I did request you bring Brother Daemon here alone. But that does not mean I am unable to bring others along for this meeting. You will see in a moment the necessity of their presence."

Michael paused and looked directly at Daemon, and for the first time Daemon could recall, he smiled at him in a fake sort of "let's be friends" way.

Daemon felt a deep unnerving within the core of him. This was wrong. Terribly wrong. Raphael tensed; he felt it too.

"Daemon, my old friend. You look well. Surprising since what I have heard, you have endured quite the perilous journey so far. It need not be this way though, you know it is futile."

Daemon pulled his smug persona back into place steadfast before responding to the wolf in sheep's clothing standing in the front of a pack of *literal wolves.*

"Mate! Gosh it's been a long time. Raph told me you wanted to chit-chat about helping us out of this "perilous" journey. Are demons here to somehow comfort me, or is it for us all to have a bit of sport here in the arena again like we used to all those millennia ago, and they are meant to be our hunting prey? No? Then I second what Raph asked. What the fuck are they doing here, *Brother* Michael?"

Michael's former smile was gone immediately. He snapped his fingers and two of the snarling demons, one of whom resembled a mash-up between a bat and a grim, old man, while the other looked to be similar to Zanul, who decided the 80s grunge fashion and thick black eyeliner were the best choice, ran to Raphael before he could react; totally blindsided, they yanked his arms behind his back and bound him with what looked like a black and red glowing handcuff.

The moment it touched Raphael, he screamed in agony and fell to his knees. His usual flawlessly coiffed golden hair flung out of place from the sheer force of being brought to his knees—Daemon was sure he heard a cracking of bones as he hit the ground.

A shudder ran through his entire body as his friend's head was yanked up to look at them all. Raph's eyes screamed, ***"Run."***

Immediately Daemon let his wings unfurl, repositioned his feet, and stood taller to face Michael. This was no meeting of salvation; this was a trick. And the pain that Daemon moments ago would've envied to make appear across Raphael's face, now terrified him deeply. Raph was only a puppet in this show, too.

Daemon needed to think of something quick. He'd left Lorelei and a most likely dying Samuel back in Stonehenge, and now he was thousands of miles away, trapped here by a demon-consorting 2nd hand of God without his powers, which were temporarily blocked once entering the arena, and a conniving pack of demons who apparently were in on all of it.

Michael walked towards Daemon, stopping a few paces away. For what felt like minutes, neither said a word. Daemon was desperately trying to sort out the strengths and weaknesses of those in the room in his head; could he take them? If he could get this demon down, the others would be easier. It was Michael who posed the biggest threat. It was highly unlikely Daemon could take him, no matter how much of a warrior he claimed himself to be. This was Michael, leader of the ArchAngels. He is the true Warrior Angel, having led battalions against Hell and has been around even longer than Daemon. Plus, naturally, there is a significant power difference between an ArchAngel and a regular angel. Although Daemon had always been applauded for his abilities, there's things even Raphael could do that Daemon would never be able to.

Well, if it meant going down fighting, Daemon would fight any angel, demon, or God for Lorelei. Michael was no different. He would die too if it meant he could return to Lorelei safely. She was it for him; *damn the war*. If Daemon couldn't be with Lorelei or if he lost her, he would bring down the forces of the Universe in any way he needed to—he'd rebel against all for her, and it would be worth it.

Michael eyed him as if he could read Daemon's mind.

"Your girl...Lorelei...She will die Daemon. Just as before, it is the way of things. She is the reason and the answer: with her demise, we can begin our great pursuit of justice and harmony. We can start anew on Earth, we can make it better than it ever was or could be. Humanity has grown too fickle, too callous, and too willing to deny any concept of God. In the end, this is too dangerous. Humans only ever got this far with our help to begin with. There is nothing more meaningful or miraculous they could achieve now. Their hunger for the destruction of one another and their insatiable desire for material objects over companionship, are and never have been the ways of God. You know this. They are too primitive. We gave them a chance—but it is time for a new, better species to prosper. A mixture of angel and humans shall be the new normal, and they will thrive. It has been seen. It is the only way."

Daemon raised his eyebrow at Michael and ran a nonchalant hand through his hair, knowing this would annoy him.

"You're sounding incredibly familiar to someone we know....Come to think of it, didn't Lucifer suggest the same thing you are saying now?"

Talking time was over. Daemon sprung into action, flipping backwards over Michael to catch him and the remainder of the demons off guard, pulsing his power to slow time fractionally. A move he knew the other angels, including Michael, didn't have. It was his specialty, and by damned he'd make them all pay for this betrayal.

Daemon landed on his feet, and went to grab Michael from behind when Daemon gasped in pain, a dagger hit between his ribs, an arm wrapped tightly around his throat with another. ***They broke through his magic.*** They caught him before he could even make a move on Michael. These demons were unnaturally fast. Demons could be bloody quick, but this...this wasn't right. With Daemon's ability to slow time, there hadn't been a demon in his existence faster than him.

Unless they are getting help with angel powers.

Michael didn't move, like he knew what Daemon would do and needn't bother himself getting out of the way. The demon at his back walked Daemon in front of Michael, forcing him to the ground, and when Daemon attempted to wrench free of his grip, the dagger at his ribs was dug further in. Coughing viciously, likely his lung had been punctured from the blade, blood splattered across Michael's feet, who continued to stand over him.

"Insolent fool. It is nothing the same as that prideful oaf. This is God's will. And it shall be done."

Daemon wiped a hand over his blood-soaked mouth and spit out a glob of it.

"If the goal is to kill Lorelei because she has the capability to stop this war, why haven't you done it already? What's the point in prolonging the inevitable then?"

Michael sighed and paced around Daemon like a panther, taking its time to go in for the final kill.

"These things happen when they are meant to happen. She has remained alive because God has deemed it worthy at this point. Soon, when the order is given, and our plan is set into action to begin preparations for war, she will be eliminated. All is part of the Divine plan. And we do not question. But....I believe it to be soon. With you out of the way, she will no longer pose a threat. Take comfort, Brother. She may be left alone in the end. If she doesn't have you, she won't have much to stop us with."

Daemon lifted his head; it was pounding, and his vision was coming in and out, the taste of metal coating his mouth, and it was hard to rationalize Michael's words.

"Me? You can't be saying that I am the key to what would make her be able to stop you?"

Since first encountering Lorelei, there was always something that didn't feel quite right. Something deep, like a string lassoed around his heart and latching onto hers, always pulling him towards her. There was no way to know when he saved her as a child all those years ago, that years down the road, he would have the call to go to her again.

A call ancient and abstract, it was this same pulling sensation that once meant only to protect, and then transformed into more: love and a reconnection of self. He felt tied to her in a way he couldn't explain. He never imagined having feelings for her. But when he first locked eyes with her, a key that had been lost long ago to his own torment-riddled self-image, clicked into place, and beneath it all was a knowing that he could and *should* be loved; and the person to love him, the person meant for him more than any other in this Universe, was her. Equally, he was her missing half.

Could this be why? Is there more to this bond than I thought?

As Daemon attempted to wrap his mind around the notion that Lorelei and him may have been inextricably intertwined longer than he thought, Michael snapped his fingers and ordered Zanul and the demon holding him, to tug his arms out to the sides, attaching the same black handcuffs around his wrists and attached them to chains in the floor. Daemon cried out again when the demon finally relinquished the blade from his side.

Struggling against the cuffs, Daemon jerked at them as hard as he could, but the harder he pulled, the deeper the flesh of his wrists melted away as the cuffs burned him. Another larger cuff was placed around his neck and attached to the pillar he'd been leaning against earlier. As long as he didn't move, the cuff wouldn't burn him. The smell of burnt skin filled his nostrils as he finally looked up at Michael with more hatred than he thought possible. Raphael was passed out and lying on the floor—apparently they didn't need him conscious anymore.

Michael locked eyes with him, kneeling in front of him. He wiped a blood covered strand of Daemon's hair out of his face, shining with his own blood and a mixture of sweat after the struggle against the chains. It would have been an almost fatherly gesture, if Michael was anything nurturing. No. He was nothing of the sort. This was to diminish Daemon further, remind him of his place. Or, the fact he had no place.

"Poor, Brother. If you only knew how needed your existence was to get us closer to the end. Why didn't you just stay to yourself?"

Michael sighed like a disappointed father and shrugged.

"No matter. You won't be a problem any longer. It's time to prepare you for your final flight."

Before Daemon could make a snide remark, Michael pulled out his sword from its halter and brought the butt of it down on Daemon's head, the last image of Lorelei's longing, blue eyes—the color of the purest crystal sky, the color of hope, happiness, and love, blazed before his eyes as he faded into the darkness.

CHAPTER 31

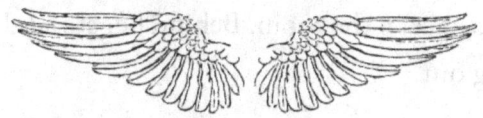

LORELEI

LORELEI'S EYES SHOT OPEN. Her head was spinning so much she needed to take several moments to ready herself for the unwelcome greeting gravity would have for her as she sat up on a plush black, leather couch. Eyes adjusting, there was no doubt this couch wasn't used very much. If ever. It was stiff as she adjusted herself to get a better look at where she was. Lorelei took in her surroundings and saw she was in a swanky office room that had a giant, black marble desk sitting prominently in the center. On either side of the desk behind it were intricate bookshelves holding a manner of odd objects and several jewels bigger than her head.

Other than that, the room was mostly filled with stunning artwork depicting all kinds of religious figures; most notable of all was a painting hung directly center above the desk: an exceptionally handsome man with short black hair, a muscular physique, holding in his arms a beautiful, petite, blonde woman. She was fairy-like in comparison to the man who looked to exude power and masculinity, while the woman radiated pure light and joy. The embrace was intimate and the passion that illuminated both figures was the focal point in the painting. It might have been the most immaculate painting Lorelei had ever seen.

Sitting up, Lorelei winced and grabbed her arm as the memory of the vicious dog demon's damage surfaced. Instinctively she felt each side, but now there were no longer gashes shredded in her skin, but the burning, cloying sensation remained. She had either healed quickly—or took a long time—her sense of how long she'd been unconscious was making her more confused. Finally sitting up on the couch, a soft cough alerted her to another presence in the room. Behind her stood the man who she saw before passing out.

Lucifer.

Panic set in when she looked all around and Samuel wasn't there. She was about to ask for him when Lucifer read her mind.

"He is safe, for now. But his wounds will no longer heal. I have made it so. You and I have something to discuss before he will be healed any further. Weigh your words wisely, daughter. They could mean his life or death."

Lucifer spun around, and the same face as in the painting above the desk faced her. Her body sang with warning; the desire to run as fast as she could away from this man filled her, but there was nowhere to run, no way to know where *"where"* was, and apparently no way to help Samuel unless she stayed to talk.

Daemon will never be able to find me now. What if he has already gone back to Stonehenge looking for me? And Samuel...what if he dies?? I can't let that happen. No. There's no way I can let him die for trying to help me in a war he didn't want anymore than I. He's just a kid. He doesn't deserve what I've put him through.

Lorelei forced herself to stand. She wouldn't face him cowering on a sofa below him. She would face him head-on. Terror may be causing her heart to beat against her chest like it also was trying to escape—but she wouldn't let him know that. Not now, ***not ever.***

"What do you want? And by the way, stop calling me daughter. You are **no** father of mine. How did you come to find out anyways?"

Lucifer gave a smirk and went to a nearby table with alcoholic beverages on it. Taking a flask of brown liquor, he poured himself a generous helping in a glass, taking a sip before responding.

"The second my top commander came slinking back here after the failed attempt at stopping you before reaching Stonehenge, he described your features to me. The moment they fell off his lips, I knew there was only one being who resembled you. I took more interest in your survival, which is why I staved off another attack for quite some time. This became a matter too personal not to investigate myself. So I watched you. What? You think Daemon's pathetic excuse for a shield would deter me? I watched as you all miserably trained in the field; oh yes, I saw your sexy little lapse of judgement as well—I see the apple falls not far from the tree, daughter. I was there, but you were unable to see me nor was Daemon able to detect my presence. I am far more powerful than anyone recognizes. The instant I saw you, I knew it was true and my suspicions confirmed. You look exactly like her."

Lorelei's skin crawled at the confession that Lucifer was there in that field. Watching. Waiting. He saw everything, and they were all fools to believe it would be any different.

Her? He must be speaking of Ariel.

Lucifer paused, and for the first time since they started talking, Lorelei sensed a sadness from him. It passed quickly, regaining his composure and continued on; but she noticed that as he spoke of her mother, it hurt him. She would have to remember this for later.

"Your current predicament: being the 'savior' and all...complicates our relationship a bit from the start. Also, there comes the issue that you are human—when your mother was an angel and me, well, you know what I am. So how could this happen, hm? A human born girl who just so happens to be the very catalyst that could bring this war to an end before it even gets off the ground. But seeing as I already have one disappointment in offspring, it would be a real kick in the ass that the world has deemed it I also have a daughter destined to be a mortal enemy. Seems like we are at a crossroads. Though, she was clever to keep you from me; who knows the wickedness you might have become if you were to have been raised by me. But to place you with that pathetic, weak mortal body...and that idiotic family...She couldn't even put you with a family with power if she were to curse you with such an insignificant existence? What a shame."

The mention of her "mother" was intriguing, had she not just learned of her true parentage mere hours before, she would think this conversation to be insanity. How could she be a human whose parents were not in fact the human ones she knew, but an ArchAngel and the first Fallen, Lord of all Sin, instead? If she were hearing the story herself before meeting Daemon, before all of this...she would have shook her head in disbelief and asked her friend to make sure she stopped ordering any more drinks.

But everything *did* happen, and she truly was the daughter of the Devil.

It didn't all make sense, she didn't have all the details, but it was written in the book of her soul. Her soul incarnated in this life for a reason, and if she hoped her true mother was anything good; a true angel of light; then she had to believe she would find out the reason soon. The crux was, would she understand it? Or would it be like right now, where it felt like her entire self-image had been flipped on its head and thrown in a blender. Lorelei felt she might burst. She knew she needed to keep her cool, but Lucifer going after her true parents, jabbed her deep inside, the grief of their losses too much to hold back.

"Don't you dare speak of my parents again, you son of a bitch. You don't know what you're talking about."

Lucifer raised his eyebrow in amusement, "Why daughter, what a big bark you have! Perhaps you are not all cupcakes and rainbows after all. Who would think that the savior would talk like such a disgusting whore. Yes, two can play in this game."

He narrowed his eyes on her. She was fuming from the anger, she swore she was seeing red.

Easy, Sunflower..easy. Don't let him get you worked up. It's how he wins. Stay calm.

Daemon's soothing voice came through like a lighthouse in a storm. She wasn't sure if it was real or just her imagination. Perhaps it was even the pain seeping to her head now and making her delirious. But Lorelei held on to it for dear life, figment of her imagination or not.

Let me find my way back to you...please...

She calmed herself and focused on her breath long enough to silence the rage for now.

"Alright. Enough games. What am I doing here and where am I?"

"You, daughter, are here in my home, temporarily. Although for now, you are incapable of traveling anywhere else in this realm than this room, unless you'd like to meet an early end. I brought you here to make a deal."

Lorelei hesitated a response. There was no way in Hell or out of it, she would ever make a deal with this psycho.

"Well, sorry to say I am in no mood for making deals today. Now give me back Samuel and take us back to Stonehenge."

Lucifer took another long sip of his beverage and shook his head.

"The deal is necessary if you wish for Samuel to survive his injuries. I will heal him, but there is a price."

Could Lorelei take the chance to trust him? No, she couldn't possibly. Daemon and the angels could figure out a way to heal Samuel, they had to, because making a deal with the *actual* Devil has got to be the dumbest move ever.

"I'll pass. Just take us back to Stonehenge, Daemon will help us."

Lorelei watched while Lucifer stalked around the room so slowly, it made her skin crawl. At last, he went over to the portrait of him and Ariel, keeping his back to her.

"Daemon is no longer there. You see, a long story short, there has been an attempted coup in my ranks. One of my own has betrayed me and joined ranks with the angels. He believes with their help he will be able to overthrow my reign and take over Hell himself. This, of course, is folly. Your Daemon has been taken prisoner by the very angels you seek aid from. You have all been deceived. Lucky for you, I can take you where he is held captive. But this, too, comes at a price."

Lorelei glared at him, each beat of her heart thudding louder and louder in her ears.

Daemon is captured?? By the angels?? But why? This doesn't make any sense. All this could be a trick, a cruel trick. Can I trust that for certain though? I could be damning both Samuel and Daemon if I don't do what he asks.

Lose Daemon. The thought hit like a knife in her throat, she nearly collapsed into tears. She couldn't lose him after finally finding him—how could she go on now when their love story had only been filled with pain and torment? If he was in trouble, there was no way she would not try to save him. She had to.

"What do you want for healing Samuel and taking me to Daemon?"

Lucifer faced her and finished the remainder of his drink before answering.

"You are free to go and try to save your precious paramour, but my son stays behind. He will be healed, I swear it. But he will not journey with you any further."

Lorelei knew she had no bargain to sway the grounds for this agreement. Samuel had to live, and she had to find Daemon. There was no other way around it.

She would sell her soul to the Devil if it meant saving them both.

"Okay, what else do you want?"

"Next, I will personally take you to Daemon, and if you and him survive, you may come back for Samuel. That is my offer. I will heal Samuel and take you to Daemon, but after a certain time, I will come for you and bring you back to Hell. And when I come calling, you ***must*** answer."

That rage tempted to overtake her again, as well as a waterfall of tears. Lorelei was totally powerless against him. There was nothing she could do to stop what was happening or save them any other way. Having to come back to Hell, and what? Leave Daemon behind? This was madness, and she was staring directly at the maddest of them all.

"But why? What would you want me in Hell for?"

Lucifer straightened his shoulders and picked invisible lint off of his silk black suit jacket.

"For now, that's not your concern. Only problem is, with each passing second, both of your friends are inching closer to possible death."

He had her there. Saving their lives was all she could do. Even if it meant giving herself over to him when he came for her later. At least their lives might be saved.

"Fine. You have a deal."

Lucifer smiled like he'd won a prize, a prize he *knew* he'd always win.

"Excellent. Let's prepare for our departure."

"Wait! What about Samuel? I want to see him before we go."

"That wasn't part of the deal. Pity child, you need to learn how negotiation works. Now, tell me, you're not prone to getting sick, are you?"

He reached out his hand, and with a wary heart, Lorelei took it, and vanished into thin air.

CHAPTER 32

DAEMON

Hours passed and Daemon awoke with the worst headache imaginable. When he tried to shift to crack his neck, relieve some of this tension, a jingling sound and subsequent instant burn alerted him to a realization: he was chained to the floor of a Roman colosseum by the leader of the ArchAngels and a revolting group of demons.

And Lorelei is probably dead by now.

He knew the odds were likely, as she'd been left in the middle of a field of blood-thirsty demons. But he couldn't give up hope now, or else all would already be lost. Daemon decided distraction and coming up with a game plan was a better course of action than letting doubt weigh in. He wouldn't give up hope. Not until the very last moment. Or until his last breath.

He looked around for Raphael, who had also been taken hostage. He sat several feet away propped up against one of the large pillars. He was finally awake, and when they made eye contact, Raph nodded to the left over his shoulder, signaling the two demons who'd taken him down were sitting behind him arguing over some nonsense about the best torturing techniques. Daemon nodded in return and turned the little bit he was able to with the iron strapped around his neck, being as subtle in his movements as he could so's not to attract their attention. Nobody noticed he'd woken yet, this could be used to his advantage. When he caught sight of Michael, his back was to him and he was whispering in hushed tones to Zanul.

Whatever Michael promised him, he was getting impatient. This too, could be an advantage. If only he pissed Zanul off enough, or perhaps got him to question Michael's loyalty—that could be what got him out of here. But a cruel reminder of the singed metal attached to each of his limbs was making every breath difficult. Even if he could get out of here, there was no telling if his powers would be restored or if they would be enough against Michael.

Zanul huffed and waved his hands in the air in frustration. Daemon quickly closed his eyes and pretended to still be unconscious as Zanul walked over towards him and cursed.

"What is the point of keeping him alive? He's right here! I want my revenge, Michael. And I want to move on to phase two of the plan. Now!"

Michael spoke plainly, but irritation also tinged his words.

"It is not time to enact the remainder of the plan, Zanul. Daemon's presence is vital here. You will see."

Zanul threw his hands in the air again and stomped off to where the other demons were squabbling. When Zanul was out of earshot, Michael spoke softly.

"It is okay, Daemon, I know you are awake. There is no need for this falsehood."

Lifting his head, Daemon purposely rolled his eyes at Michael.

"Always the show off, eh Michael?"

Michael walked towards Daemon, stopping a few paces away, one hand placed neatly on the hilt of his sword. Daemon's skull remembered it well.

"The time has come, Daemon."

"The time for what? For you to kill me?"

Michael shook his head, "You shall see."

Daemon roared with anger as he tried to reach out to Michael; a valiant but pointless attempt. The smug look on his face and the cryptic answers were beyond infuriating. Michael didn't even flinch at the attempted assault, only stepped to the side and stood in silence. Like he was waiting for something.

When Michael stepped aside, in a rush of black smoke and wind, Lorelei appeared before him. Disoriented, he looked around confused, but she was there in the flesh. Daemon's heart burst at the sight of her, tears formed in his eyes and the moment they locked eyes, his world felt centered again. She was alive! If Daemon could jump, or move at all, he would jump for joy. Every fiber of his very soul burned to be relinquished from these chains and to rush to hold her in his arms, to never let her go again. The thought she was hurt or even worse, *dead*, after leaving her in that field was close enough to demolish him altogether. He didn't know if he would ever see her again.

But just as so much hope and love filled him, so did fear.

What the fuck is she doing here?? And how did she get here?

The look in her eyes seemed to say it was a long story. One he hoped he had time to hear one day; but for now; they were in serious trouble.

"Daemon! Daemon what have they done to you?" She yelled and ran towards him, but when she was passing Michael, he reached out and held her back with one arm; she struggled against him and tried to fight him off.

Michael's demanding tone rang through the coliseum.

"Zna iaial."

As he spoke, Lorelei's body froze. Literally froze in motion, only her eyes were left blinking, muffled screams coming from her sealed mouth. Michael lowered her to the ground on her side and stepped away.

"LET HER GO, MICHAEL! She doesn't deserve this!! She has no power to do anything to you!"

Michael began to step forward but Zanul and the other demons rushed over in delight at the appearance of the human.

"Oooo yes, look at this delicious thing! Who knew I would get a new command *and* dessert." He finished saying this was a wink at Daemon.

"She is not for you, Zanul."

Zanul groaned. "Awww come on? Does this mean we're going to get the blasted thing over with?? It's time for my rule, Michael. So we can get on with this war already. Lucifer must pay for his neglect of me. He must. This human girl should have no power, just as he said."

Michael looked down at Lorelei with an emotionless face.

"Oh, she has more power than you think, my friend. More power indeed."

Daemon finally spoke up, yelling at the idiocy happening before him.

"Ha! You think you are going to take over Hell from Lucifer? Right, and when that happens I will know the saying about Hell freezing over, Zanul. How did you even know she would come, huh? Is there something else you know?"

Michael shook his head.

"No, but I knew she would do anything to find you. And I needed her here in the end."

Daemon screamed at him, "But why? If she is here and you already have me, what more could she do to you? What good is she for now? You already got what you wanted; you'll get your war."

Michael walked towards Daemon and circled him. Daemon tried to look behind him but couldn't due to the chains. Turning his attention back to Lorelei, her eyes called to him and spoke volumes of the fear she was feeling, knowing he was feeling the same. He failed her. But still, she only looked at him like there nothing in the world she loved more. It made his heart yearn for her. Tears were slowly rolling down her cheeks, dripping on the colosseum floor in delicate splotches.

Daemon could feel Michael standing behind him when he spoke next.

"We know who she is now. There is no denying the lineage, and it will be dealt with accordingly; this deception will not go unpunished. Sister Ariel will see that she cannot deceive the Almighty."

For the first time, Raphael spoke, "Ariel? What does Ariel have to do with this??"

Raphael's voice was panicked, he never questioned Ariel being involved or getting hurt. But Daemon knew the truth, and when Raphael found out more, he would never be the same. When Daemon thought Michael might reveal more, one of the demons hit Raphael across the face, and he was once again unconscious. Michael nodded in support and returned his attention to Daemon.

"She serves the best purpose. The most Divine purpose. She is here to witness what happens when you defy God's will, and what can happen to those you love when you make those choices. The punishment for a sinner. You, Lorelei Alexander, shall relish in the fact that no human, nor Fallen, shall endeavor to stop what is meant to be. For as it is said in the Bible, "...*the wicked will be punished with everlasting destruction...And evildoers will be* **cut off**, *but those who wait for the Lord shall inherit the land*."

Michael pulled his sword from his hilt, and the blade came slashing through the air. Muffled screaming, Lorelei's eyes met Daemon's while she watched in horror: **as Daemon's wings fell to the ground.**

Chapter 33

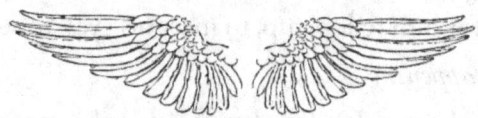

Lorelei

THE SCREAM THAT ECHOED the colosseum was tortuous to hear. It was like everything else on the planet stopped to hear the cry of agony unlike any other. Her nightmare she had back at the inn days before, was coming true right before her eyes. It was nearly the same location, the columns she saw Daemon strung up to. How were there angels and demons conspiring together? If nothing else, this confirmed Daemon's suspicions of her intuitive and psychic abilities. Perhaps all her dreams were prophetic. But this being a horror she could do nothing but watch, was no coincidence. It couldn't be. It was too specific, too cruel.

But a dream was just that. You could wake up and leave it behind because it wasn't real. This was all too real, and neither of them would ever be the same after. In history, once something world-shattering occurs, it leaves a mark, an imprint of its story carved in stone for all to see; this was one of those moments—branding itself into a special place in Lorelei's mind, forever branding her with the truth: *She was **no** savior.*

When Daemon's once glorious wings hit the floor, the scream still ringing in her ears, tears cascaded down her cheeks, mixing with the immense amounts of blood that now coated the ground beneath them. The blood spread so close to her face, being forced to lay on her side, she wondered if she might be drowning on it before too long. No matter Lorelei's relentless screaming, she could make no sound, she could move no part of her body to make her way closer to Daemon. She was frozen. Helpless. *Useless.*

Daemon was slumped over, his body barely hung by the chains wrapped around him. There was no way to tell if he was even breathing. She willed with all her might for him to look up, to meet his eyes, to see if he was okay.

This can't be happening...

However much Lorelei fought against the constraints of this immobilization, or how much she begged for Daemon to look up, it was pointless. And she hated herself for how useless she was. How could she ever be the 'savior' when she can't even save Daemon? Or Samuel for that matter? How would she ever go up against beings who were as old as Earth and superior in every way? She was human. And even with her true parentage known, she had no powers enough to stop this war. Or save her friends.

All she could do was see snippets of complicated moments that didn't make a lot of sense up until now. She had no way to know how to enhance those abilities, and even if she accomplished to learn how to cultivate it, or even use more of the Enochian spells and grind to a level of competence, that didn't do shit for actually protecting anybody right now. That kind of stuff took time. Time that had long run out.

Right there lied Daemon, wings cut, dying—Samuel lay dying elsewhere and she wouldn't be sure if Lucifer was telling the truth about saving him or not. She could only hope he would keep his end of the bargain. Lorelei was alone, and incapable of doing a thing for either of them.

How could anybody like that, do anything good? If she were truly a good person, she would've figured out a way to get them out of this mess before it got to this point. They were all so naive. This plot, this war, these *enemies*...were far greater than she could have imagined. As it was clear now, they had enemies on **both** sides. Heaven and Hell. It wasn't just pitch-forked depicted demons out to ruin humanity; it was also the angels who came whispering in the ears of mortals about salvation and 'Peace on Earth.' The ones who were supposed to be the good guys. They too, were now an enemy.

I should've known I couldn't do this...I should've known I had no business trying..

Lorelei's tears rampaged her face, making her eyes sting. She finally took her eyes away from Daemon, who was unmoving. She avoided looking at the silken black feathers that now lay in a pool of blood, while finding Michael who was carefully wiping the blade he used for his savage action, as if it was such an inconvenience for the blade to be splattered with blood, and not a barbarous, vile act. The heartbreak at realizing there was truly no mercy shown by God when his soldiers were permitted to do this, if God indeed was unaware...what little hope Lorelei had, vanished in a blink of an eye.

Michael met her gaze and leisurely strutted towards her, waving a hand and saying another phrase in Enochian, and she was released from her prison—her head cracked as it fell to the ground; she pushed herself up to a sitting position, rubbing the side of her head. The dizzying effects of a sure concussion caused a ringing in her ears. Looking back to Daemon, she called out to him.

"Daemon...Daemon can you hear me?"

Michael stood in front of her, and held a hand out to assist her. She tucked her arms to her body and held herself in a hug, ignoring him. Wondering if Michael would let her pass to go to Daemon or not, she forced herself to stand and waited. Her eyes were filled with hatred at this 'sacred' being standing before her.

"Lorelei, I am sorry you had to witness such a thing, but it was the only way. You and Daemon must understand, no action goes unnoticed. Daemon was the reason that propelled you so far forward on your quest. If he had not saved your life all those years ago, we would not be standing here. And if he had not re-involved himself later to assist you, to let you know of the prophecy of the girl who had the power to stop Armageddon, then again...none of this would have transpired. You and he are linked beyond this frivolous infatuation. When Daemon went against orders to end your life, sparing you instead, he enacted another part of the prophecy—one that until now, we did not realize the significance of. His companionship, guidance, support and ability to fight alongside you; that was what would drive you to stop the war. This was not merely a punishment, it was a needed remedy. With him...the way he is now...and with your half-brother also gone...I am afraid there is not much left to be concerned with. You are no longer a threat. None of you are. The Human Element the prophecy speaks of, is folly. A forsaken crutch in the scheme of so much grander to come. You, and your species—are *not* the element this Universe needs to persevere, Lorelei. Do not be so fooled."

"Now that we know the secret of how you were kept from us, we will proceed with the correct measures for ensuring that something like this never happens again. ArchAngel Ariel will be dealt with, and the rest of the angels who share a similar sentiment. We will proceed with the war as planned. And you can go back to your life. You are free. I have been informed your death is no longer necessary."

Lorelei narrowed her brows and stared him down. Now he was threatening her mother. Even not knowing her, she couldn't help feeling a pang in her chest at the thought. Michael would stop at nothing to end whoever stood in his way. Nobody was safe. And definitely nobody was free.

"What about Daemon? And how do you know about my brother?? Never mind, that part isn't important..."

Lorelei paused and looked to where Raphael was, who was also unconscious.

"And what about Raphael? What are you planning to do with him?"

Michael looked back at the other ArchAngel and shrugged.

"We have no use for him. The majority of his powers have been stripped, save the basics. He will continue to have his healing abilities, so you may heal Daemon if you so desire. I have no care what happens to him. Let's call it...a gift to you. A condolence. You have suffered much already, there is no need to suffer further. You and Daemon may live out the remainder of your lives together in whatever way you wish, however long you have left. Raphael is hereby a Fallen from this day henceforth, we are being merciful by allowing him to maintain his abilities, and since we are on a deadline, the ceremony we usually perform for Fallen will be...waived. For now. He is no longer permitted to return to Heaven."

The callousness dripping from Michael's tone set Lorelei's teeth on edge. How could someone who you served alongside for centuries, be cast aside so easily?

"Fine, he stays with me and Daemon. Now what?"

Lorelei watched and flinched as Michael came closer to her, looking her up and down in a patronizing manner, until he laid a hand on her shoulder, patting it.

"Now, you heal. And move on. This is your second chance, Lorelei. I would suggest you take it."

Lorelei nearly forgot the demons pacing impatiently behind them, huffing and groaning, rolling their eyes when Zanul—who she didn't see before—winked at her and waved playfully. The memory of his burning lasso made her instinctively grab her previously injured arm, which only seemed to please him. But his enjoyment only lasted a moment. The shock of seeing him after what Daemon said of using the Finishing Spell was making her more and more confused. *He should be dead.* Instead, he was walking up to Michael and shouting.

"ALRIGHT! We get it now, let's move on already, Michael! We have business to attend to. Although I very much enjoy seeing so much pain and suffering of an enemy...this is not the only part I signed up for. Now you've made us wait here long enough. When will a group of your soldiers be ready to invade Hell?"

Turning towards Zanul, Michael towered over the demon and a look of annoyance flared in his eyes.

"You....demon....have proven enough use. But unfortunately, there will be no angels aiding you on this fruitless endeavor of taking over command from Lucifer. You are no match for him, and there will not be a need for Hell much longer. I appreciate the information you relayed concerning Lorelei and Daemon, how to find them and all...but our alliance goes no further."

Zanul was fuming, jumping around, cursing, telling Michael to go places she wasn't even surewhat they were. The other demons joined in, and soon they were circling Michael like a pack of hyenas, yipping and yowling, some even began pulling out weapons.

"I see...your grievances are noted, Zanul. Yet I suggest, if you wish to continue to live a prosperous existence, you and your friends leave without further agitation. Seeing as my angel healers brought you back from death, I believe we are equal."

With that, Michael snapped a finger, and the demons vanished. The stillness and silence of the arena now in full, foreboding effect. Lorelei stood stunned, waiting for what to do next when Michael didn't bother to face her again, and spoke over his shoulder.

"Take care, Lorelei Alexander. Try to make the most of these last days, savor your blessing, that you may experience them."

Before Lorelei could retort, Michael spread his wings and lifted into the air, leaving her standing in a river of blood. She waited until the last flap of a wing she could see, and ran as fast as she could to Daemon, who still hung slumped over. Her boots were covered with his blood, she had to wade through like water. She fell to her knees, stepping precariously over a wing, another tear falling as she reached a hand to caress it one last time; it shimmered that beautiful matching emerald color under her touch, the same of his captivating eyes. Her heart broke to see the beauty and majesty of them, stained and soaking, never to beat again. Kneeling in front of Daemon, she lifted his head up to look at his face, moving gently his silver bangs out of his face.

"Daemon, please...I'm here, wake up. I'm here...I love you...we're going to be okay...I promise...I love you...I love you...."

She just kept repeating that over and over, like a broken clock that kept chiming long after the time passed. It was impossible to do anything less. She hugged his neck, kissed the top of his head, and positioned herself to sit, nuzzling her face against his own while she looked around her. Raphael was still limp on the ground, Samuel was stuck in Hell with her ruthless father, Daemon was permanently maimed, the angels were behind this insanity, and the world would still end soon with no way to stop it. All because she was the Chosen One. **The Human Element**. But in the end, none of those titles mattered. She was a failure. A nobody. *Just a human*. Hugging Daemon closer, she buried her face in his neck and wept.

The world may be ending, but Lorelei's world was already shattered.

To be continued...

www.ingramcontent.com/pod-product-compliance
Lightning Source LLC
Chambersburg PA
CBHW010536100726
47903CB00011B/3023